# THE WAY
# WE WILL BE

## BATTLE OF
## THE PLANETS

### GEORGE FRANCIS WILLIAMS

# THE WAY WE WILL BE: THE BATTLE OF THE PLANETS

Thanks go to my wife and sister-in-law for significant help and encouragement.

There are many quotes and misquotes from The Bard, as well as from well known poets such as Ted Hughes.

ISBN 9798793784191

Discussion: FB@TheWayWeWillBe

## Trigger Warning and Disclaimer

This book is a work of fiction intended for adult readers. No scenario or outcome is intended to be relied on as a forecast and no responsibility is accepted for their use as such. Characters in this book express a range of political and religious views which are not necessarily those of the author. It contains tangential references to living and dead persons, businesses and organisations. Known villains aside, all references are intended to be neutral or positive and no offence is intended to such persons, businesses, organisations or countries.

# CONTENTS

# FOREWORD

I started writing this book many years ago, but the majority of plot and writing was composed in the Autumn of 2020, following which there was a review by a few beta readers and a pause in writing when I considered whether or not to proceed. In Autumn 2021 I was deeply affected by the unexpected death of Sarah Newcombe, having attended her wedding celebration just two weeks earlier. Her funeral took place around four weeks later. It was indeed strange to meet very old friends and acquaintances twice in the space of six weeks, yet under such very different circumstances.

I am particularly grateful to Will and Eva for giving permission to use Sarah's artwork for this book cover. The main plot of the story is unaffected by those sad events, but there are some subtle additions I have added reflecting some of my experiences.

The prelude set in 2040 describing conflict between Russia and the West, including the narrow avoidance of nuclear war, was also written long before Putin had started preparations for an attack on Ukraine. As I prepare for publication, a part of me is wondering whether I might have set this story 18 years too far into the future.

Indeed many developments which I describe here in the novel, which I had considered futuristic when first setting out my story, are now being at least discussed. For example, autonomous killing devices are discussed from an ethical perspective, but the reality is that the technology already exists, even if it has not yet been deployed. I introduced the "bubble" concept into the writing long before anyone had heard of Covid and, while its application in this novel is wider than the Covid definition, the extension is now far easier to envisage.

I hope you will enjoy this story. I hope it will be read and debated widely. I am especially keen to support reading groups who wish to study it. I will be offering groups who wish to engage in discussion the opportunity through social media including "Ask Me Anything" sessions for a limited period following the launch. Please see FB@TheWayWeWillBe for more details.

George Francis Williams
The Way We Will Be
March 2022

# PRELUDE

*Always listen to your dreams; they might just be telling you something.*

### SCENE LONDON 20 JUNE 2040

There had been a week of heavy rain, unsurprising for England at any time, and much less so in current times. In some parts of southern England a whole metre had fallen within five days. Irrigation systems installed in gardens were switched off and businesses installing them closed. Old Father Thames swelled along its banks. Staines-on-Thames became Staines-in-Thames, Runnymede ran only with water, and many of the other towns and villages along its banks were now lying underwater.

In perfect timing, storm 'Circe' arrived from the east. The surge she created met the Thames at high tide. Warnings were issued but the Thames Barrier could not cope. Water poured along the lower river overspilling the banks. She was still strong approaching central London. East London and Essex suffered even worse that the centre, with Canvey Island fully underwater and the nearby area needed only St Mark's Basilica to fully resemble Venice.

Several tube lines flooded and the overground struggled to cope. The Docklands Light Railway continued running until withdrawn for safety concerns over the high winds. In the Palace of Westminster the Parliamentary Terrace and several hospitality rooms were flooded. The Fire and Rescue Service was stretched beyond breaking point as the crew became sailors overnight. Several districts of London lost power.

Around southern England the motorways suffered too. Following a series of accidents the M25 and M2 were closed. The Moon reported :-

"Long delays on the A303 at the new Stonehenge tunnel. The tunnel itself was intended to save thousands of motorists from hours of queues on summer holidays. The new tunnel may have escaped the floods but it couldn't escape the seasonal protesters, angry at what they say is desolation of ancient tombs. Police are now investigating reports that several car drivers were hauled from their vehicles and beaten up with one elderly driver dying in hospital. We say it's time to get tough and stop these protesters once and for all."

By 23 June the rain stopped, and by 30 June the flood waters had started to recede, by which time the temperature in London had risen to 38 degrees centigrade.

The papers were full of doom with The English Standard reporting "The stench of sewage and flood water filled several parts of the City and docklands. In Peckham riots started after local supermarkets started running low on dairy products, pasta and toilet paper. Government sources reported this was due to panic buying and the loss of refrigeration. Insiders point out that most of the major supermarkets had also suffered serious cyber-attacks on their logistics systems."

Satisfaction with the Government was already at an all-time low. Plotters were ready, armed with laptops and fake news including purported leaked videos from inside No 10. No one single group aimed to exploit the chaos; but anarchists, far-right groups and jihadists were all, in their different ways, ready to take advantage to advance their cause. The common theme was clear: the Government must go.

A suspicious lorry was challenged on the Mall. It refused to stop and soldiers fired on it. The driver was shot dead, and the lorry veered off into St James' Park. The resultant explosion shattered windows as far away as St Anne's Gate. The monarch was evacuated by helicopter to Windsor and was later taken to

Balmoral by their security detail. Critical infrastructure started to fail. Riots started to break out across London prompted by reports of food shortages.

The Hours commented: "An investigation by this paper has revealed that not one of the ring leaders from any faction involved in the unrest was actually in London that day. They were sitting comfortably behind computer screens, either elsewhere in the country or in some cases outside it. The carnage was carried out by their foot soldiers. Cloud based accounts vary, and it is difficult to tell truth from fiction. A number of online supposedly factual accounts and images appear on closer inspection to be the product of deep digital fakery. This is a serious matter, and all the more reason for the public to place their trust in the traditional press over self-publicising pressure groups. What is needed is firm leadership and, though as press we are loath to support censorship, more control of internet-based extreme content is essential."

The Daily Fax reported in a similar vein:

"Sources close to the security services believe that renegade groups in Russia and China were the source of the main cyber-attacks on British commerce and infrastructure, and the stirring up of dissension online. Given that the economic impact runs into several hundreds of billion pounds, we implore the Government to take retaliatory action immediately and to limit foreign influence on social media propaganda."

The riots intensified and were no longer about food. The army was already distracted with the task of maintaining emergency flood defences. As there were too few soldiers available to cope, armed police patrolled the streets, forced on occasion to use deadly force. Some were instead overpowered by groups of protesters. Stores in Knightsbridge were ransacked, Regent Street was vandalised, and protestors abetted by an insider now stormed the Palace of Westminster, already compromised by flooding. The rioters stormed in through St Stephens Entrance, overwhelming security personnel completely, while some managed to gain entrance from the Thames. The main body of them charged in as far as Central Lobby where they split into two. Both debating chambers, Lords and Commons, were invaded, while Members of those Houses were still in debates. Some of the militants came armed with iron bars, or spray cans, smashing and destroying as they went. No statue was left untouched, no picture left undefaced.

"Workers' revolution snuffed out to deadly effect" screamed the headline of the Labourer's Friend, which to be fair to that publication did have a modicum of truth. The main impact of that reporting however was to inflame the situation still further.

Among those who entered the Palace of Westminster were four with more insidious intent than the general protesters. No one in there noticed the back packs on four of their numbers amid the noise and confusion. Not, anyway, until they exploded, scattering their former owners and those nearby into several pieces . The culprits could later be identified only by dental records. There was one suicide bomber in each chamber, Commons and Lords, at approximately the same time. One in the Elizabeth Tower destroyed not only Big Ben but the clock-face too. The final one in Central Lobby mainly killed fellow rioters as opposed to the members of the public and press who more usually frequent that icon of British democracy.

Five minutes later even greater damage was caused as a light plane crashed into the side of the building. It was carrying sufficient aviation fuel to ignite the whole structure. There were a couple of hundred survivors, but most inside perished one way or another, whether staff, visitors, law-makers or the rioters. Miraculously, the Chapel of St Mary Undercroft survived intact.

Nor were Whitehall and the levers of Government left alone in the worst attack on the seat of Government since the Civil War. The Treasury, Foreign Office and Cabinet office were all attacked, each of them succumbing to the mob. The buildings were left largely intact but would require significant repair work before being habitable. This could have been Paris in the 1790s, but it was London in the summer of 2040.

## STATEMENT BY THE PRIME MINISTER (ALL MAJOR NEWS CHANNELS)

"I regret to inform you that a combination of the forces of nature and foreign enemies have caused significant economic and physical damage to our country. Many of our hospitals are without power, food distribution is currently unreliable, and a new variant of flu is spreading quickly. The experts inform us that unless we take measures immediately we could see close to a million deaths. I am therefore tonight ordering all non-essential workers to stay at home. You may only leave your home to purchase food or medicine for yourselves and your families. No civilian may enter or leave the country and all scheduled flights are cancelled. It is necessary to take this action to protect our country from the threats it faces. I know you will understand why such measures are needed, and they will not be kept in place a minute longer than is strictly required."

## SCENE RETALIATION

London would not be the only place to suffer civil disorder. Countermeasures were put in place by the military to retaliate against those responsible for the emergency situation.

A leaked Government memo read "We sent in Michael (Mike) Montgomerie to calm the situation. He is well aware of the ultimate main source of the trouble: Russian cyber manipulation intended to destabilise the country. He has extensive experience, and despite his colourful past, he is a man to be relied on.

In addition he has counter jihadist experience, which could be of use given our assessment that extremist groups are also attempting to take advantage of the situation, piggy backing off state actors, albeit with a somewhat different agenda."

**MICHAEL MONTGOMERIE FILE:**

**Age:** 45.

**Languages:** Russian, French, Spanish, Arabic.

**Personal motto:** "To the victor the spoils."

**Previous assignments:** Attachment to US Delta force, NATO signals, South America (saw action).

**Conduct:** Previous warnings for multiple inappropriate sexual liaisons.

**Strengths:** Expert in cyber and counter cyber warfare.

**Family:** Great grandfather on his mother's side was a Russian military colonel. Grandfather on his father's side descended from French Huguenots in Chatillon. Grandfather on mother's side was the British ambassador to the Paris.

**Security risk assessment:** Low.

**Intelligence:** Extensive contacts within Russia with a key insider asset (see linked entry below).

"Chief asset was recruited on a mission to St Petersburg two years ago. MM exploited the asset's grievances against the Russian state which had been passed down from father to son since 1917. Asset has extensive cyber knowledge. Asset's weakness is an inherited arrogance and suspected misogyny. Suspected to have had multiple sexual partners from a relatively young age, possibly including prostitutes. Asset currently works for Russian cyber security."

**GLOBAL INSTABILITY: SOMETHING MUST BE DONE**

The asset, for all his faults, proved particularly invaluable in the retaliation against Russian cyber-attacks. One by one Russian power stations turned off, including the last remaining nuclear stations. Outright explosion was avoided but one reactor nearly melted down, reviving memories of Chernobyl. Across

Moscow the people took to the streets demanding action and retribution against the West.

The Kremlin threatened nuclear war, but US commitment and firepower were enough to diffuse the more extreme threats. Moscow was content to hit back with further direct cyber-attacks, this time on the financial sector. Hundreds of thousands of financial and credit card accounts were exposed on the dark web. Criminals all over the world soon took advantage, and many found their identities stolen. Without access to financial resources, the victims were left with nothing at all. It would have been worse but for Operation X-ray, Michael's unit for counter-cyber warfare. The Russian and Chinese bot farms were neutralised. Eventually extra online shields were erected against the foreign attackers. The response was fatally slow; by the time the defences were up much damage was done. It would take some time to rectify. Never again could the Government allow systematic threats of this nature.

"Something must be done," declared almost all national publications.

The cyber security of the country would need to be improved by all means necessary. If that involved some restriction of personal liberty, so be it.

## SCENE AFTERMATH

Even two weeks later some found themselves completely unable to regain their previous identities and connection with their financial assets. Governments everywhere were simply unprepared for the task of verifying everyone's online identity and struggled to assist victims by linking them with their online identities. Some were able to recover their identities by making in-person visits to their banks but the branch network had diminished to such an extent that most fell through the net. Queues outside city centre banks stretched for half a mile. Those who did recover their accounts often found large amounts missing and unaccounted for.

"As a society we have out-sourced not just our cash but our whole way of interacting with the world, to the internet. We have even out-sourced our memories to the net, and developed virtual amnesia when the net was unable to retrieve our data. Whole families have been unable to buy food or fuel. Travel cards have become inactive, cars have been immobilised and phones useless. What we need to do is to take a good look at ourselves and what we have become. And now that the Government appears to be in utter chaos, what we need is a clean sweep, and a new administration based on real democracy which can do the basic job of Government: provide for our security by all means necessary." Thus wrote Space Magazine in its leader column.

But the worst was yet to come. Within a week came disease; a new strain of hepatitis emerged from the raw sewage caused by overflowing drains. This variety could also be transmitted by human contact and was often fatal if untreated. The mainstream hospitals overflowed and make-shift ones were mobilised. Nurses and even doctors needed counselling themselves after witnessing the mayhem.

Community and food-share schemes based round 'bubbles' of volunteers were set up to aid the disadvantaged. The bubbles took up the challenge by also providing counselling and mental health support. These bubbles started growing, expanding and connecting, as they became more important to people's lives. In many cases, they would become people's main form of social contact. As central civilian command fell apart, so a new political force emerged from the most elite bubbles, one ready to save the nation and the world.

### INTRODUCING WILL: SCENE A COLLEGE TRIP

Will was at the end of his first year at College, studying mathematics, with a view to a possible switch to theoretical physics at a later stage of his studies. He had just turned 19.

Usually term would have finished by now and he would have returned to his family home, but the University had deferred the start of the Easter Term by a few weeks due to health concerns. They had chosen the delay to the alternative of online learning after consultation with the Student Union. Will's examinations were over, but he had not yet had the results. He was not at all an exceptional student by the University's standards, though he was hoping for a first (or "Wrangler" in University parlance).

He had little inkling of the upcoming events, or he would perhaps not have even got up that morning. He may not have realised that that day of all days would be the start of world-changing events. It would have been easier to have pulled the covers over his head and pretended nothing was wrong. If he had known about the events taking place in London later that day, he would have risen at 11am, run around Christ's pieces, and returned to College for a shower and lunch before strolling down the backs. Running was the only non-cerebral activity Will regularly engaged in at University. However today was different as he had committed to the post-exam trip to the capital three weeks ago and he had no idea what was about to happen.

He rarely spent time in London except for changing trains, mostly to and from College. Once he ran the London marathon, in a leisurely four hours, but that was it. While London was undoubtedly an exciting city and the seat of power, he found the underground in particular bewildering, dirty, noisy and overcrowded. He struggled to see why anyone would want to pay higher prices for anything from coffee to gallery entrances in the capital, when it was unpleasant to travel to and around. When he did go to London he preferred to be part of a group, preferably travelling by coach, to have a very specific purpose in mind, and to make the most of the excursion.

He had been looking forward to this particular trip which included a tour of the Palace of Westminster, still the seat of power for the country at that time, at the invitation of a Member of Parliament who had graduated from the College.

The thought of the mock gothic building, the stone floored Westminster Hall, even watching a debate from the visitors' gallery made him well up with pride in being English and in the openness of the democratic process. That was until news of the unrest filtered out on social media.

"We have to change plans," explained the trip guide after consulting with the other student leaders. "There are protests in London. We will visit South Kensington where you have the choice of the V&A or the Science Museum instead. Unless you want to join the protests, of course."

Will loved history but found modern politics boring. Student politics was the most boring of all. It was the woke that sent him to sleep.

However, the change of plan suited Will, as he loved the Science Museum, just as much as he hated rioting and disorder. Most of the students who joined the protests were global climate change activists. He wondered why they would protest at a Government and country that had taken the issue so seriously compared with other larger polluters in the world that had dragged their feet on commitments to reduce harmful emissions to the atmosphere. More to the point, he found the fundamentalism disturbing. They bandied around terms like "sustainable" without defining exactly what they meant. Did they not understand the second law of thermodynamics; disorder always increases, so nothing is sustainable for eternity? We're all toast in the long term. Worst of all, student climate protesters tended not to have practical policies. The problem was serious enough, but it required something more than slogans, and the activists always seemed to avoid the awkward issue of who pays for the changes.

Instead of engaging with student politics, he had been studying the physics of ionised particles, how they behaved in the sun, and how they behaved on earth. He was captivated by the attempts to recreate the inside of stars in spherical donuts. It held out the potential to create large amounts of energy without using fossil fuels. Now that was a practical solution, provided that it could be made to work. It therefore seemed to be a better investment to continue his studies rather than attend tedious meetings.

He noticed a girl about his own age looking a bit lost. She was wearing hat which concealed her hair. He walked across her and asked if she needed help.

"I'll be alright, I'm sure," she said. "I just helped a young child who got lost herself. Then the group I was with went on without me!"

"I saw a group of what looked like students just three minutes ago," he volunteered. "Two of them had hospital-branded bags from Guys and St Thomas. I could help you catch up with them."

"I'm sure I'll be fine," she said. "Which way did they go?"

Will couldn't exactly remember but pointed vaguely in the direction of the Medical Sciences section of the museum hoping he was correct. He wasn't, but he was at least trying to be helpful.

"You could try phoning them?" he suggested.

"Thank you so much for your help but I don't carry a phone," she said.

Who in this day and age went round London without one?

"I want to live in the present, and I don't like people tracking my every move," she added in explanation.

"Don't you feel lost without one?"

"That was a little impertinent, wasn't it? Don't you feel imprisoned with one?" Will was a little taken aback. Was she mad or did she have a point? How could she be someone of his own age clearly studying a scientific discipline and yet reject technology?

Five minutes later she crossed back outside the corridor, having established Will had no idea where her group was. Then he realised he had lost his own group.

Three hours later the tannoy alert went out for him. He had a phone of course, but had forgotten to charge it and it ran out half way through the visit. He was to all intents and purposes just as lost as the strange girl he had just come across. That detail is unimportant to our story though; what matters was that Will had decided his future. Over the course of his immersion in the Science Museum he had resolved to become an energy engineer and perhaps even solve the problem of nuclear fusion here on earth. That was how he was going to save the planet from carbon catastrophe, by finally removing the need for energy production from fossil fuels. The problem of how to exploit it had been going on for decades, but it did feel like there was no better time than the present to invest in more research in that area in order to address the world's energy and carbon issues. That required someone of Will's unique abilities. He was determined to help get the country there before the Russians did, but what was really important was to end emissions once and for all, right across the planet, using scientific endeavour and research.

## SCENE BACK AT COLLEGE

Fortunately for Will and his mates, the journey back to College was unaffected by the trouble in London, the coach being a twelve year old model still running on diesel, and being driven by someone astute enough to ensure the tank had sufficient fuel for the return leg. The first Will noticed something which impacted him personally was the following Monday when he tried to pay the end of term College bill.

"Username and/or password not recognised."

That was strange. He should have sufficient money in the account. Then he remembered that credentials and cash were two separate things. Had he mis-remembered the password? No, the password was stored on his browser so he wouldn't forget it.

He clicked to re-set his password. Then he tried logging in to his account.

"Username and/or password not recognised."

That was serious. It looked like his bank account and College email had been hacked.

He wandered down to the porter's lodge. They weren't really supposed to deal with IT issues but on the other hand, they could always be relied on for good advice.

"Aye, you're the fifth gentleman today that's come in here complaining of that," she replied. "I'll send you to Dr Babbage who'll sort you out."

Will knocked on the oak door.

"Will here, sir," he replied. "Seem to be having a few IT issues with my account. I can't even access my bank."

"Ah. You mean you can't pay your college bills?"

"I have the money sir, I just can't get at it."

"Good to hear you're solvent, which puts you in the minority of students. Probably because you don't rack up bar bills. Anyway, I'm glad you came in person," replied Babbage. "I've had a few phone calls asking for resets to your college email account that appear to have originated from Russia, judging by the accents. I suspected that they were not completely genuine. For that reason I'm only doing in-person restores from now on. Like any self-respecting scientist, I don't trust what I can't see."

"I see, sir. My parents are tee-total, so I try not to drink too much. Thank you for your understanding."

"You can't trust anything except flesh and blood that you can see with your own eyes."

He typed furiously on his keyboard.

"All set. Your password is "1MustStudyHarderS00n', understand?"

"Yes sir," he replied, relieved.

"And be careful, Will," he replied.

"Why?"

"Everyone who comes here gets spotted by fellow students and they may well guess it's a re-set job or that you've been hacked," he replied. "You're in danger of a ponding if you're caught."

"Thank you sir."

Will had no desire to taste the dubiously flavoured pond. The last student to suffer such a fate had to have his stomach pumped out. He had nearly suffered that fate last winter, when an attempt to pond him failed due to a thick layer of ice which his assailants were unable or unwilling to break in order to accomplish their mission. He checked the coast was clear and darted back to his room, where he finally managed a password reset and logged on.

"Overdraft limit exceeded."

There followed many unsuccessful attempts to contact his bank. This was going to be a very difficult term. Will was, however, the fortunate one, being able to confirm his identity in person. His parents, somewhat less tech-savvy than himself, and living far from their nearest physical bank branch, found themselves permanently locked out from both their email addresses and their banking facilities. As a result the monthly financial support he obtained from them vanished and he was entirely reliant on his loans to finish the term. His heart went out to his mother in particular who couldn't understand why her world had turned upside down and why no one seemed able to help her. Before she was able to reconnect online, and struggling with anxiety even in the best of times, she committed suicide unable to cope.

## SCENE RUSSIA JUNE 2040

It was not only England that suffered. The protests in Moscow spread to St Petersburg, Yekaterinburg and Novosibirsk. The country had only a few months' earlier emerged from lengthy social restrictions due to a pandemic. The disease had been global but the Russian and Chinese blocks had been less well prepared and had therefore needed more draconian action. A population whose mental health was already at a low ebb was in no mood for further inconveniences.

Food shortages struck the country and then came the cyber-attack on the country's nuclear power stations. Russia knew exactly where it had come from and understood it as a reprisal.

Colonel Michael called his main official contact, Captain Ulyanin, in an attempt to call a halt to the cyber-attacks and online incitement. Over a few days of negotiation the two sides started to understand and trust each other, until Ulyanin was suddenly removed from office by the new revolutionaries who distrusted him. Fortunately the situation calmed as everyone realised that further provocation was not in anyone's interests. The nuclear station which had nearly melted down was back generating within a few weeks.

## INTRODUCING KATERINA

Our heroine Katerina Kotov was a teenager still at school, and an only child. She had wished for a brother or, better still, a sister, but as her mother explained she and her father couldn't have any more. She was about to join her friends for first communion, something she and they had delayed for a few years due to the pandemic which had caused food shortages and social restrictions in Russia as much as elsewhere. Her family were not especially religious, but it had been a tradition handed down through her mother's family.

"Why do we have queues again now? I thought we were over the worst of the disease and that we could settle back to our old lives." she asked her mother, thoroughly exasperated.

"There's some global unrest, dear, don't worry," her mother replied.

Wanting further reassurance she picked up her tablet and checked Rus-Net news service.

"The West is attacking our motherland. The British, on the instruction of their American masters, were responsible for the devastating attack on our electricity system which closed down many parts of the country for several days. They are doing so when they know we are recovering from disease and disaster and when they know their actions will cause the death of innocent women and children. Russia has done nothing to deserve or merit this unjustified aggression. We should meet force with force, and the westerners must live to regret their actions."

The following night her mother came:

"We need to escape to the country tomorrow morning, just for a while. It's too dangerous here with the instability," she said. "We will use our dacha. We have tinned and dried food there, and our own generator. You only need to take a few personal things. We will be back soon enough."

"What about school, what about first communion? It should have been three years ago."

"School can wait and so can first communion. A little longer won't hurt. You can confess to God in your heart."

"What about the sins of the west who are attacking our country?" she enquired. "Shouldn't we respond? So many hospitals and businesses and homes have had no power for days. It makes me so angry."

"We must learn to forgive if want to be forgiven," explained her mother. "I felt welcome in England when I worked there. London has a special place in my heart, and it will in yours one day. You should learn to forgive and love them too."

"Why don't I have a sister or brother like the other kids?" she asked her father the following day, as they were travelling away from the city towards relative peace. The unfairness of her isolation was starting to affect her. "I'm missing my friends. I've missed not being with them for most of two years, and now we're relocating. It's not the same on webchat. At least you and Mum have each other but I don't have anyone my age."

"It's your poor Dad," replied her father. "I'm just not up to it! As for your friends, well, your true friends will wait for you." He gave her a half-resigned smile.

"Nonsense you are a great father, Professor Kotov. We have our beautiful and clever Katerina. She is multi-talented, top in every subject at school. We have to learn to accept what God gives us and I am very proud," exclaimed her mother. "Maybe in future science can help us to have bigger families. I'm trying to find new ways myself at the Health Research Institute."

Turning to Katerina, she remarked, "I have high hopes for you. Perhaps you will join me and discover things I did not."

Katerina glowed. Indeed she was very beautiful, tall, with long dark hair and a waifish face , though shy and reserved with it. Obviously she was not to blame for having no brother or sister and she could hardly blame her father for an accident of biology. Perhaps she had a real purpose in life.

"I'm missing your dancing," remarked her father.

"I'm focussing on tennis now, Dad," she said. "It's been easier to practise this last year. One teacher told me I was too tall."

"Well I enjoy seeing you do both," he said. "Once I thought you would grow up to perform with the Russian State Ballet."

Katerina had never had any such ambition.

"So which is more important; religion or science," she asked her mother, changing subject, knowing full well her father avoided all mention of the subject if he possibly could.

"Science and technology lets us live our lives in more ease and comfort," explained her mother. "Religion tells us why we're living it in the first place, and the comforts it gives are spiritual not physical."

The "why?" seemed too big a question, but she could understand science and technology.

"I want to grow up to be like you Mum," she said, "Sometimes I prefer the science to church and sometimes I prefer the church to science. You're right about the ballet; I can still watch it even if I can't perform."

The very thought of performing in front of anyone scared her. Science could be performed without exposure to public ridicule. All that needed to be decided was the branch of science. Her mother's work in Reproductive Health excited her; that is what she would study.

About London she felt torn in two; her mother spoke so highly of the city, particularly the culture and social life, yet she detested the people who had attacked her country. Yes, she must visit, but she would be very wary of the English or indeed anyone from the west.

After a few weeks the situation eased and the Kotovs returned to their home in the city, now renamed St Vladisgrad. Katerina breathed a sigh of relief. She suggested an outing to celebrate the relative freedom.

"Can't we take a walk, and perhaps visit the library?" she enquired.

"Why of course," declared her father, "why not take one of your friends too, as you haven't seen them for so long. Mariya perhaps." Co-incidentally, Mariya was not one of the circle of friends preparing for first communion – she had taken hers six years before, and was a bit older than Katerina but they got on well and she was a good friend of the family.

"Oh what a good idea. I got her a job as a trainee nurse at the Hospital in my old unit – she's a lovely girl," declared her mother.

The matter was settled and Mariya called around at 10am.

The library was in a sorry state. It was only two weeks before it was due to be closed, to be replaced by a coffee shop and online advice centre, albeit one under close supervision by the party. Throughout the pandemic it had acted as one of the few permitted social spaces outside the church, allowing people to meet at a safe distance, maybe discuss politics or art in a relaxed way. The new regime had other ideas, however, and intended its closure, with a view to more supervised social interactions in the future.

As a teenager Katerina was keen to explore. Her use of online resources was monitored by her parents, like any child. The library offered the chance to explore knowledge without that oversight. She needed to make the most of the chance to explore unsupervised. While her father was distracted discussing a new Hermitage exhibition with the chief librarian, and her mother was perusing medical science textbooks, she gave Mariya the slip and quietly made for the foreign fiction section. She made straight for English Literature; admiring a copy of a first portfolio Shakespeare, then moving on to more modern authors and poets, such as Ted Hughes. Her grasp of English was quite adequate to read and comprehend the words. From fiction she moved to European Art, marvelling at the range and diversity, losing all sense of time.

By one o'clock, the Kotovs had not been re-united with their wayward child.

"Mariya, have you seen Katerina anywhere?"

"No, Mrs Kotov. Do you want me to find her?"

Mariya knew the place better than either of the Kotovs, and also had an inkling where she might be.

She wasn't the first to locate the young errant. A young man, perhaps five or six years older than herself, had been examining books in the IT section. Noticing her alone for some time he approached.

"Moyo pochtenie," greeted the man. "No one looking after you?"

Katerina blushed.

"I'm sure I don't need looking after," she replied.

"A young girl as pretty as you certainly does," he countered, grasping her hand. "It's not Miss Kotov, daughter of the good professor, is it?"

She nodded, but froze, unsure what to do, new to the experience of being alone with any man close to her own age. He was about to attempt to steal a kiss on her cheek when Mariya appeared. The man beat a hasty retreat.

"Katerina your parents are worried," Mariya chided gently. "It's not safe to go off like this. I'm not sure what to say to them."

"Oh I'm so sorry," said Katerina. "I had no idea of the time, and that man took me by surprise. I think he knew my name, as he called me Miss Kotov, and knew Dad is a professor."

She bit on her thumb, hard, in an attempt to quell her nerves. "I see. Did you encourage him?"

She paused, noting the mark on Katerina's thumb, and Katerina blushed even harder.

"I didn't say anything either way, yes or no."

"What's that you were looking at" asked Mariya. "Ah. From Russia with Love."

The cover pictured a woman and an armed man.

"I can dream."

"You certainly can, but that was no James Bond who accosted you back there. You could report it to the authorities as attempted sexual assault. Now quick or your parents will be cross with me too."

Mariya returned with Katerina to her mother. Her father had by that time wandered off towards the history section where he bumped into a young man in a hurry.

"Professor Kotov, I think?" The presumptuous young man introduced himself. "I believe you know my father?"

Kotov remembered.

"Ah yes. Fine fellow. Member of the club of course. I hear you're very good with computers, and have a bright future ahead of you."

"Thank you very much sir. Was that your daughter I saw in the library?"

"Very likely. She was lost for ages. I should keep a closer eye on her."

" I think you should; she's rather exquisite. I should like to get to know her very much better, Professor."

"You like her do you? That's very good to hear. Well, your father is first rate, a former president of our group, and I would be very pleased if you two were to get together, as they say now. Do remember though she is quite religious in her outlook. She will respond only to the most traditional courting."

"Of course, Professor. I wouldn't dream of any improper conduct prior to marriage." The young man smiled.

"Ah well, perhaps there will be bells at St Peters then," replied Kotov. "Good luck."

Later Katerina met up secretly with Mariya.

"You know I didn't encourage him. I thought he was going to force a kiss on me. Do you think I encouraged him without knowing?" enquired Katerina. "I'm sure you know these things."

Mariya frowned.

"I don't want to encourage anyone at all," said Katerina. "Perhaps I should wear headscarves like the old women do in church."

"Oh I hope not. Everyone will think you've gone retro or religious. You're not super-religious now are you?"

Katerina shook her head. "Not really. I mean I'm doing first communion soon just like you did, but that's not it. I just don't like the attention. I don't want to feel I'm leading them on."

"Well remember this," concluded Mariya. "A man has no right to force his attentions on you under any circumstances and you don't have to put up with it."

"Thank you Mariya. You're too kind to me. I should employ you as my matchmaker."

"It would be pleasure but the downside of that role would be fighting off suitors and compiling the short list!"

They both smiled.


## SCENE AUTUMN 2040 AND POLITICAL UPHEAVAL

Before too long both Britain and Russia were under radically new Governments. By the end of the year most European Governments had also fallen. The agenda of the new administrations was clear: to survive at all costs by tackling climate change, pandemics, cyber-crime and warfare, and eliminating social injustice through stricter forms of social control. The role of public health protection was enhanced, and a Government master database on citizens was created to rationalise hundreds of separate databases which were unable to talk to each other. All this was underpinned through the bubbles which had become state mandated.

At first the bubbles were voluntary but as time went on they would become effectively compulsory as more and more privileges were reserved for those shown to be complying. It wasn't long before a public health guru worked out their potential use in times of global virus outbreak, in terms of restricting social contact in order to contain transmission.

The newly formed interim Government, operating mostly virtually, produced a White Paper. Its Executive Summary stated:

"We propose to re-form society based on a voluntary bubble basis consisting of twelve adult individuals whose online identities will be physically verified, to increase Cloud-based trust. These individuals will have state-approved identifications to allow confidence in online transactions. Each bubble will have a president, who him or herself will form a part of a higher bubble of control, culminating in the Community Council control in each locality or city. Bubble membership will be through selection based on advancement in profession, but not on actual profession type. Indeed we will encourage a mix of skills and professions within each bubble to facilitate multi-disciplinary solutions to the challenges of our time. No one will be forced to join a bubble; it will be completely voluntary.

For our young people, we will have special arrangements. We need to share the responsibility for raising the next generation, so that the best of society's habits and customs can be instilled for the great social good. In this way we will encourage all children to be brought up under the supervision of local Community Council, rather than with their biological parents. This will limit the impact of inherited wealth giving children an unfair competitive advantage.

It has been rumoured that we are planning to introduce tracking devices for individuals. We would like to assure all citizens that we have no such plans. We believe in liberty and individual freedom, and no one will be under any compulsion whatsoever in our new society provided that they are not endangering the public good."

The newly formed organs of Government registered these bubbles and encouraged the formation of new ones, with bubble hierarchies linked ultimately to Government. The elite bubbles were presided over by Council members, while those lower down the chain were first supervised by those from the elite professions who themselves were part of a supervised bubble. Nuclear family associations were discouraged and state welfare of children would become the norm. As the system expanded oversight would be increasingly effected through artificial intelligence and the remit of the groups would expand gradually. The intent, from the outset, was to replace the conventional family, though only the architects of the plan were fully aware of the vision. All of this would, naturally, take some time to materialise but the genesis of the new world began then.

It was not long before the establishment was overthrown completely. The Lords were abolished, the Church of England disestablished, and a new Government emerged operating on new principles. The church was permitted to continue in a non-state role, but the bishops were side-lined. Many envisioned the eventual demise of the church itself.

Michael was smart enough to retain his position through the political upheaval, where Ulyanin had been denounced. He vowed to spend the rest of his life protecting the country from threats whether human or natural in origin. It would take time but he also needed to rebuild links with Moscow. He needed to be careful; some of the ring-leaders from the left had formed the new ruling coalition and they had to be watched. They also had spies. No-one was to be trusted. He would ensure he was not frozen out or cancelled by getting personally involved in helping to set up the new bubble structures.

An enormous firewall was established across the west to deter cyber spying. In Moscow the authorities took similar action, to evade espionage from the likes of Michael's unit. They threw up their own cyber defences and invented the concept of the Seven Star, for very similar purposes to the West's bubbles, but typically composed of seven rather than twelve members. The new Russian agenda was less hostile to organised religion than the new western Governments, but there were conditions. The church must pay suitable homage to the state and be free of western influences. The real enemy was seen to be the US and the UK.

The impact of cyber defences and firewalls, albeit sold as a temporary measure, was that almost all internet traffic and ecommerce between Russia and the West ceased. It would be several years before world-wide co-operation returned, and when it did it would do so in a completely new society, with a break-up of the internet giants. Libertarians and free-speechers were out-lawed, or worse simply cancelled. These people were simply an obstacle to creating a safe society. This phase in our development would come to be known as the last culture war or the de-enlightenment.

In Swindon a bright teenage geekish programmer, Ben Volbert, decided to create a new game and gave it away for free. "*Planets*" was to unite everyone on this one planet we all inhabit, from East to West. Perhaps because it was neither commercial nor political, at least ostensibly, it was one of the few points of contact between East and West.

It was designed to be physically astronomical but culturally diverse. The unearthly settings would avoid bias towards any one country. The mixed nature would ensure widespread appeal. There would be a rich variety of scenes, a game with which no player could ever get bored. He had help and financing from Michael's new Military Intelligence unit, who had good reason to promote it, with a strong multi-disciplinary development team to lend support. Included in the team was Michael's St Petersburg young hacker, acting independently of the authorities there.

On the day of the launch, Saturn, Venus, Jupiter and Mars aligned. It was soon to become the most popular game on planet Earth.

## INTERNATIONAL PEACE SETTLEMENT

Another significant event happened the day of the game launch. International tensions had reduced slightly, but the United States was still concerned. A round table peace conference had been called in Europe to put to bed any further talk of military conflict between nuclear-armed countries or damaging cyber-attack which was now known to have some potentially crippling effects. The Verona Accord would become the bedrock of future agreements on policing a new world now so reliant on online transactions and communications. The agreement was signed the very day of the launch of the new game, though no one at the talks would have connected the two.

There was another significant agreement at this venue. The parties agreed that international cyber-crime was a serious global threat and that a co-ordinated approach to identity checks would be needed. They agreed security and policing needs over-rode the rights of the individual and that all those permitted to connect to the web would in future need to iden- tify themselves uniquely. International co-ordination would be required to prevent nationalistic or block based webs develop- ing independently. However some blocks insisted that until this was put in place, they might need to keep the heavy curtain across their firewalls that they had been forced to erect. The Chinese even insisted on implanting chips in their citizens for identification purposes, to complement their facial recognition systems and to establish unambiguously the identity of any online user. Thus was born the first germ of an idea; the cloud citizen. It would be a few years before dreams were realised, but this is exactly what would happen.


## NARRATOR SPEAKS

Now you know the background, the terrible culture wars that gave birth to our story, and the online game that will play a strange part in these proceedings.

I came across various manuscripts within a secret location on *Planets*. They consisted of a main narrative, together with Will's Data Log, a number of secret reports, and most important of all images from a paper diary kept by Katerina. How they came to be there no one knows, but it can only have involved one of the game administrators.

This is a story about Will and Katerina, two young people from very different backgrounds, emerging from their teenage years at the time of the culture wars, of global pandemics and of global political revolution. Most of the events of this tale took place seven years after the events just described when the true nature of the revolution had become clear to all. I have been faithful to my mission, which was to discover the fate of the pair, and the reasons that led them to their actions.

With modern technology we can translate easily into all languages and idioms, but words can have two meanings; context and history are everything. As far as possible, this account is grounded in real places. It doesn't travel backwards in time, because time only moves forward. We will move from history to the future.

I cannot tell you exactly where I came across these manuscripts, and the other sources of data. I have a feeling there are more out there, and I want to be first to bring these stories to you. What will you make of them? That's up to you. Maybe I can bring you more in the future. For now, I just give you a taster, in as few words as possible. As a wise man once said, "Brevity is the soul of wit." But I do warn you to read very carefully indeed. We have guile, poetry, science, fantasy, love and death in this tale. Remember, we know what we are, but we do not know what we will be. And - as has also been said - there are more things in heaven and earth, dear reader than you will ever dream of. But enough from me: let Will and Katerina , now adults, take over. After all it's their story. We will start with an extract from her diary.

# KATERINA'S DIARY

## KATERINA'S PANDEMIC PRE-DIARY NOTES

Now we have a lockdown due to a new pandemic, so it's time to keep a diary. Mum and Dad say this pandemic sounds worse than anything they've experienced before. I had to give up ballet dancing as the authorities did not deem it constituted essential physical contact. Everyone had said I was really good at it. My teacher said I had the ideal shape. But the classes have all stopped and I don't think I'll take it up again when they restart. I'll still watch it though. It's such an elegant art form. Here in Russia we have the best performers in the world, so we should celebrate our national successes.

How long is this going on for? I'm going to die. And now we are moving to the countryside to avoid the city. School is online, and I hate it.

I'm glad the lockdown is over, but it brings other problems. I'm not sure if I want to go back to school now. It's so difficult making friends all over again. But if I don't go back, I won't go to college, and without college there's no job, and without a job there is no chance of making a real difference to the world.

I don't understand why I'm an only child. Everyone else at school has a brother or sister. Perhaps it's because I'm too difficult or too ugly. I don't have lots of friends like some girls. The boys think I'm swotty, and too pious, and some seem jealous I'm top of the class, so it's really difficult to fit in. The other girls from church are all friends, but they have to be, so it doesn't count. I wish I was popular instead of bright, and didn't have to try so hard. Life would be so much easier.

★

At last, we have a date for first communion! Everyone else at church my age has done it except me, so now it's my turn. I think I'll belong more when I've done it. I'll have a huge great party. It will be my turn to be one of the in-gang.

### KATERINA'S NEW DIARY 8 MAY 2040

First communion was exciting and now I get to use this new secret diary, which was a present from my parents, alongside a prayer book. I've torn some of the pages out of my old pandemic diary and will keep them in the inside pocket. The party had to be cancelled though. Health restrictions are to blame. They would allow the church service but not the socialising afterwards. I hope we get back to normal soon.

I did get something nice from Mum as a present. She passed down grandmother's bear-skin hat. She received it as a wedding present but Dad was happy for her to pass it on. I don't think Mum wore it much, as it's not as cold these days as it used to be. I shall keep it safe; maybe the weather will get cold enough to wear it sometime in the future.

The bishop said that just as this diary is locked firm, so should the believing girl's body be locked firmly until marriage under God. He told the boys to guard their eyes and avoid turning their heads towards the girls, to avoid the sin of lust. Can't girls lust too? And shouldn't boys stay a virgin just like girls? And shouldn't they just stick to their wife when they get married? Well of course that's the teaching they say they keep to. But when the last Czar had an official mistress, and decided to name the Opera House after her, did the Church object? Not in public, anyway. What sort of message does that send? It sounds like there's one rule for the girls and one for the boys.

I loved tasting the blood of Christ for the first time. It's only the best wine they use for these occasions. From Georgia I believe. It's the first time I've tasted alcohol, but from now on I can drink red wine and white wine and vodka and all sorts. But not too much. We were warned about drunkenness too. From such, all kinds of unholy behaviour might occur. It can be the slippery slope towards sins of the flesh. I shall take care not to tread that wide path which leads to hell.

I should use this diary to record my prayers and confessions before God. I will write in front of the mirror. God's word acts as a light and a reflection on my soul. If I write in front of this mirror, I can observe myself as others see me. I can observe my impurities, so as to correct them before others need to correct me. That way I can be the least burden to society.

He also told us to be confident in the faith. "By this sign conquer" he quoted from the Emperor Constantine. We are to be brave in fighting for the faith. I am sure I saw a military colonel in the congregation today. I wonder what that would have meant to him? Does he pray before starting each military operation, perhaps? Or is he there merely to observe the bishop - perhaps to encourage the bishop's patriotism? Dear diary, such questions intrigue me. Maybe you can help me answer them.

## 9 MAY

Should I tell you all about the things that have been happening in Russia recently? I fear, diary, I am so angry. But I am also a Christian, so I should forgive our enemies.

**15 MAY**

The priest today said we have to forgive others or we won't be forgiven. He read a passage from the Bible about a servant who got forgiven but wouldn't forgive in return. There does seem to be a lot to forgive though. What about sins against our country, like the propaganda broadcast by the west? Does everyone in Russia have to forgive, for it to mean anything, for we are all sinned against? The priest didn't say. Dear diary, I am angry again, and that's exactly what the priest said I shouldn't be.

The wine wasn't as good as last week. Are they running out of the best?

**29 MAY**

Today I'm still glowing and reflecting on my new status as a member of the church. I keep thinking back to my first communion. I've also noticed boys at church glance my way. I'm glad the bishop said my body must be locked until marriage. He reminded us all of Katerina of Alexandria who refused the advances of the Roman Emperor and died for her pains. What a role model. If only I could be like her. Now I'm sitting here writing, completely naked, looking into the mirror. I'm not beautiful. I will have no serious suitors let alone an Emperor. The boys take one look, maybe a second, and then their eyes are drawn elsewhere, to other girls in the church, doubtless more pious than I am, as well as more beautiful. I'm too pale. I have spots on my forehead. God, please remove these spots. I got laughed at in school on Friday. I was told by one boy I was too skinny. Perhaps they like fat girls now.

**5 JUNE**

I skipped church today, but at least diary I am not skipping you. The spots on my forehead are still there. God is displeased with me or he isn't listening. I shall wear a headscarf from now on until they have all gone. I have an old one that used to belong to my father's mother. It's a rich dark purple. It was quite an unusual colour at that time, but it is my favourite colour. It evokes complex thoughts, and I feel good wearing it. If I'm laughed at, so what?

## 12 JUNE

The priest spoke about Joseph and his fancy multi-coloured coat today. He was good at having dreams and working out what they meant. He wasn't good at modesty or being popular with his brothers though. I think the message was that God speaks prophecy through dreams, but I don't know how that works for me. Last week I dreamt I was spot-free and getting married in church. Today the spots are still here, exactly where they were last week. Perhaps God is not listening to me, or sending dreams to tease me. Or perhaps I shall leave the church to those whose righteous prayers are answered. The priest ended by denouncing the gay pride movement which had appropriated Joseph's coat as its own symbol. I do wish the church would stop going on about that; it makes them look boring.

Maybe medicine is the answer, not prayer. Our neighbours prayed for children when they got married, but two years later they still don't have any. Mum works in science to help others have children. Maybe that's what I should do too. I've already told school I want to apply for medical college when I leave.

## 24 JULY

Dear diary, I am not very faithful to you, am I?

On Friday I went to the library. Dad likes English novels, so I was curious. I went to that section and picked up a spy novel. Of course, the spy is handsome. I had a strange feeling skimming through it. This spy seems to have no morals at all with women, the sort I should avoid, and yet I found myself drawn in. Dear diary I have to confess to feeling slightly tempted by just the mere thought of such a man. That is so wrong. I must have weakened my resolve to have nothing to do with men, and in my moment of weakness nearly lured a boy into kissing me. I was wearing my scarf, so he wouldn't notice the spots. I saw him from a couple of shelves away. I must have smiled at him, while viewing the book, because he stared hard. I should have turned away like the bishop said, but I didn't. I must have drawn him in. He came right over and almost kissed me. I shouldn't have let him get close. I want to confess my sins, but will anyone forgive me? Mariya says it was his fault not mine, but she is just being kind to protect my feelings.

Last night I found some old nails. I used them to scratch my wrists until a little blood came. It felt good to have them pressing against me. I cleaned it up before mum could find it, but I'm worried she guessed.


## 3 SEPTEMBER

It's been so long now. I've been neglecting you dear diary. I have had such trouble since I last sat in front of my mirror and spoke to you. There's less of me to see now. I can't seem to enjoy eating. Mum stands over me now until I've eaten it. She's started watching me afterwards when I go to the toilet, to make sure I don't try and get rid of what I've eaten.


## OCTOBER

Dear diary: it feels strange to start college. The work is so hard, but I've made new friends. They seem to like me except for teasing me about my scarf. They say I'm like a woman from a southern province and I should throw it away. The mirror tells me to keep it.

**NOVEMBER**

Life is getting strange and confusing. Perhaps if I still went to mass the priest would explain, but I can't now; I'd be too embarrassed to confess. I shall join the Christmas confession queue, and not pretend I'm something I'm not. Sometimes they make stuff up to confess beforehand and natter about it to each other, to try to avoid owning up to anything embarrassing or which would really challenge how they live. "I gossiped behind Mrs So-and-So's back." "I haven't been making my children clean behind their ears." Or the men confess to secret lust. Never physical adultery, (though the priests say that the lust is just as bad). Anything that sounds respectable, but not what they're really thinking or have done wrong.

I can't understand the reports from abroad about Governments being overturned, and Russia is threatened now too. Dad is appalled about what's happening in London. He said that London was the one place in the world that would never have a revolution. He worked there once and he spoke so well of it before. Now though it sounds chaotic.

**DECEMBER**

The changes have come here too and it scares me. The course is changing too. We are learning more genetic science for reproduction. It sounds interesting, but some in the Church is saying it's wrong. How can it be wrong to help people though? Maybe they have got this wrong and the scientists are right after all.

**31 DECEMBER**

Went into St Petersburg to see Ded Moroz and the Snow Maiden. This hasn't been done for years now due to lockdowns. Last time I went there was snow nestling on the onions of the cathedral, but tonight they created artificial snow just over the square. I'm not sure how they did it, but it looks odd with the churches not covered.

## 7 JANUARY 2041

Yesterday was bliss. I ate no food at all until the evening and I felt so much better. There are so many parts of the world where children are underfed that I feel only joy in denying myself what they had no choice in receiving in the first place. The only problem is having to eat today, but I can pretend to be ill or something to get out of it. This morning mum and I went to church. I confessed last night, but I ended up arguing with Father Bulgakov about reproductive science. The church says the scientists are wrong about this; we should just leave it to God to decide. He said it was like the tower of Babel, with man trying to show himself to be as good as God. I am fond of the black priest. He has a wonderful insightfulness, and I always feel good when I'm with him. He is pure and unsullied; completely dedicated to God. I can't agree with him on this though. Surely it's our duty to help eliminate suffering in this world, and if we can do that by getting rid of faulty genes which cause disease or disability, why shouldn't we? But the good father says otherwise, and he's well-spoken of within the church.

In the end I said I agreed with him just to get his blessing, and I don't want to hurt his feelings, but really it was a lie. Then I told him I fasted, but I didn't tell him how much I enjoyed it. He told me it was a sign of my dedication to God. He even said I could be a Saint in the making. Oh dear, if only he knew the truth. I love this priest but I can't help disagreeing with him. Dear diary: in future you will be my confessor. You won't argue back and tell me all my studies are wrong, will you? God knows all, so he knows my diary, doesn't he? The key which keeps this diary locked is no barrier to Him. Let this be my confession and let my bread and wine with family be communion.

## APRIL

I skipped mass today. Dear diary, I said I would confess all to you, so here I am. Will it be only Christmas and Easter? No diary, I shall make a real effort to be more faithful to you.

I am sensing revolution in Russia again now. The communists are regrouping under another name. In reality they are a whole bunch of people, most determined just to get rid of the church and plunder her assets. There are nationalists too. They are saying Russia has given too much ground, that the west is terminally ill, we have fallen behind China, and that the country must change. They say that they will respect democracy and even enhance it, but that society has to change. We have to balance freedoms with the control that a Government of the people needs in order to maintain a healthy and success society. Science builds success. If they're right, I'm going to be very useful to them as a reproductive doctor.

## JUNE

The revolutionaries "New Russia" have swept to power. They operate under a broad coalition. They are inspired by the Soviet era, with central planning and control. Under central command the country was stronger, they say. All the organs of Government are changing, including the ministries and the military. The new ministry of the interior has uncovered shameful behaviour by several priests, including my dear Father Bulgakov. I do hope he's really innocent. How can a man of God do such things?

## JULY

Father Bulgakov has confessed all on state television and the images are now all over the Cloud. It was too awful to watch. To think I confessed to a man who had such secrets. I still feel love and admiration for him but at the same time I can't ignore what he has confessed to. From now on I shall never set foot in church until the day I marry. The one thing I will not do is break my sacred vow to remain a virgin until that time. Maybe, with the work I am doing, it won't even be necessary to marry at all to have children. Maybe instead I will have a child created in hospital and not my body. Surely that would be so much safer, anyway? Only time will tell.

**SEPTEMBER**

England announced it is moving its capital to a city I've never heard of. The process will take two or three years according to the officials. That follows Scotland announcing it is moving its capital to St Andrews, thanks to the international fame of its University. I'm confused about England and Scotland. Is Scotland in England? I'll have to ask Dad. It's all change. The new Government here has been talking of moving the capital too, to Yekaterinburg. I feel greatly honoured. But what is their reason? To commemorate the ancient Christian martyrs or to honour the place of revolution? I am not sure.

**OCTOBER**

I asked Dad about the Scotland–England thing. He told me that lots of people get confused, but if you ever asked that question in Scotland you might not be welcome there much more.

Now it's a whole year since England's revolution (sorry, England and Scotland's revolution), and three months since New Russia came to power. They will leave the capital in Moscow for now. I visited there a few times as a young girl, and it was so exciting seeing the cathedrals and the underground station and Red Square. Since we travel so little these days, I'm not sure when I will next go there.

## NOVEMBER

One more thing. I've started playing a game called *Planets*. I've created an avatar with a white pen as my symbol. It's taking up a lot of my time now. I will of course still find some for you though, dear diary.

## WILL'S LOG BOOK EXTRACT

### Meta data "science museum"

**Reason:** Cancellation of other planned trips due to disruption.

**Data collected:** There are 120 regular and uniform polyhedral, many on display.

**Quote:** "Through pure luck, or another's misfortune, I end up at the Science Museum. I'd love to go every day. The mathematical objects are particularly fascinating. Heaven was interrupted only by a young lady needing directions and carrying no phone who broke my concentration."

★ Meta data "hacked" (text search).

It's happening to everyone and it happened to me. It's horribly frustrating having to get everything back that belongs to me and to prove who I am. They need to devise some of fast hassle-free way of getting your ID back and tracing any money that gets stolen. Maybe I should come up with an idea.

★ Meta data "politics" (text search).

There's a new party in power now. I don't really know much about them but they sound more organised and really living in the twenty first century unlike the others. They understand the way the world is changing, and they know how to address climate change. I'm glad I voted for them. Now we can start to see action not words. This is going to give me the chance

I need to put my science to good use by working for the Government to save the planet.

**Plan:** Apply for work in the climate department.

**Outcome:** Success. I start Monday.

# ACT 1

# CLOUD LIFE

**SCENE SWINDON SPRING 2047**

"We congratulate the Government on finally completing its plans to move England's capital to Swindon. It is the culmination of years of transforming our society from one based on finance, to one based on tech. London will always be the greatest city in the world for culture, but Swindon, lying at the heart of the technology belt, represents all that it means to be successful in the twenty first century. It has been the fastest growing city for the last fifteen years. From being the workshop of the Great Western Railway, through being the pioneer of cable services, to now hosting the Cloud's vital infrastructure, Swindon is the ideal choice. To crown it all, Swindon City have just been promoted to the premiership again. Swindon is truly on the up." Swindon Weekly Advertiser.

Will looked out from his outside window across the new capital with pride. He had one of the best views from this part of the city. He left his top floor flat, rushed down the "M" stairwell, and strolled down to the courtyard below to, briefly, sit and contemplate under the shade of the Japanese cherry tree.

He was lucky to live here. The complex was constructed as a quadrangle during the second Walcot regeneration less than a year ago. It was designed for maximum well-being and minimal energy consumption, in line with the ideals of this age.

"We are proud to present Walcot Lodge in a central location in our soon-to-be capital, with all essential facilities in walking distance. It is almost completely enclosed on all four sides except for a large gate designed for emergency vehicles, above which is space for service rooms and the building control centre. Each ground floor room has a common area for each staircase and could seat four or five comfortably. It has potential for 312 flats, arranged in 26 stairwells lettered A to Z with 12 floors. Ideal for bubble communes. The building is designed to be self-sufficient in power over an annual cycle. Each apartment has the latest technology and outward facing direct drone delivery hatches designed to obviate the need for concierge services. Heaven is complete with shared roof-top gardens to allow you to connect more closely with nature. The perfectly manicured quad garden is complemented by a variety of shrubs, trees, and a sun-dial, a fitting antidote to the modern age and designed to calm the mind. Gardening services are of course included as a part of the annual management fee." So read the agent's marketing literature.

The common areas were deliberately too small for whole bubble meetings in comfort. Instead bubbles were encouraged to use centrally controlled environments, with facilities provided and monitored by the Council. It had the added advantage of encouraging weekly walks to the external bubble meeting location.

Michael had started out at the top of M staircase, normally reserved for a bubble president, with Will as a relative newcomer (he had joined the bubble only a few weeks ago) on the first floor. For some unknown reason, Michael had asked to swap so Will had the prestigious top floor apartment, with the best views and oak panelling. M staircase had an entrance to one of the "heavens." The roof top garden did not cover the entire roof but shared space with solar panels and communications equipment. Each stairwell was occupied by a single 'bubble' or social group. Currently only twenty four of the twenty six stairwells were occupied, with 'J' and 'R' currently not taken. Only complete bubbles were permitted to join under the terms of the planning conditions.

Sometimes Will reflected on the proximity of his apartment to the old Wills factory which once upon a time manufactured cigarettes. "Was it your factory?" he was often asked in jest when he mentioned it to strangers. Not only did he not smoke himself, he didn't even know anyone who smoked now. Indeed it was not even permitted in most private residences; such was the importance of physical health in public life.

The 'head gardener' referred to in the marketing was in fact shared with a few other complexes, and his underlings consisted entirely of garden robots. The gardener's role consisted mostly of setting them to work, fixing them when they went wrong, and dealing with complaints from residents. Will used the quad for exercise but also often went to sit on the bench under the cherry tree to contemplate. Today he had something to actively worry about, and he found the garden focussed his mind in a way his home office could not.

## SCENE ENERGY

Will held a number of roles, but the most prestigious was Swindon Community Energy Coordinator. The task was to forecast short term electricity balances and ensure local energy stocks were sufficient. He had to oversee the control systems and intervene when critical decisions needed to be made on prioritisation in the event that local availability of power was insufficient to meet ideal demand.

Today Will's luck was at a low ebb as indeed was his mood, and with it the more positive side of his nature. His problem was this, that local energy storage levels were especially low. It was a bright day, and the temperature in Swindon had hit 34 centigrade. Solar power was on maximum output but cooling demand from the intense heat today exceeded the very power that was supposed to be generated from the sun's rays by all the panels in the city. The solar irradiance was diminished by a slight haze over the south of Swindon stretching as far as the recently relocated Science Museum.

The system issued an automated notice.

"High risk of demand reduction." All energy users @ 16:34:05.

Will examined the Demand Variance Log. As usual it was the food refrigeration services that were the culprits. Cutting them off would impact food safety.

Air conditioning to residential buildings like his own might need to be rationed. Walcot Lodge had its own power reserves given the elite bubbles residing there, though that information was not well publicised. It consisted of a small hydrogen generator and a very small store of compressed liquid fuel stored below the lawn, and would not last for long.

From the comfort of the garden and his personal communicator, Will took an online poll of large demand users. There was little desire for humans to wilt in the intense heat, potentially causing excess deaths. There was currently a big transport demand for power pods which had to be satisfied if their users were not to be stranded. The train service could not be reduced; that was a reserved central power coordination matter in any case. Will made a decision: limit the local in-cloud processing capability for half an hour. In hot weather the servers managing cloud transactions themselves consumed too much cooling power that could instead be spent on refrigerating food and keeping humans cool. Surely a limited break would not hurt too much? People over profit.

"Demand control imminent for commercial Cloud Servers." Cloud users @ 16:55:23.

First Windmill Hill, then the remaining business parks, ground to a halt.

The communicator rang. "Do you know what you've done; you're costing us over $100,000 an hour in lost business. Can't you cut off residential first?"

"Sorry sir," is all he could muster.

There would be repercussions tomorrow, when business would take to social media.

"Community energy stalls Swindon's economy. If this is how we treat the new capital, I'm emigrating to Norway."

"Quite right mate. What's the point of modern Cloud living if there's no Cloud to live on?"

"They're all stuck up about carbon targets. Blow the climate and let's get our power back."

Tomorrow's another day. The bubble was planning entertainment, and he was desperately in need of diversion. He just hoped that news of the energy consumption of those planned entertainments would not turn out to attract the same kind of social media attention that his decision on power prioritisation had seen.

## MINUTES OF BUBBLE MEETING 14 APRIL 2047

**Bubble name:** Swindon elite 1.

**Proposed Decision 1:** To engage in a virtual Antarctic excursion at the Oasis.

**Proposer:** Will.

**Voting record:** Not unanimous (see risks).

**Timescales:** Not confirmed, but will require a few weeks' planning.

**Rational:** Education on the impacts of climate change.

**Costs:** To be met from central resources.

**Risks:** While virtual, this experience consumes significant amounts of power may be some reputation risk associated, and decision not unanimous.

**Proposed Decision 2:** To engage in a physical trip to Kingsgeld, an off-cloud town.

**Proposer:** Michae.l

**Voting record:** Unanimous.

**Timing:** Imminent subject to confirming booking details.

**Rational:** Education on the dangers of living off-cloud.

**Costs:** Met from bubble members, but expected to be small.

**Risks:** Some risk around contact with locals living off-cloud.

The traditional food and beverage may offend some..

Some carbon emissions through transport, though Kingsgeld is nearby.

## WILL AND MICHAEL

Colonel Michael was trying to get through on the communicator. Was Michael at large or in the complex? Michael and Will had become friends through work before Will joined his bubble. Will called him "Captain" despite Michael's more senior rank. Michael was not only bubble President, but a member of the prestigious Swindon City Council which oversaw all bubble arrangements in the city. Being the capital, the City Council was also the most prestigious Council in England, and tended to trend set. It also virtually hosted the Online Parliament.

Michael was a man with fingers in many pies. Chief among his collaborators was the People's Optical Link Organisation: Military Intelligence National Transmissions (POLOMINT). That was the organisation which tapped into enemy block communications and activities, and worked with the Special Signals Regiment. Global energy intelligence had been added to POLOMINT's remit some time ago and, as a result, Will and Michael had started co-operating professionally over energy issues which had in turn led to Will's invitation to join the bubble.

East-West international borders had been almost completely sealed after the Culture Wars until a few years ago. That hampered all kinds of international cooperation including energy and climate change progress. Michael's work had helped achieved some glasnost with the Russians, building on the work of the Verona Accord. He used not only POLOMINT's cyber skills and military hardware, but also his assets inside the country. Indeed he had been one of the founders of POLO-MINT and the first head of the Russian desk.

"You need to see this," said Michael. "I've been monitoring this for a while."

He showed some footage of operations in a large Siberian peat bog, taken from the UK satellite in stationary orbit above. Will knew instantly what it meant.

"That's shocking. They're draining the bogs ready for peat harvesting. It's been collecting carbon for four hundred years, and now it's about to be released. How dare they do so much damage in such little time. I go to global emissions forums with these guys and they keep such a straight face while all the time they are fooling us."

Will's expression itself became a dark shade of peat.

After a few seconds he added "I'm intrigued about how you got this, the imagery is so sharp." asked Will. "I can even see a spot on that fox."

"We can see everything," replied Michael. "But since you ask, it's a High Orbit Geostationary satellite, or a Spy-sat to you and me. It hovers high over western Siberian. The Russians know we have it, but not how sharp an image we get, or what we can do with the info. If they did, they'd probably construct some kind of countersurveillance capability, but fortunately they don't."

"I see. How would they do that?"

"Probably jam it, or even shoot it down, which of course would lead to retaliation. But the key thing is that it's my job to find out things like this. It should be yours to be interested in it and decide how to take it up with the world energy forum's carbon committee. I'll let you join me up here with the satellite sometime. It's a great view and fun to zoom in on what's going on. But what's important is to hold them to account for their actions, and I know you want to do that too."

"Quite right I do. Did you know that peat stores a third of all soil carbon world-wide?" asked Will.

"Actually I didn't but it makes sense now. I can see why I was tasked with this by the minister. I think we need to meet up in the common area and form a plan of action."

"Right. See you soon."

The military satellite view sounded fantastic. How exciting to be so high and see the dawn ahead of everyone else. He imagined what use he could put such a view to. Will might not be a poet but he was certainly a dreamer, and more often than not he had his head way beyond the cloud; focussed more on shining stars than the golden daffodils which were by now just fading in the borders of the complex's gardens.

They met up in the common room shortly afterwards.

"Remind me how you got your interest in Russia, Michael, and how you started with the military?"

"I spent time in London, including work on detachment with MI6. After a while I needed a break. The place was getting a bit hot for me. So, I quit for a couple of years to play baseball in New York. I was the best Yankee they ever had. After that I came back and rejoined the service starting with a spell in NATO signals," said Michael. "That's when I really got interested in Russian politics, but the background in their culture started earlier."

What he kept quiet about was training with US special forces while supposedly majoring on sports, given that his strong links with the US were not public knowledge.

"One of my great grandparents was Russian," he continued. "I wanted something to do travelling around on trains when I was young, so I read War and Peace."

"Wow."

Michael had one of the most brilliant minds Will had ever come across.

"In Russian."

"Right. I watched the Me-Tube ten minute precis of that one. In English."

"The Russian came in useful," replied Michael.

"How did you learn it? You weren't born in Russia?"

"No. I learnt the best way. It was in London before I first went to the US. I slept with a Russian girl."

Will had no foreign languages. He wasn't that great on body language or romance either, and as a consequence was going to struggle learning new languages with Michael's technique.

"I can't see myself doing that," he said.

"You just need the right knack," replied Michael. "Anyway, it was business as well as pleasure."

"And you learned French too? With a French girl?"

"No she was Canadian. From Quebec but living in the States. That was after the Russian girl got engaged to a guy from back home."

"So was the Canadian business or pleasure?"

"State secret."

"Is it true you were the model for James Bond. Your prowess in life's most important areas seems to suggest it."

Michael reflected.

"Apart from being about a hundred years too late, he got a double first in oriental languages; I got a double third in idling."

"What sort of idling?" enquired Will. "Doubtless a very useful subject."

"Stroking the college first boat by morning and stroking trainee nurses from Addenbrookes by night," replied Michael.

"But what did you graduate in?" asked Will.

"Well I know what I graduated to," replied Michael.

"Yes, and what was that?"

"Trainee doctors at Guys and Tommies. Men's eyes were meant for gazing, after all."

"OK. So how did you get into military intelligence? Casual relationships aren't in fashion right now, as they're seen as a security risk."

"Times have changed since then, and getting in was easy at the time. I was already in the Officer Training Corp. Shortly before

I graduated I had tea with the Master. He had strong links with the service and arranged an introduction. After that I swapped in between intelligence and special forces a few times."

"I see. So you had to avoid Russian doctors during your extra-curricular activities?"

"Only Russian **agents**," replied Michael. "I can spot a honey trap from a mile off. They use them a lot. It's an old trick but it still works."

"There's no way I'd form any kind of liaison with Russians, doctor or no doctor," Will said, not sure in his own mind if he really meant it or not. "Everyone should play by the carbon rules and those who ignore them need to be found out and exposed." He alluded to the draining of peat bogs.

Michael laughed.

"It wasn't just Russians I 'liaised with', and you know you can't equate the people with the Government," replied Michael. "They're good honest and honourable people, mostly. It's just their Government that's corrupt, at least in our reckoning. My job is to make love not war, wherever possible. That's what got us the thaw in relations which in turn has benefitted the economy."

"If you say so," he replied, "though I doubt I'll get the chance to meet any Russians myself. What I really want to know is how you slept with so many women, in the days when you could. Actually I'm curious about how many."

Michael chuckled.

"I can't remember, and the uniform helps."

Will reflected. Michael might have had fun in the past, but at the same time he was not at all comfortable with Michael's casual sexism. It might have been marginally acceptable in the twentieth century, but hardly today, when personal relation-ships were more strictly monitored. And Michael's approach had only worked short-term; he had never been married, and was currently single, as indeed were all the bubble members. Will however wanted more for himself, as he felt his current life incomplete.

## A STRANGE MESSAGE EXCHANGE IN VLADISGRAD

"Miss Zhukova, apologies for having to introduce myself. I am Count Paris."

"Well that sounds rather grand. How do you know me?"

"I know lots of things Miss Zhukova. May I call you Mariya?"

"Of course, but I'm intrigued about what you want to know."

"I am after information about Miss Kotov. You know her?"

"Yes we are old friends and we are in the same Seven Star."

"Of course. Now please tell me how I could win Miss Kotov over? I am an admirer of hers and I am determined to win her."

"Well that would be very difficult. She is quite shy with men, and she is devoted to her work."

"Yes I'm sure. Her shyness just makes me want to try harder. What are her passions?"

"I'm not sure I should be telling you that."

"Why not? Is it a state secret?"

"Well I suppose she likes ballet and poetry and art and all things English."

"And what does she like that's Russian?"

"Other than the ballet? Vodka I believe. I'm not sure why you're asking; it's as if you are a spy of some kind."

"A spy like James Bond perhaps? Thank you Mariya. Yes, that has been most helpful, and yes, I work for the Russian Government. But this is more personal business I am interested in and once again I thank you personally."

## SCENE AT THE COUNTY GROUND

"I've got last minute bubble tickets for the match," announced Michael. "It's Oxford United. Anyone interested?"

Will had never been to see Swindon, and the last football match he watched was at college.

"OK, sounds good. I've lived here long enough without going."

"You interested?" Michael asked Peter.

"No, I have an appointment at the vets for my snake."

Will grimaced. How Peter got permission to keep it was a mystery.

"Right. Just the two of us."

"I can make it," chimed in Ben, who was entering as they were speaking.

"OK. Not many of us, but we'll have to cheer harder then."

Will was quite curious and a little anxious about going. He couldn't name a single player from either side. He wasn't sure how he would cope with the crowds. The three of them walked over together, setting off 15 minutes before their timed entrance. The turnstiles he remembered from his earlier days were replaced by transparent security compartments, each large enough to hold an entire bubble. At the stewards' direction each leader would present their ticket and enter with his bubble, not always the full twelve. Inside the compartment, the system checked the identities and health status of each member present, before releasing the bubble members into the stadium. From there fans could move to their assigned area.

The seating was compact and in sets of twelve. It reminded Will of old fashioned church pews, except that it was the team being worshipped rather than God, and instead of oak, the construction was part plastic part Perspex. The seats would indeed be quite cosy if the sets were fully occupied. However apart from the away fans, most bubbles had one or two members missing which allowed those present to spread out. Will's party consisted of just three of the bubble, so they could space themselves quite comfortably. The pews contained small speakers, designed for announcements and the referee's feed.

The partial separation created by the barriers between the pews did little to dampen the atmosphere. Indeed, since home and away fans were now mixed, there was a good deal of banter. Three nearby pews were occupied by the gold shirts of the opposition supporters. The general commotion was unfamiliar to Will used to a more ordered social and working existence.

First the Oxford United players jogged out from the tunnel, followed by the Swindon team. As the number 9 ran out a very audible hiss emanated from the away supporters.

"He's just transferred to Swindon from Oxford," explained Michael. "He was their star player last year, so they're quite upset."

The match got off to a bad start for Swindon, with an early goal thanks to a defensive error.

"Swindon Town are going down. Swindon Town are going down." The Oxford supporters seemed quite confident.

"I thought they were Swindon City now," remarked Will to Michael.

"No one calls them Swindon City. Swindon Town or the Robins. Never City."

"Oh, I see."

After 20 minutes, Swindon equalised. By the end of the match it was 3-1. If Swindon Town were going down, Oxford wouldn't be helping them there.

Away supporters were allowed out first, to catch their train which was being held for them, but Will's bubble was allowed out soon after.

"I enjoyed that," said Will. "I've never really followed football, but I really started to get behind them at the end. We must do it again."

## SCENE THE WEEKEND IN ST VLADISGRAD

Katerina stared blankly into the air on the pod-bus home from the hospital, before momentarily slipping into slumber, missing the view of her favourite museum, and the world's largest, the Hermitage. She heard only Tchaikovsky in her ear-pods as the lids closed around her tired eyes. Travelling without her virtual reality headset could have given her the chance to enjoy the view. Instead her mind wandered, and in place of the view from the pod-bus her imagination supplied instead human swans over a shimmering lake. At least it was the weekend now and she could be herself.

The week had not gone well. It seemed that she had missed something during genetic matching for two prospective parents both of high social standing. At first she thought it was unimportant, but thinking through she could see the risks of damaging a future human life in a most grievous manner. She knew it would become clearer the following week what the consequences of her actions were, but for now she had to block it out and hope for the best.

Her cat, Oscar, came for some attention as she entered her apartment, before escaping through the cat-hatch and making his way downstairs for exercise. He knew when she needed space; he was that sort of cat, intelligent, empathetic and very affectionate.

She was about to work on her poetry which she wrote by hand in the back of her diary, when she had an incoming message from Mariya.

"I've heard you have a secret admirer," said Mariya.

"No way. No one's remotely interested in me," Katerina laughed.

"It's true; and I believe he's very determined. Remember that time I caught a man trying to kiss you in the library years ago? I think it might be him. He spoke to your father afterwards, you remember? I recall he joked about seeing you two married in St Peters and St Pauls! I think your father was quite taken by him."

"If it's the same bloke then I'm sure he'll find me without me having to look for him. How he made a positive impression on Dad I really do not know. The only impression he nearly made on me was strictly without permission."

Katerina suspected Mariya of keeping tabs on her and secretly relaying information back to her parents as to her welfare. Mariya and her mother certainly talked, though her mother was, sadly, now developing early onset dementia. At the end of the day, though, she trusted Mariya and looked up to her as an older sister.

The next question was: could she tell Mariya about her potential mistake at the hospital? Technically Mariya worked for the hospital too so she ought to report back anything she heard to her superior. However it was very unlikely she would do that. It was slightly more likely she would report back the failure to her mother, who would give her a hard time, and that was infinitely worse. But it was essential to talk, so the risk must be taken.

"I need someone to talk to, do you have time? It's about my job at the hospital. You won't blag if I tell you? Why don't you come round?"

"Sure. If there are problems I need to know, Katerina. I've heard you're doing really well, so I'm sure it's no big deal. The job means so much to you, following in your family footsteps, and you're being recognised. With your dream of going to London to meet your English spy, you'll want everything to go smoothly of course, so let me help if I can."

Katerina laughed loudly.

"You're sounding like mum! Anyway, I can't talk about this online, it has to be face to face."

## SCENE KATERINA'S FLAT

Mariya came round as soon as she could but it took her a bit longer than expected. This gave Katerina time to stop worrying about the problem, rationalising an explanation for her actions. She therefore focussed on her hoped-for trip to London until she remembered she had some old-fashioned entertainment she wanted to experience with friends.

"I've got some illicit English film. James Bond's 'Never Say Never'. It'll teach us all about espionage in London and how to entrap a spy at a casino. You won't tell, will you?" She winked.

"Intriguing," laughed Mariya. "I'd better watch it with you so I can figure out what you're up to. And no, I won't say a word."

They watched uninterrupted.

"I'm definitely not letting you go to London, now," exclaimed Mariya. "Your mother would never forgive me if you got abducted, or worse still came back in love with an English spy."

"It was my Mum who gave me this!" replied Katerina. "I don't think she mentioned it to Dad."

"I've definitely seen a new side to you. I always thought of you as so cerebral."

"Never judge a book by its cover!"

Like English bubbles, the Seven Stars (the Russian equivalent of bubbles) often lived in close proximity. There was a quick confident knock on the door; Sonya from next door called round mid conversation. Katerina was always pleased to see her. With her chipper view of life, she was the perfect antidote to Mariya's more cautious outlook. The two companions complemented each other perfectly.

"Hey, how are you Mariya? Looking out for Katerina I see."

"She's more than capable of looking after herself I'm sure. I was just trying to tease out from her if she had a secret lover."

Sonya turned to Katerina with an expectant look. "I won't tell anyone. I just need to know. Promise!"

Katerina shook her head. "No way. I wouldn't how know to handle one if I did get one."

"Men are so easy," Sonya opined. She opened up her hands as if releasing the secrets of engagement with the enemy. "Your mother should have told you. I understand she had a lot of admirers when she was younger, I'm surprised she didn't have a good mother-to-daughter chat."

Katerina shook her head. Her mother hadn't mentioned anything of the sort to her.

"There are just three rules."

"Go on, I'm curious. You're just finishing your training as a psychologist, so you should know better than us!" said Mariya.

Sonya paused. These words of wisdom were to be taken most seriously.

"I assure you it's all practical training! First, a man is right even when he's wrong. Never contradict him. It's better he makes his own mistakes or find things out for himself than for you to tell him, because that would wound his pride."

It flew in the face of her instincts as a scientist and doctor, but she listened carefully.

"Second you need to show some kind of vulnerability. Make him think he's needed and he can help you. Make him feel that by looking after you he's being a real man."

"They both sound like lying a bit," replied Katerina.

"It's all sound practice, I assure you," replied Sonya. "Finally, remember men are turned on by what they see, not by what they hear."

"I see."

"They're so easy to get to bed if you know how, they think with their instincts not their brains," she continued. "Keeping them there is the harder bit. I would give you some lessons, but I'm not so good at the last bit."

"Oh dear, you really are a bad influence on Katerina," remarked Mariya. "I think what you meant to say is that your technique is ideal for attracting the fleeting attention of shallow and unsuitable male candidates."

"Better keep her away from me then," grinned Sonya. "I wasn't even born legitimately. Rumour has it my mother was one of the FSB's honeypot girls. We have it in our genes!"

They all laughed.

"One more piece of advice, this time from me," added Mariya. "Never marry anyone who works for the British state or even has friends in military intelligence. You won't have long to live!"


## ODE TO SPIES

Secrets are your stock in trade
Willing traitors getting paid

Philby, Burgess, Blunt and Blake
You were all a big mistake.
Many are not who they seem
Playing for the other team.
What's the impact of the spooks?
Atomic secrets Herr Klaus Fuchs.
Do we have here eyes and ears,
Feeding info through the years?
Who can be this new young suitor?
Handy with his old computer.
All is clear in just a while,
When we meet his cunning guile.

## SCENE A PUBLIC HOUSE IN KINGSGELD

Next Sunday was special. The bubble met outside the Congregation (bubble meeting rooms) at noon. Their transport, the "BubBus", appeared (so named as it could carry a whole bubble safely and in comfort). Will dutifully queued to join, finding a pod near the back.

The destination was an ancient nearby town, Kingsgeld, which had separated itself from the Cloud some time ago. The town was dwindling of course, and younger residents were being given the chance to join civilisation provided they committed to Cloud Protocols and joined a bubble.

It was only twenty minutes by road, but it seemed a lifetime as he gawked out at the unfamiliar environment.

The journey itself was on simple country roads and passed the old golf course. At an average of twenty miles per hour, they overtook two slow-moving pods and eight cyclists en-route, not to mention a couple of pedestrians. It did feel odd for Will after more than two years of not leaving Swindon at all. Ten years ago this would have been an unremarkable journey. He got used to staying within the city during the most recent lockdown, and just couldn't find a reason to travel. Once out of the city, that sense of freedom of being Not-in-Swindon elated him. The memories of many car and train journeys returned from where they had been locked up these last few years. He would travel again, and further afield, when opportunity presented.

The Busbus stopped at an open area surrounded by old-style houses. People were walking freely around in small groups, not caring about social distancing and without personal protective equipment. There was a strange lightness to the place, not at all what he expected when travelling off-cloud. Will had felt a little anxious at first, which contrasted with the town's residents' calm and relaxed demeanours.

"In line," shouted Michael. It could have been square bashing. "We have exactly one hour until lunch. Do not approach strangers too closely here; they are well intentioned no doubt but you can't be sure of their infection status. Without identifiers, we don't know who they are. Remember there are no facilities here and we won't eat until we get to the pub. And stay in sight. You should not use your cloud communicators here except in emergencies. It's the off-cloud protocol for this area."

"But the phones still work?" asked Will.

"Yes. Everyone needs a phone, Will. It's just that here there are protocols about how and when to use them."

"Don't listen to Michael," whispered Tim. "It's perfectly safe. I've been here before several times, alone, and I'm still alive. Just because central authorities don't know who they are through online verified identification, doesn't mean they're not all very pleasant people."

Kingsgeld was dominated by an historic building once the scene of action in a Culture War, that had resulted in a temporary halt to the monarchical Government. Enemy troops used it to shield themselves while under siege, and the building still retained a cannon ball fired at them, which it had put on display. Will wandered inside it with curiosity in what seemed to him an alien world. A church building, and an old one at that. More memories came flooding back.

**EXTRACT FROM WILL'S LOGBOOK:**

## Meta data "church"

**Church visit date:** February 2039.

**Temperature:** 6 degrees C.

**Reason:** College function.

**First impression:** Why is it so cold and dark?

★

**Church visit date:** April 2047.

**Temperature:** 30 degrees C.

**Reason:** Off-cloud cultural expedition.

**First impression:** What a great way to keep cool without the use of air conditioning.

## ST MICHAELS

The church appeared to be named after the bubble leader, undoubtedly the reason for choosing this place for an Out-Cloud away day. None of the bubble had strong religious views, with the possible exception of Rose and Peter who were stout atheists.

"Kingsgeld was once larger than Swindon," explained Michael, "but when it rejected Modern Living people drifted away, as the residents saw the benefits of a better way of life."

Will puzzled over this; from what he could see of the town it was unlikely ever to have had more than sixteen thousand inhabitants even before the second Culture War.

"Now be careful. Don't touch anything, don't speak to anyone, and keep your distance from the Outsiders and Refuseniks. Don't make eye contact until we eat. Last year we had to reprimand someone who is sadly no longer with us. Afterwards we will eat in a traditional English pub. It's safe — it's been cleared and cleaned. Protection still on of course, until you actually eat.

We have a portion of the pub sectioned off. They operate semi-cloud for ordering, to cater for visitors like us, so submit your choices in advance on the Bubble Trip Communicator. It's the only thing you'll use that device for this afternoon."

"Don't worry captain," said Tim. "There'll be no need for heroics to save us from predatory Refuseniks. I do believe some of the good inhabitants of this distinguished town journey to Swindon to work, and assist us Cloud citizens with many tasks our modern technology has so far failed to automate with any degree of success."

"It's a perfectly valid choice, for those who choose to believe it," observed Peter, also like Tim on the political left.

"The issue here is about choosing to co-operate against common threats or choosing to face them in isolation," replied Michael. "No man is an island. Yes they may do some work for us, but without fully integrating we can't trust them because we don't know them. That's always going to make things more difficult. It's not that these people are inherently bad but by not co-operating with us we can't know as much about them and therefore can't trust them in the same way."

Wisely, no one challenged him.

They filed carefully out, Will last. He noticed a strangely dressed young woman approaching. She looked like a period actress from some nineteenth century romance, except that she was not wearing a bonnet or hat of any kind, which allowed him to observe her shoulder-length curly red hair. Heading for the church, she carried not a personal communicator but a black book. The others were just in sight but moving at pace. Curious, he thought he would attract the woman's attention.

"A present for you," he presented her with a daisy plucked from the long grass.

The girl blushed. "You're from Swindon? Are you sure you should be talking to me socially? I thought you were taught social distancing from those outside the cloud when in non-cloud areas?"

"Have we met before?" he enquired, a dim recollection of her features coming back to him.

"I don't think so. Should I remember you?" she replied.

Physical distance had to be maintained. Will walked on, hoping not to get left behind with potentially awkward explaining to do.

The bubble rested at a park and drank coffee.

"What do you think, do you find it scary?" asked Tim.

"Guess so. More weird than scary. It's so close to Swindon but it could be on a different planet."

"They say this triggered Jack, the guy who killed himself last year, but I don't believe it. I've come several times on my own and there's nothing to be concerned about," said Tim. "It's just a fiction to keep us grateful for being Cloud Citizens and to keep us where we can be monitored more easily."

Will didn't see how being off-cloud for a few hours could trigger anyone either, but what did he know?

He sauntered back towards the church, where the young woman was coming out. He noticed again the lightness of spirit, the living in the present, and her infectious laugh. She was a real head-turner. He became immediately conscious of his somewhat unkempt appearance and recalled he had not shaved for two days.

"You again! I thought you had gone back to Swindon," she said.

"Soon. I want to explore more."

"Oh it's dangerous here, you wouldn't want to come back." Now she was really teasing.

"I could come back for you," he replied.

Her eyes popped out at this one.

"No, you really wouldn't. You have far too exciting a time, living on cloud and doing anything you want."

Will paused, looking slightly stunned.

"So, tell me what you do?" she continued.

"I'm a community energy co-ordinator. Government job. Represent England on some international committees."

"I see. What exactly does that entail?"

"Oh, it's quite complicated, I'm sure you wouldn't enjoy the detail."

"Oh, is that right? How can you be so sure?"

He hadn't expected that response and now he was on the back foot. The tactic of avoiding technical and complex conversations hadn't worked. So, he changed the subject.

"Can I be so bold as to ask your name?" he enquired.

"Why would you need that?" she asked.

"No reason," he said, admitting defeat. He sensed already whatever he felt for her was unrequited. "I trade carbon as well," he added weakly, more in desperation.

"You trade carbon? Is that coal or diamonds? Do you go down a mine to do that?"

"Diamonds." He winked.

"I'd love to see them, but maybe another time." She paused. "Just in case you ever need to know, the name's Rosaline," she added.

"Quite a beautiful name."

"Well thank you. And you are?"

"Will."

"Will. As in the last testament, a commitment to future action, or just short for William? It's quite a versatile name. Are you versatile?"

"It's short for William Green. I traded twenty billion dollars' worth of carbon last year," he said. "Green by name and green by nature."

"How interesting but am I meant to be impressed? What did you gain, apart from money?" she asked. "Did you get in touch with your inner self? Did you find peace? Now I see you again, I think perhaps we have met before. Didn't you send me in the wrong direction in the museum when I was a student in London?"

Will had forgotten. This was not going well.

"You looked too preoccupied with your little models. I'm surprised you even had time to notice me."

The prospect of certain defeat in love has no deterrent effect on an ardent young man, but the actuality of defeat is quite devastating. She had completely captivated him in five minutes; no girl had managed to do that before. Yet she seemed utterly unattainable. Retreat was required. She had the better of him in every way.

His communicator alarm went and, saved by the bell, he made his excuses.

## SCENE A BITTER EXPERIENCE

They reconvened at The Highwayman, Will dejectedly following his cousin Ben. He knew Ben had graduated from online games developer to POLOMINT and worked with the military closely, often with Michael. Ben had overheard the unfortunate encounter with Rosaline, but chose to say nothing in front of the others.

They had been given instructions on traditional eating habits. The ordering may have been cloud-based but the food came with real-life waiting personnel, not the robot service more common in Swindon in the limited number of hospitality venues which were still open.

A dog sat in the corner asleep. When the party came in, he looked up and started licking his nether regions. Dogs love having sex, but they never fall in love, reflected Will. It was like their eating habits; completely transactional. Life must be so much simpler for them.

What no-one in the party except Richard and Michael had grasped was how long this rather traditional process of eating a meal would take to complete. Not only did they have to sit, but communicators were completely banned during the meal except for ordering, and the food took an age to come. For Will, it was reminiscent of formal hall at college, only in rather less grand surroundings. The venue was perfectly legal in its semi-off-cloud existence, but appeared to be too small for effective social distancing. He had grown accustomed to very different social habits over the last seven years with waves of pandemics and social control. Where was the sense of personal space?

Will's food, when it eventually arrived, consisted of several slices of what was described as beef, which came in a giant "Yorkshire Pudding." He had ordered a novel vegetable choice including Jerusalem Artichokes, at Tim's recommendation. The food was heavy and hard to digest. The party were brought glasses of brown liquid described as "bitter." Will took one taste and pushed the glass away. There were much better ways to imbibe alcohol.

Inevitably one of the bubble discussion points aroused rancour.

"Do please keep your murderous products out of smell's reach," complained Tim to Richard, even though they were at opposite ends of the table. "When I agreed to come I didn't realise I'd be so close to meat I could smell it."

Tim was a vegetarian, though not a vegan. He made up for in dairy what he lacked in natural meat.

"All good and natural. Perfectly good for you. As long as you don't have it done burnt," Richard responded. Maybe it was the sight of slightly pink meat on Richard's plate which caused most offence.

The dog strolled round and stopped at Will. He bent down to stroke him, and the dog licked his face. Fortunately no one else noticed. He would have reached to his pocket for disinfectant, but for fear of drawing attention to the hygiene mishap.

"I was just pointing out that once used to be a cow," said Tim.

"The milk in your coffee came from a cow too," replied Rose, who usually said little in these debates.

Many thought her moody and introspective, yet others felt intimidated by her not least by her physical height and acerbic wit.

"The cow wasn't murdered in order to give it up, though," retorted Tim.

"The cow didn't want to give up her milk. She wanted her calf to drink it. You might want to think about that in your cheese course."

Sometimes allies could be so annoying. Tim scowled but nothing was going to separate him from nice mouldy cheese. Neither would anything separate him from a discreet indoor herb collection consisting mostly of hemp which he often shared with Rose. It was of course legal if disclosed, just disapproved of. Michael knew and himself disapproved strongly, but did nothing.

"The cow didn't suffer to give me this milk or my cheese. What I meant was, with our visors off and taste buds fully open, I just don't want to be anywhere near your meat-eating. I wasn't calling Dick a murderer," said Tim. "A highwayman, perhaps?"

"Actually Tim, that is quite close to what you did say," noted Peter, who like Rose was usually on Tim's side. Tim scowled.

"Each to their own but I'm the only one licensed to kill round here," added Michael as he wolfed down his rib-eye steak.

"What choice of single malts do you have?" Tim enquired.

"It depends what takes you fancy," replied the bartender. "We have an eighteen year old Laphroaig or a twelve year old Auchentoshan. I think we have more in store. Shall I check for you?"

He ended up with a twenty four year old Talisker. Liquid nectar never fails to please.

After two pints of the bitter Will had so detested, Michael loosened a little. "It's an acquired taste," he explained to Will.

"Best rib-eye I've enjoyed since Buenos Aires," he said. "And that was thirty years ago."

"Where's that?" asked Will.

Michael chucked. "It's in the Argentine. I went there as junior advisor after the second Falkland conflict to negotiate a long-term settlement. Stayed on after to explore South America. Took in Ecuador, Bolivia, Peru and Chile."

"So which was your favourite?" asked Will.

"Peru without a doubt. We white-water rafted down the Urumbamba before jungle trekking. My party came off another raft in a small jungle lake and faced down predatory caiman before getting safely to shore. By the time we rejoined civilisation my skin had been half eaten away by sandfly."

An experience Will had no desire to emulate, not that anyone could travel like that these days.

"After that I met up at Cuzco with the guys from Task Force Green. We had a merry evening in the Cross Keys and hit on a plan. We would race. The first to finish the Inca Trail, running."

"And, who won?" enquired Will.

"I was the first of our group" replied Michael.

"How long did it take?"

"I took nine hours," replied Michael "and got taken straight to hospital with exhaustion. The rest got lost. The guide who was pace setting thought they were all following me."

"So the guide didn't get lost then." Will was curious.

"Oh no. He'd done it himself the previous week in five hours. I heard since he'd got it down to four and a half."

"Goodness. What's the record?"

"Three hours forty five minutes. Anyhow, after I recovered I made it back to Lima to treat myself. It was fiesta time and they love to party. I found a free local guide to the city for the next few days. A really lovely girl."

"Racist and sexist," chimed Tim. "You were just exploiting your western privilege to undercut the professionals and get a cheap lay."

"What would you have done then?" asked Michael.

"Talking of girls, I spotted you with Rosaline," said Tim, turning to Will.

Will reddened. "Is there anyone who didn't?"

"You won't get anywhere with her," Tim continued.

"How come?"

"She's of the order of St Clare," Tim declared.

Will looked puzzled.

"Heterosexual but closed," whispered Michael in his ear. "Religious."

"How come you know so much about her," asked Will.

"That's my business," retorted Tim. "I'll just admit to having received the same brush-off as you."

"It does strike me that perhaps we do know some of these off-cloud people after all," observed Rose.

Michael frowned. "Well, we might think we know them, but we can't prove we know them, and that's what counts."

This could be another contentious one.

"Tell me about how we ended up on jury service," asked Will, changing the subject quickly. Michael could reveal too much after a couple of pints despite his background. "I hear we've got a case coming up we have to adjudicate on, to determine if an avatar is real or ghost."

"As yes, the Artificial Intelligence test," said Michael. "It's an important aspect of Cloud security. Ghost IDs can be hijacked by cyber criminals too easily, so we need a way to eliminate non-natural entities."

"A guy from the forerunner of POLOMINT came up with the method last century," said Ben. "Name of Turing. Bright bloke but gay and the Russians saw him as a threat to their encryption so they assassinated him with cyanide. Put it in his apple, or something."

"You can't poison an apple," objected Rose.

"It seems they found a way," said Michael. "Devious people some of them."

"But why did he invent the trial system?" asked Will.

"No idea. Anyway, they tried to make it look like suicide, but we weren't fooled."

Death: murder, suicide or accident; how can we be sure? Ben thought he knew but chose to stay silent.

Before they departed Will noticed the dog bounding out of the pub. He appeared to pause on the long grass by the pavement, holding out his tail straight, before nonchalantly sauntering back into the pub.

He had recovered his energy following lunch and he wanted to find Rosaline again. The ambience of The Highwayman must have lulled his common sense into forgetting the emphatic nature of her discouraging signals.

"I'm running back to Swindon. Ben's in charge." announced Michael as they were getting on the BubBus. Will was aghast at the thought of Michael trying to run slightly inebriated. He guessed he did it because the military took daily medical checkpoint data. Those not in the military only got them monthly.

"I'll run back too." What Will really wanted was to return back on his own steam and own time, to give himself a second chance of seeing her without the distraction of potential viewers of an uncertain exercise. Failing that, it was a good way to get over his rejection.

Michael gave Will a look; nonetheless Will had been a fair runner in the past.

Everyone else filed on and got back uneventfully. Before they left, Michael reminded them to prepare for the next trip: Antarctic on Ice. Touring virtually from the comfort of the Oasis.

"I've heard it's unpleasantly realistic," commented Tim.

"I've heard it consumes more power for one experience than the average Swindonian uses in a year," chipped in Rose.

"Just remember to wrap up warm," were Michael's final words on the subject.

"I'll just warm up now with a jog round the square," announced Will.

"Be quick then."

The Bubbus set off, minus two of its original occupants.

Will jogged around looking out for the girl, but she wasn't to be seen, so five minutes later they set off together. Will, despite being out of form, managed to get back to Walcot Lodge just ahead of Michael.

"Well done," Michael acknowledged. "You should have joined the military. I'm glad I'm exempt annual fitness tests now."

"No thanks. I'll leave that to you guys."

Ben caught up with Will in the common area after Will's shower.

"Didn't quite work out this afternoon then?" he ventured.

"She was captivating yet unattainable. So frustrating."

"That's the risk you take going off-cloud. You may see things you want but you can't get. You know in your head it's totally impossible but your head hasn't told your heart. You can't leave the cloud and she won't join it. She knows that, and you do too really. She was being kind to you by not leading you on and you should have seen that."

Will jolted at this, but deep down he knew it was true. Surely in life there is no greater torture than unrequited love.

That night Will dreamt about her amid waves of extreme indigestion. He slept on and off. The next few nights weren't great either. That was Will's first trip to an English pub, and rather left him wondering how it was that the tradition had become so popular. As it happens, it wouldn't be his last, but it had been his last pint of old England's traditional beer.

### ODE TO UNREQUITED LOVE

Let me have the ball and chain
Let me have that full-on pain
Spare me not the wooden rack
Breaking bones within my back
Spare me just a broken heart
When from her I must depart.

### SCENE A STRANGE MAN IN ST VLADISGRAD, APPEARING SUDDENLY

Vladischat was safe, or meant to be. Only members of St Vladisgrad Seven Stars were permitted to join; all citizens committed to the motherland. She signed on to read her secure messages.

The typical ones bored her intensely. Despite her many female friends and interests, Katerina did not feel contented in life and Vladischat was anodyne, though she still used it. It was not a lover she longed for but an escape from the intellectual prison that was the Russian Seven Star System. She needed someone or something completely different. The Church was different, but for now not her thing. All else was conformity.

Today there was a new invitation to chat and from a man. It was perhaps not that unexpected for a childless unattached female such as herself to get approaches from men. Childless meant potential parent, and the laws of nature usually require one of each natural gender, not to mention the state permissions required by the law of the land. These chats were usually monitored for social and political compliance. So an approach from this "Nik" she had already heard about, was not unexpected, though not entirely welcome all the same. Was he the secret admirer that Mariya had mentioned? If so, was he none other than the impertinent man from the library all those years ago? Mariya had thought so. Other than being a St Vladian, she knew nothing about him. Would he prove too intelligent and urbane? Reluctantly she accepted the chat request.

"How can I help you today?" she enquired.

"Let me introduce myself. I am Nicholas and am descended from Tsar Nicholas himself," declared Nik.

Intelligent possibly, but he wasn't the most modest of suitors.

"I'm not sure how I can help you with that. I work in reproductive medicine, not history or genealogy. But as a matter of interest, how come your family survived the first Russian culture war, let alone the second?"

The events of 1917 were referred to in Russia as the first culture war while those in the UK and US had somewhat different interpretations of that phrase.

"We'll come to that question of how you can help me soon enough," he replied. "You certainly have what I need. But to answer your question, my family fled to London where we had business interests. Then we moved to Paris. We made money to replace some of what we lost. We helped Vlad get to power and got wealthier as a result. We came back, richer than when we fled."

"And now?" she enquired.

"I'm in Cyber warfare for the Government, and doing well. Also I'm on track for the Vlad Council. I have some powerful connections."

The Council of Vladisgrad was prestigious. Only senior members of the party achieved that. The Council itself was the second or third most prestigious in Russia, and took turns to host the National Assembly.

"I imagine you have come to me as a suitor. So tell me, are you permitted to have children, and if so how many?" she enquired.

"I have wealth and connections. I can choose with whom I have children and how many. I am of course very careful only to choose as co-parents those with real potential."

"Ok. How do I fit in with that?" she replied. Did he have connections at the hospital she wondered? Perhaps she should be cautious.

"Drink with me," was the simple reply, "let me get to know you." By which he meant, of course, in the virtual sense, given the current regime of social control.

Ten minutes later the best Belenkaya arrived in a miniature bottle at her hatch complete with a glass. This strange man had no need to enquire as to her location; he clearly knew all about her. She dared not question how. At least he had style and class.

When her bottle came she poured it out while he watched. They slammed it down together, old style. "Is this allowed?" she enquired. Surely a prospective Council member would know the rules. "We may be meeting online but it seems too much like a date, and as you know they have to be authorised."

"It's all allowed for me."

"But we can't actually meet, without a good reason or permission."

Nik grimaced. "Yes we can meet. Permission can be obtained. Events of mutual interest take place all the time and we might just bump into each other. It just takes patience. Trust me, and we can enjoy each other's company in privacy and person just as much as we wish."

She decided, somewhat reluctantly, to trust him.

"And again," he ordered. The second one arrived at her hatch at breakneck speed and was downed as fast as the first. There's time for the third too ...

It was nearly 10pm. Time for *Planets*.

"I need to go," she said. "I have a game-date."

"Ooh. Which game?"

"*Planets.*"

"And let me guess; you joined seven years ago when it was free, when the authorities permitted anyone to join without registering with them?"

She blushed. He seemed well informed.

"I want to see."

"It's private."

"Well, let me take control of your login and see what I can do for you. I'm told I'm rather good at it."

Katerina gasped with astonishment. That was definitely illegal.

"Are you sure you need to do that?" she replied. "What exactly are you planning to do?"

"Would I hurt you, when I'm on track for the highest office in the city?"

Put that way, it seemed churlish to refuse.

Another bottle arrived and several glasses more were consumed. Nik appeared not to slur his words. She saw him drinking, but could she be sure it was real drink? She began to lower her guard, revealing more of her online identity.

"I still need the credentials," he retorted.

She hesitated. But, this was Vladischat, he must be safe. These calls were monitored, weren't they? If there was an attempt at subterfuge surely online security would intervene? Somewhat nervously she revealed her authentication for the game.

"Nice," he replied. "You have achieved the status of Red Queen on Oberon I see. You have done well. Such a fine position and not long to go until you get to earth on your chosen path through the game. But personally my taste is White Russians not Red Queens."

"Thank you." This man was either the business, or arrogant and had no idea of his place. Which was it? If he really was white Russian nobility it could explain his arrogant behaviour. That very conduct explained the need for the Red Russian revolution in the first place.

"So, you work in reproductive science. How interesting."

She nodded. "Reproductive medicine, with plenty of time for research."

He nodded.

"I can help you if you help me," he continued.

"So, how do I help you? What do you want? I really do have to go very soon. Anyway, how do you know what I need?"

He might be an admirer of hers, but she was not becoming an admirer of him. So far Katerina had not warmed to this man at all.

"Oh, I think you have a few little issues at work you need fixing. But what a shame that you need to go - I was enjoying getting to know you," he assured her. "I really want more time with you. Free tomorrow at the same time?"

"I suppose so."

"Excellent. See you then."

He disappeared. Katerina was not looking forward to a second round with him tomorrow. How come he knew what she did? She was wary. She would definitely not be drinking next time.

She went into the kitchen and pulled her sharpest knife out. She toyed with it in her hand, pressing the flat edge onto her left forearm, before putting it back in the drawer.

She awoke in the middle of the night from a dream. A brown bear had rampaged the camp killing a red giant, and she was being blamed for it. She saw a vision of herself being thrown down a deep well and blacking out. Pinching herself, she logged back into the game just to assure herself it was a dream and not reality. All was well, at least for now.

## SCENE SWINDON BUBBLE MEETING

It was Sunday again and that familiar routine. He was up by 10am, and took a short walk to the meeting rooms. As usual he placed the communicator in the locker, washed his hands, checked in his bio (weight, urine sample and breath-test), and found his space at the bubble meeting.

The twelve met almost on time. The register was duly taken. Everyone had their own role.

"I'd like to open this meeting, which has a special consultation meeting added on to the normal agenda. The purpose is to introduce the latest Reproductives Bill. This proposed legislation is designed to meet the Block's social and environmental responsibilities through the safeguarding of the next generation. The aim is to bring in stricter licensing of reproductive activities." With these words Michael opened the meeting.

Tim (the lawyer and disabled access officer) was first off. He usually was. The most outspoken of all of them, he was a passionate social justice warrior, a man of fine speech, who nonetheless had sometimes irked the authorities in the past with vaguely disguised political literature. He had been suspected of Russian sympathies, latterly disproved. He somehow managed to end up on the winning side in the end, demonstrating quite acute political skill. As a committed vegan earlier in life he was now more relaxed in his diet, permitting himself fish and dairy products, and self-described as vegetarian or pescatarian. He had become a pioneer of sustainable food and credited by many with changing social attitudes. He had indeed pioneered the development of the bubble system, from one purely focussed on security and public health, to one with a far broader social remit. Despite his drive and contribution he could be a little pompous and it was thanks to this characteristic that he was not the leader of this group,

Tim had also been responsible for the Federal Bureau of Honesty as an additional measure to ensure the integrity of cloud identifications, prevent identity theft, and keep alive cloud citizenship which could not now be achieved without bubble membership. It was the link between that organisation and the bubbles which would soon give rise to the Turing Test, as this elite bubble would at a future date be asked to decide on the truth of a fact. Before that, there would be important democratic business to attend to, and Tim stood to deliver his speech using his considerable oratorical skills.

"It is a hard thing to legislate against our natural inclinations. Kings may pass laws but they cannot easily police the insides of homes. The world may be heating up, over-crowded and too loud, but which of us wants to compromise, especially when it comes to our families? Now I ask you, in passing responsibility for licensing parenthood to a black box AI program, are we not breaching the basic human right to reproduce and indeed the right of an unborn child to life? What of those unborn children conceived naturally, who will as a result of some potentially flawed computer program be terminated before birth? This proposed legislation must be stopped immediately before passing into law."

"I agreed with the previous socialist Government that the nuclear family unit needed to be challenged, to be broken up. It represented a hang-over from tribal culture. It risks perpetuating those basic instincts when it is society's job to engineer them away. I agree the next generation should grow up in an educational environment free of such influences. But I can't agree with deliberately using science to select a genetic characteristic for what the state regards as good. Which of course is to say what does "good" really mean?" agreed Peter. "Are not all AI programs really just a reflection of the programmer's bias, or at least of the bias in the data on which the program was trained? This is a dishonest piece of legislation and we should heartily reject it."

"We have to rally against this racist piece of legislation. Designing babies, our future, DNA by DNA will just lead to identikit societies. Who wouldn't want the perfect offspring if you're only allowed one? Who is really to say what the perfect offspring is in twenty years' time? Our world has changed so much for the better in the last two decades, who's to say it won't change again, for the worse, in the next two? It's Darwinian Eugenics by a new name." Tim pressed his point further home.

That, however, did not mean all moral matters were settled.

"Not at all," countered Will. "Do you want to perpetuate pain and misery? How could you bear to tell the parents of a young person born with a congenital condition, that they could have had a normal child, but for your hopeless idealism. That we could have cured them at a time when it was still possible but we failed to do so due to these sensibilities?"

"Trust you to support the Government," said Tim. "You might as well belong to the ruling party."

"Our Will is a Pillar of the establishment," snarked Peter.

Will ignored him. Peter and Tim would continue to push their line until everyone agreed with them.

The elite bubbles were never chosen for political uniformity. That was the point. A sufficient degree of social control could be exerted even within a wide permitted spectrum of views.

"We have to think of the greater good too," said Michael. "The Cloud looks after us, but we have a duty to support the principles it upholds. It is a part of the responsibilities that we accepted as cloud citizens when we took the pledge."

This last remark did not go down well with everyone. There was significant room for disagreement on what the pledges actually meant.

"I'm sick to death of these changes and proposals." Richard, the Food Officer, could be guaranteed to take the argument down a notch when it got too heated. "I recall the days when you could just go to a pub and meet a nice girl, maybe she would move in, get married, all that. Under these rules we have to get an online permit before even going on a date, and if you do get together you get told whether or not you can have children. Dreamed up by clever civil servants and 'Anti Human Rights Barristers'. It's pathetic. Let's cancel all the lawyers."

Richard was no academic nor was he eloquent of speech. He lacked Michael's charisma and looks, but he still spoke from the heart. There was never any love lost between him and Tim or Peter, or Rose for that matter. He had been invited to the group for his business acumen, but in many other ways he did not belong. Effectively coerced into the Cloud, he would have preferred a simpler life, but was bright enough to know where his interests lay. He had started life as a sheep farmer in Wales but now operated in the Wessex food processing industry making widespread use of the genetically modified crops he had previously opposed. At least he knew which side his GM bread was buttered. It was that skill, rather than erudition, which had merited his place here.

"I'm sensing mixed feedback here. Remember, the Russians are doing it," replied Michael. "It's one of many changes they are making in their utopian society. Every day we track their satellites and drones; air land and sea and we monitor their state communications. We see and hear everything they do and thanks to some good intelligence we know what they're thinking and planning. They keep improving and they are starting to out-manoeuvre us. They are intent on gaining superiority over us within a generation, and they intend to use controlled parenting and genetic techniques as just one of their techniques to achieve those goals. They didn't get technical advantages in their world from sitting back and letting the dullards take over, and they don't always stick to international rules. If anyone thought they had a moral compass on climate change, I have enough evidence to the contrary not far from the Ural mountains, which I've already shared with one member here."

Will nodded.

"Well if you're backing offspring limits, I sincerely hope that you don't have any secret children we don't know about," commented Tim. "I'd hate for you to be exposed as a hypocrite."

"None I know of."

"And the ones you don't? How about that Fanny from South America?"

"She had my details and I never heard. Anyway, all legislation only applies to the future, not the past. You should know that as a lawyer."

They voted in secret and finished the meeting. There appeared to be a majority in favour, so that was one elite bubble in favour, at least. All except Richard stayed on for coffee and chat, now that the formal business of the bubble was complete. It was the informal side, while not mandatory, that provided some of the most valuable benefits, just as the common area was one of the most valuable areas of Walcot Lodge. It was where members dropped their guard, and where Michael could make the most observations of his flock. All physical bubbles did the same; those lower level bubbles which were unable to meet in person and which did not live together had less prestige, and consequently had far fewer privileges. It was the physically co-habiting ones which attracted most attention, were most difficult to get into, and which provided the most benefits, particularly as far as employment advantage was concerned.

Ironically, caffeine itself was a "monitored product." Not illegal, but its consumption was reported on the individual health records for central review. Ignoring a warning to cut down adversely impacted social credit, while, on the other hand, its consumption at bubble meetings was positively encouraged as a stimulant to conversation.

## SCENE COFFEE AND COMBAT

"How did you get on today in Iraq?" enquired Ben of Michael, just as sipped their coffees.

"Not bad; took out twelve Daesh fighters. No damage to western block assets. Possibly some collateral, but we're still trying to assess."

"You mean innocent Arab by-standers, don't you?" demanded Tim. "And as for operations against Daesh, you aren't always that successful are you? Last week you admitted you lost twenty drones against them with only one confirmed kill their side. Why is it we have so much against them?"

Will knew this last statement to be true; last week Michael was in a particularly poor temper for no apparent reason. He arrived slightly late and left bang on the hour, not even staying for coffee; somewhat welcome given his mood that day.

"I have some news about our military strategy against Daesh, for anyone that's interested. We're moving to autonomous kill next week," said Michael. "That will improve our efficiency and reduce losses."

Despite their friendship, Will was taken aback. He understood that algorithmic killing had been banned in war by the Second Geneva Convention ten years ago, even before the culture wars and before the technology was mature. Had it been employed during the culture wars it might have led to Total World War. Algorithmic killing was outlawed against not only humans, but also against declared civilian personal Cloud data centres. Online life was valued as much as carbon-based existence in these military engagement  rules.

"Is this legal?" he asked.

"The Tech Lawyers say yes. Daesh have never ratified either the first or second Geneva Convention," argued Michael. He had no time for lawyers; he was a fighter pure and simple. "That means we don't have to follow the conventions in war against them."

"So, how does that work? How can you be sure you're tar-geting the enemy? What if you hit innocent non-combatants and peace-lovers by mistake? That would be deeply immoral and very stupid," enquired Rose, the women and non-binary officer.

"We're confident we won't."

"How can you be so sure?"

"State secret," replied Michael. He wasn't going to reveal how good his surveillance satellites were.

The debate between the two would continue for some time.

"We have a right to know," demanded Tim. "We're not going to just take your word for it. That's been done before with disastrous results. Just look at political history from earlier this century."

"Well, I could tell you, but I'd have to kill you after." Michael's stock answer.

"It's disingenuous to say Daesh haven't ratified the convention so we can do what we like. In point of fact given Daesh have not been recognised as a state they had no opportunity to sign and therefore the exclusion of non-ratifiers cannot apply. Anyway, that decision has to be brought before the bubbles for a democratic vote."

"Afraid not. The Supreme Law Council has ruled, and it sits above the vote of the people. It doesn't constitute a qualifying change of law. You of all people should know that!"

"Shouldn't we just sit down and have a civilised cup of tea with them?" suggested Tim.

"They're animals; their sense of right and wrong has been seriously corrupted," countered Michael. "They don't deserve to be considered human."

"I consider that highly racist," retorted Tim. "It's the classic othering of the enemy used to justify dubious military exercises. You charge them with crimes while ignoring your own."

The meeting continued in the same vein. Death by excruciating boredom. Will now hated the new engaged democracy and its pretence at listening, when all it really cared about was spying on its own citizens. He had supported the concepts originally, but the practical outcomes were not what he expected.

At the end, Michael had another controversial unofficial announcement.

"You might be interested to know we're bringing out voluntary personal embedded GPS," Michael announced. "It's really useful if you're out of Cloud area. US forces have used it for decades. The papers are coming out for the next formal bubble."

"We've had enough of being spied on," complained Peter. "You can track us anywhere anytime anyway while we're in Cloud country through our National Virtual Identifiers - NVIDs. This is quite scary really. What on earth are you people up to?"

NVIDs were an essential part of being a Cloud citizen. They were allocated at registration when the citizen swore to uphold the Cloud protocols and principles.

Will and Peter went back a long way, and their debates at college had been endless. Neither would admit defeat or error; it was a badge of honour. Tim had also been a mental sparring opponent. He was more erudite but less analytical in his oratory than Peter. At the end of the day, Will felt more comfortable debating against Peter than Tim.

"Oh, GPS is nothing to be worried about. It's only if you're going off-cloud. It could have helped track you on our trip to Kingsgeld. It can help with health and wellbeing. None of the data is used except for your own personal benefit. And it's entirely voluntary." Michael had all the answers. "We've got it in a useful range of products. Wrist-watch, one-size-fits-all rings, you name it. Wearable, not implanted like personal identifiers. If you don't like it, just take it off. If you were in China, it's different. They started to implant a GPS as well as your identifier seven years ago on a mandatory basis. There is no hiding anywhere in that society."

"I'll take one," volunteered Will.

He tried on a ring. Not exactly a thing of beauty, but it felt comfortable enough. While designed to look like jewellery, it was in reality made of strong but malleable fabric. As soon as he put it on it was registered to him. Strictly for his own good of course.

"The Russians have had voluntary GPS for years," continued Michael as Will tried it out. "They started implanting it in new Cloud citizens last year, on a voluntary basis. In western Russia there's no option to remain outside the cloud once you're eighteen, unless you have elected to become a monk in the church and agree never to have sexual relations or become a parent. It's only Siberia and the east you can be free of surveillance. Even that will change in the next few years."

This after-meeting had been quite intense. Will enjoyed the opportunity of sticking up for Michael who he saw as his inspiring older brother figure, and he enjoyed the intellectual challenge of the bubble. It satisfied a key part of him; the need to constantly test his mettle against his intellectual equals.

What he lacked, and what the bubble did not give him, was a significant other in his life. It was the hole that Rosaline might have filled, but had failed to apply for. Bubbles were not dating circles; they were arms of the state. Playing *Planets* might be his form of emotional relief, but he needed much more. However hard Michael tried to show him how to approach women he still felt shy and awkward. At least these days most of the contact was online and so introductions could be easier; even forty years ago most couples just met by chance at work or through friends. For the shy or socially awkward, it perhaps gave a slither of hope, but it just hadn't worked for him yet.

## SCENE ST VLADISGRAD SEVEN STAR

The Seven Star met at 8pm exactly. Lateness was frowned on for this elite and intellectual group. Katerina was to talk about reproductive science in the service of Russia and how it enhanced the mission of fighting the decadent West. Natasha, Sonya, Anastasia, Mariya and Anna would all be expecting a fine presentation. Anastasia in particular would ask questions, being the country's leading Zoologist and an expert in reproduction in the animal kingdom. There might well be scope for cross-over insights between the two disciplines.

"We must first understand the history of reproductive science in humans. It had its genesis here in the Russian Republic, building on the Soviet experiments of the 1930s. It used the best, and discarded the worst, of world-wide science. Just as we can use the best, and discard the worst, of the genetic material we have. This is what reproductive science is really about. In the Soviet era medical mistakes could be disposed of quickly. This came at some cost to the natural mother and conflicted with conservative social forces. Now we have no need of those solutions. Even in those times, it was not always clear when mistakes had been made. That resulted in disloyal citizens with defective judgement. That is why we had the purges. In future, there will be no need."

Katerina paused.

Olga interrupted, "But our science was developed as a counter to the West, and to maintain or increase our birth rates while their own fell. Just as we demonstrated superiority in chess until artificial intelligence dominated the game, so we can demonstrate superiority in science, at least until science itself is a task which can be automated or its routine functions performed with silicon intelligence. Let's just ask ourselves: 'Who did the west copy when they tried to make safe and cheap nuclear power work?' Us of course. 'Which country has the best mathematicians in the world?' Russia, of course. While the west stalled and grew inward-looking, preoccupied with a liberal blind alley, we progressed. Only Russia has the discipline, the courage, and the skill we need in today's world. Look at the retreat of the west. They have a shrinking population, and shrinking land in which to put that population as sea levels rise and swallow their coastal flatlands. Look at their social cohesion; they tolerate all sorts of dissent and varieties of opinion. They may have won the last century, but we will win this century."

A stern eye from Tanis reminded Olga they only had an hour

for the whole meeting and that political digressions, even if sound, needed to be limited.

Tanis was the rapporteur, and Katerina's line manager at the hospital. In the communist days she would have been a party boss. Nothing escaped her notice.

Katerina continued.

"So we developed our gene editing, and our cloning. We may not have been the first to create a human being, but we were the first to correct a deficient one, using sophisticated gene editing. And we were first to fuse the DNA from sperm and egg under controlled conditions, or at least partially control conditions, to create flawless new citizens."

Katerina reflected as she spoke. Success or failure in her role came in the 'still partial human element' in the process, matching the genes up to the parental requirements. It was the part she specialised in. Sometimes this meant trade-offs, selecting for one characteristic at the risk of some kind of weakness in an area not prioritised in the parental wish statement. This in turn reminded her of her recent shameful failure in this regard. Fortunately for her the mistake was still not evident to the management, and Tanis was clearly not yet aware. Tanis would discover, but only after the meeting. For now, Tanis looked content.

"See these examples."

She flashed on the shared three dimensional display unit. Several photos of near-twins, developed for research, bearing uncanny resemblances while not quite sharing all DNA. The photos came with biographies, and those in each case pointed to stark life differences or reduced lifespan itself. In some cases, mental health issues, self-harm and depression could be avoided. There were gender-specific issues too. For example, dependent on parental choice, early baldness could sometimes be avoided.

"How about parental matching?" asked Anna. "What process do we use to ensure optimal outcomes."

The matchmaker's dilemma, recast.

"Matching algorithms have worked well. They are constantly being improved. Of course state consent is still required, mostly, but there are few refusals in St Vladisgrad where the couple have met through an approved socially-controlled matching program."

It would be difficult, she thought, for state permission to be denied provided that the parental offspring limits were observed, that the parents were in good social standing, and the algorithm had provided a match. Of course, it was health history records and not just DNA which led to the match in the first place.

"We have more data now. The algorithm was first used twenty years ago and the initial results look very promising. Seven of the first hundred matches are in the St Vladisgrad inner ring (the elite of the elite Seven Stars), and twenty officers in the Russian army, while most of the rest are studying with top grades. Only thirteen were cancelled."

This news was warmly greeted. This Seven Star, as all Vladisgrad Stars, was intensely patriotic. Russia was strong, and would become stronger. The decadent would perish, indeed already had. The enemy would be beaten without a shot fired; the shame of earlier periods of the country's history, the Communist Party, the nationalists, the corruption, all put behind them. Though, as Katerina knew, all was not quite as rosy as it seemed.

Anna had one last message.

"It's being reported that there are stalkers on Vladisnet, deceptive men who try to trick you into giving them your reproduction credits. They target the elite, hoping for financial gain."

Katerina kept quiet.

"It's really important you don't talk to them; they can hack from very little, they can hypnotise, they can rob you of who you are."

"Quite right," agreed Tanis. "If anyone wishes to see what happens to those allowing themselves to be exposed online, I can show them after."

A pronouncement of this nature from her was intended to end debate. Caution over curiosity; they all agreed. The motherland first.

Katerina thought of Nik. Was he a danger to her?

She slipped into reflection mode and from there to dreaming. DNA is the source of life but also the source of so much trouble, as all Russians compete to try to get theirs into the next gene pool by all means possible. Words started coming into her head.

**SCENE ODE TO DNA**

Four letters make up me
They are C, A, G and T
(Not the drink), the poetry
From mummy and from daddy
In Holy matrimony
Or a laboratory,
Sets the way we will be.

**WILL'S DATA LOG EXTRACT:**

## Meta data "girl/girls"

Consulted Michael on the topic of girls. He seems to have had plenty of previous experience which he claims to have boiled down to a simple approach based on his view that it's all about which half of the brain to engage. It is necessary to test his advice, to determine if the methods will be successful for this subject.

★

**Subject name:** Rosaline.

**Result:** Negative.

**Conclusion:** Avoid being condescending in future (see detailed text note below).

**Personal outcome:** Utter humiliation; described as "out of my league."

**Lessons learned:** Don't get hopes up.

Experiment conducted on the bubble excursion to Kingsgeld. I found myself in the rare position of being warmly attracted to a girl. She was self-confident and smart, while being off-cloud yet carefree and happy. Note to self: when trying to avoid right brain topics, avoid being condescending.

# KATERINA'S DIARY

## 7 JANUARY 2047

Dear Diary. I have a really big confession. I lost you. I don't know what happened, but life went all of a whoosh. I think you disappeared when I moved into my first tiny apartment. Everything had to be squashed, and maybe there just wasn't room for you. Then last year I went and made it all worse for myself. Yes, the cat. I found it on the street struggling to move, and had to take it home. I took it to the hospital and it stayed in the office for a few days where I could keep an eye on it. I named it after some famous film awards. Did I tell you I like western films? I do, but I keep quiet about it. It seems to be frowned upon these days.

There's so much other news to tell you. I've grown up since we last spoke. Here in the city there's so much to enjoy. I discovered poetry, and music, and all sorts. I'm going to start writing poetry, dear diary, but I want it all to be secret. Maybe I'll use you to keep it safe and well away from the Cloud.

I don't want to bore you with all the details of what happened. I trained of course, passed and came top of my class, then started work in the hospital in reproductive science. There were a few blips along the way, but you don't need to know about them; they aren't important, and I'm happier again now.

I want you to know that this is the only place I make my confessions now. From time to time I wander into a church – though most are closed now – but only to admire the architecture and icons. I don't know where God is, but he certainly isn't there anymore. No one's there, really. Even Mariya doesn't go anymore.

The state has its own ceremony now, which is a bit like first communion, only for everyone. Well, everyone who wants to join. I suppose that's a bit like the church really. Instead of pledging our lives to Christ, we pledge to obey the rules of the Cloud and allegiance to Russia. The Cloud is international, but we're supposed to mostly keep to the Russia-China block. Instead of the bishop laying on hands, we have a small electronic device implanted. It's a really quick operation, just a local anaesthetic. They reassure you it doesn't mean they can track you anywhere. All it does is allow you to identify yourself to the Cloud or your communicator. It means there can never be any confusion about who someone is online if you allow authentication through the identifier.

All this sounds a bit much but as a result I've got a new groups of friends to help keep me living well. It's not a church, it's called a Seven Star. We meet and talk about things. I moved into the same block as them last year, and that's when I found you and knew I just had to start with you again, when Christmas came. We meet and eat together once a week, so it's sort of like the mass, and the initiation is a bit like first communion. I'm not sure the church likes it but they haven't banned it for church members yet. All they've said is that the church's monks can't join in. Married priests and church members are allowed, it seems. So I can still go to mass if I want to, it's just I've grown a bit tired of it.

**FEBRUARY**

I'm being good now diary. It won't just be at festival time I come to speak to you. I want to tell you all about my plans to see London. Now, you have to remember that my father spent time in London many years ago. He was working at the Hermitage, but got offered a secondment to the British Museum and he took it. I know he had a really great time there. Mum went out there too for medical training, and speaks fondly of it. I know it's changed since they were there, but I can't wait to go in person, if I'm allowed.

## APRIL

Mariya is such a blessing. I was so scared I'd made a stupid mistake at work. She came round to cheer me up, but Sonya gate-crashed and we ended up watching an English film. Sonya is such a flirt. I think she has boyfriends, and several of them, but of course these days she can't admit it.

She's so pretty, and all the boys fall over her. I don't know if that is good or bad? Some days I'd love to have men flatter me and chase after me. Other days I'm glad they look through me. I don't think I'd know what to do if I got attention. Seek advice from Mariya, I think. Not from Sonya. She's fun and I like her, but I'm keeping true to my vows.

## I MAY

Dear diary, I have an awful confession. Last night I was feeling bored, you see. I had an incoming message and I was curious. It was all on Vladischat, so it was all meant to be safe, censored, controlled. It was a white Russian calling himself Nik, I think. He certainly loved his vodka. He had some sent round, and we drank. Then we drank some more. He claimed he worked in cyber warfare and was on the Council. I was an idiot. Somehow, I let him into my *Planets* login, or else he hacked me. What is worse he seemed to know all about my little indiscretion last week, even while Tanis my manager seems quite unaware. How does this man know? Only God is omniscient. What am I to do? I think he might have been telling the truth when he said he was important. He certainly seems to know a lot. But why did he want to take advantage like that? But really it's my fault. I should have resisted him, not let myself get drunk. He wants to meet again and I think he's trying to get me to help him hack the system at work. I hope he doesn't really have power, or I'm in a lot of trouble.

## 2 MAY

Dear diary, I have another confession. I couldn't tell you last night, but I cut myself. It's only right. I don't have Father Bulgakov to confess to and order my penance any more. I need to use the knife. If I build up, slightly deeper and longer each time, I'll teach myself to be more careful. It's a bewildering world we are living in now. It's meant to be all-seeing all-knowing, but I feel lost. I know the leaders mean well, but I don't trust them like I used to trust the church.

## 6 MAY

I've got a Seven Star tomorrow and I'm speaking. Help me diary! It scares me. I'm sure someone will come up with something I haven't thought of.

## 7 MAY

Survived presentation. Disturbing news from the meeting though. It seems this "Nik" might be quite dangerous. I hope I never meet him again, or it will be the death of me. Oh for my happy days of innocent childhood. The days before a stranger tried to kiss me.

But what I will do is focus on my work. We are a great country, and it's my job to help create the DNA of the next generation who will make it even better. The country could do without my own DNA I think. "Nik" seems to know where I live. At least he didn't want to try to sleep with me. I don't know whether he wants to co-parent with me or just steal my online secrets. He would be too appalled with my body for intimacy, I'm sure. He claims he has social privilege and

I don't doubt it. With that power he could surely attempt to meet me in person if he wished. Very possibly he can track my movements. Yet he has not yet proposed such an encounter, just said it's possible if we want it. One mercy, at least. I'll just have to hope I don't meet him by chance at some event, in the way he seemed to be hinting at. I wouldn't be surprised if he was able to engineer some apparently random meeting as a pretext to accost me.

## KATERINA'S TRAINING RECORD AT ST PETERSBURG STATE MEDICAL

## ACADEMY

**Graduation date:** 2046.

**Classification:** First.

**Specialism:** Reproductive science.

**Prizes:** Rebrikov Prize for Gene Editing.

**Notes:** Student experienced fainting when observing a dilation and curettage  medical procedure. Has been excused further work in this area. The following day required treatment for apparent self-harm. Some ongoing food disorders, but has largely been able to overcome these with the help of therapy.

## POLITBUREAU MINUTES: TOP SECRET: I JUNE 2047

"Relations with the Russian Orthodox Church (ROC) were debated. ROC have been complaining about treatment of Fr B, but have indicated a potential softening of their line on reproductive science if the state agrees to modify position in return. Agreed it is counterproductive to return to Soviet policies, and it may be more efficient to agree a compromise. ROC will stop public criticism of our policies provided that we promote the church's view in relation to sexuality. They will allow members to benefit from reproductive science if married, and it was agreed to provide up to two permits to such couples when certain reasonable conditions are met."

"There was some discussion of state security. There are suspicions that one agent in cyber security (NK) may be a double agent for the west. This individual has back door access to communications channels we are unable to monitor for now, but we are working to infiltrate what we suspect is a clandestine forum of dissidents. As the suspect does not realise he is under suspicion, he will be allowed to continue for now, albeit closely watched."

# ACT 2

# PLANETS LIFE

## NARRATOR ON *PLANETS*

I need to remind readers of how this game came about. It was all Michael's idea, ably assisted by our young English hacker Ben and his even younger counterpart in Russia, Nik, a mercurial character in league with British intelligence. The original purpose of the game was to provide a cover for espionage activities, albeit that Nik had a view to potential profit into the bargain. The strategy was partially successful, before enemy blocks started becoming suspicious about its true purpose, and continues to have some intelligence value even now.

The first Unique Selling Point of the game was giving players choice through the ability to sign up for different "trajectories" through the game at the outset. This gave users different objectives and destinations. For example, earth might be either the starting point, or the end point, depending on your pathway. There might be accelerated routes between planets or moons millions of miles from each other.

The second feature was the continuous nature of the game; it ran twenty four hours a day seven days a week. You can either play 'real life' or you can programme your game avatar (your online player linked to your logon ID) to take decisions according to a set of rules and behaviours, i.e. the game avatar personality. Real life play tends to be more successful at winning points and gaining levels, hooking players in longer in the game and therefore improving ad revenue, but skilled avatar programming can also be successful. You might not immediately be able to tell if a given character is being controlled by avatar or directly by a human at any particular point in time, a delicious twist to game play.

By 2047 the game had, unexpectedly, become a commercial as well as intelligence success. Instead of withdrawing the game, which had mostly fulfilled its original intelligence purpose, it was discreetly re-branded. Technically, it was a private commercial company, with the game designers holding some of the stock. In the rebrand there was a public offering to diversify ownership. At the same time, controls were put in place from 1 January 2047 to prevent fully anonymous users signing up to any online platforms, such as *Planets*, circumventing threatened bans on the game from Russia and China. These controls obviated spying activity for new participants and prevented blocks from banning access. All traces of former espionage activities were removed to cover up its previous use, and to reduce the risk of compromising intelligence sources previously acquired through the game. That didn't stop the game being regarded with a little suspicion in many quarters, and rightly so, as legacy accounts still preserved anonymity.

The new controls on the game meant that the new game avatars can be registered to an NVID, with the intelligence agencies from each block able to see that registration. However the game avatar personality could still be programmed according to player choice, or have connection with a real-life person's characteristics, at the player's discretion. Indeed, the avatar itself could be programmed or reprogrammed relatively easily. The sweetest angel sitting next door might be a demon in the game. Or vice versa. And it might all change tomorrow.

The intention of registration was clear and good; to reduce prevalence of identity theft and fraud. The reality of course was a loss of privacy for players. Crucially, campaigners and the game's creators argued that doing this retrospectively, i.e. forcing the NVID to be revealed to security agencies for each existing game avatar, would be an unfair breach of privacy. Players, when signing up in the past, had not expected their real-life IDs to be revealed. Western agencies feigned objection to retrospective identification, all the while having secret access via a back-end process known to them but not to other agencies.

The upshot was that only new users could be forced to sign up in such a way that the NVIDs could be revealed to Government and hence tracked. It was those old unverified users which eastern blocks took most exception to as they wanted to fully control and monitor their citizens.

Some of the content had created culture clash and in some cases had caused offence. This was addressed judiciously by subtly altering the trajectories according to the social profile of the player. This became easier to achieve post registration, as users were obliged to divulge more personal information about themselves in the process, which was used to assess cultural, moral preference and sexual orientation in the widest sense, and in turn used to create sensitive experiences. Earlier players, such as Will and Katerina, had chosen their paths from a narrower and less sophisticated menu.

Many studies had been conducted on the impact of the game on mental health and social development. Some praised its ability to connect individuals from different backgrounds. Others criticized its compulsive nature, and claimed it acted as a chamber reinforcing personal prejudice. Will for example logged in each day. The bubble monitored his time online, but crucially could not ascertain how much of that time was spent on the game as opposed to other activities. Katerina was more disciplined and kept more strictly to her own five hour rule.

The trick it seemed was collaboration with other players, but to collaborate well you needed some kind of relationship outside of the game itself. This was one of the reasons *Planets* came to be so highly regarded; it was the best networked, not the brightest, who tended to win.

### NOTES FROM WILL'S PSYCHIATRIST 14 FEBRUARY 2047

"The patient was referred by his bubble on account of falling asleep during meetings. The president suspects an excess of online gaming, especially *Planets*. The patient admits to having an unregistered account but says he limits play to four hours a week, in line with official guidance. He also claims that use of the game enhances his professional and social networking opportunities. He has admitted that he is not in a relationship and would consider using the game platform to find a partner or even co-parent. I asked him what strategies he used to leverage that network most effectively, but his answers seemed vague. I asked him about collaborator feedback through the game. He replied positively that the last rating was a 7 and the feedback praised his 'close attention to the pressing issue of climate change'. I suggested taking regular breaks from the game, not playing past 11pm at night, and engaging in mindfulness. His bubble can assist with the latter activity. He agreed, though the body language suggested a lack of engagement. I was left wondering if he was listening properly."

## SCREENSHOT OF THE SAKHAROV PLANETS FORUM

@CountParis: I have detected a plan to attempt to hack our IDs. The Government plans to introduce visual street surveillance using new technology. It seems it can penetrate some building walls. Enforcement would be focussed on locations they suspect of harbouring resistance.

@Rasputin: Do we have potential countermeasures?

@Euler: a metal sheet or grid over the communicator area should be sufficient. Has progress been made on other pressing concerns?

@ CountParis: I am making progress on infiltrating the eugenics program. This game is the gift that keeps on giving. Not only is it helping to fund operations but it gives me opportunity to find weak links in state security. I have a valuable lead and have further steps to take shortly which I believe will yield results.

@TheProfessor: Do be careful with her.

@CountParis: Certainly sir.

@Euler: I'm pleased this game keeps our operations in the black. Is there other news?

@Rasputin: I hear that the good priest Fr B has now died of exhaustion or physical neglect. Details are patchy but I will find out more.

@CountParis: So sorry to hear. I'm not remotely religious, but he was a genuine man who had his uses. Let's observe silence on his behalf next time we meet, when I aim to bring news from the West. Do be careful until then. There are spies everywhere.

## PLANETS USER LOG EXTRACT I APRIL 2047

**Subject:** "Katerina Kotov."

**Privileges:** None.

**Date joined:** 7 January 2045.

**Govt registered:** No.

**Avatar image:** Eikaterina of Alexandria.

**Ave wk online:** 5 hours.

**Collaborator rating:** 9.8.

**Level:** 3.

★

**Subject:** "Will Green."

**Privileges:** None.

**Date joined:** 25 December 2044.

**Govt registered:** No.

**Avatar image:** Richard the Lionheart.

**Ave wk online:** 10 hours.

**Collaborator rating:** 4.

**Level:** 2.

★

**Subject:** Withheld.

**Privileges:** Admin.

**Date joined:** 31 December 2040.

**Govt registered:** No.

**Avatar image:** Count Paris.

**Ave wk online:** 2 hours.

**Collaborator rating:** n/a.

**Level:** Complete.

## ODE TO THE PLANETS

Holst said that you all were nine
Far one, small one, Pluto's fine.
Then a theory says there's eight
Students, teachers to frustrate:
Mercury you're hot as hell
Venus beauty born in a shell
Earth it is that gives us life
Mars is god of war and strife
Jupiter has bright red spot
Saturn's rings are just as hot
Uranus smells like quite a rotter
Neptune you are god of water.

★

Now the planets are a game
Success in it will give you fame
Or lead you on a merry dance.
To find a lover; there's a chance!
But careful who you meet online
The unknown stranger may be fine.
Or might be out to trick you quick
Doesn't it just make you sick?

## SCENE THE DREADED RETURN OF NIK NEXT EVENING

Nik was, unfortunately, true to his promise. He had showed a slightly unhealthy interest in Katerina's gaming habits, for her liking. She had been on *Planets* for six years; indeed she was close to achieving planetary freedom, as Nik had surmised last night. She wanted nothing to threaten that.

"Moyo pochtenie. Good evening Miss Kotov."

She had only ever been called Miss Kotov once before in her life.

"Evening."

"Vodka?" he enquired.

"No thank you."

"Not even a vodka martini? Shaken?"

"No I'm good thank you."

"Ah shame. You won't mind if I do?"

"Of course not."

His polite formality sat alongside his plain arrogance quite uneasily.

"Now, I was getting most curious about your position on *Planets*. You must have realised by now I am a little acquainted with the game myself."

"I had wondered."

"So you see I am most intrigued to know how you have been getting on."

"Well, I can show you."

She opened her login so Nik could see from her viewpoint. As Red Queen she lived in the house of the Red Giant, directing the maids and watching the camp. It had taken her two years to achieve this role after she first arrived.

"Nice. Let me see more." He was insistent. She showed him the best view. The whole layout. The main hall, the feasting table, the armoury, the complex of bed chambers and the dungeons full of chains and instruments of persuasion.

"Is this the sort of home your ancestors lived in?" she asked very innocently.

"I designed this scene myself originally," he snorted. "No one has improved on it yet; my successors, red Russians no doubt, mostly dumbed it down."

"Oh, I see." The penny was beginning to drop. "You were one of the original game designers. That's starting to make sense."

"Now I have seen your bed chamber, and seen your progress so far in the game, I need your help in the reproductive science system. I'm told you are the best, now your mother has retired. I have the permit but I need to know who is available."

How did he know that?

This started ringing alarm bells, not just at the suggestive language but the somewhat more insidious attempt at unauthorised access, circumventing the usual procedures.

"Just a view of the data."

She could not do that.

"I'll have to think about it."

"Don't take too long."

What she didn't notice was that Nik by now had a view of what he really needed; her avatar credentials for *Planets*. He was not a master of cyber warfare for nothing. The trusted network allowed him to slip in and steal exactly what he needed.


## SCENE *PLANETS*

The next day she had an unpleasant surprise. She returned to the *Planets* but could not access. Nik messaged and it was clear he was behind this; she hadn't expected a hack attack from someone she knew; most attempts were from robot farms way into the Dark Web.

"I need the Reproductive database."

"I can't give it, sorry," she replied.

The screen darkened. In the distance she heard thunder. "Want your Red Queen to stay alive?"

"That's blackmail."

"Well, what do you want? To keep your job? It's quite well paid, isn't it? Brings a lot of social privileges. I hear you want to travel to London. That's not possible for most people. I have contacts, remember. How would your Seven Star feel about it if they knew about the mistake you made at work?"

"So what exactly do you want to know? If I know I can tell you. I can't give you direct access. Really, I'd like to help you, but I can't give you a logon there. It's not mine to give."

"I'll give you twenty four hours."

She awoke early and suddenly that night with a sharp pain in her foot. Her dreams came back to her and a cold feeling swept her body. She was dressed for a ball and doing the Foxtrot with some aplomb. Her dance partner was equally as impressive and skilled, but then he turned and she saw his face.

She got up and logged on; she had lost her logon on *Planets*.

The dream played on her mind and filled her with self-loathing. She went to her drawer where she kept her equipment for such disturbing events, all pilfered from the hospital. She inserted several sterilized needles into sensitive areas. After twenty minutes she removed them and downed three vodkas; the inner pain receded. At least this time she hadn't used the razor blades.

## SCENE THE COMMON ROOM IN WALCOT LODGE

Tim and Peter were relaxing with a non-caffeine drink when Rose walked in. She was indeed a rare visitor to that area, being a solitary type. She found formal meetings trying enough as it was. She preferred to spend time on her own, mostly. For this present foray we have only to thank her need to borrow coffee and her inability to wait half an hour for a delivery. An in-person request was harder to refuse than an online one.

"Will should have some," suggested Peter meanly, knowing it was the top flat. Rose would text instead, surely, instead of climbing the stairs. The disappointment for Peter and his diversionary tactic, was that, by chance, Will passed by the open door to the common area at that exact same time, overhearing quite clearly.

"You called?" asked Will, popping in.

"I need coffee. Completely out."

"I've got some in the common cupboard. I'll just get it for you."

Peter scowled.

"Coffee makes thinking and thinking wins games," explained Rose. "I don't care how much it's monitored." She poured some water into the kettle ready to boil.

"You should try systematic deductive logic instead of games," countered Peter.

Rose scowled and accidentally knocked over the kettle. Fortunately she had not yet boiled it and the only damage was a water spill.

"My iron wit will beat you dry," Peter quipped.

"Can *I* help with your thinking?" suggested Tim. "I'm quite good at it, I'm told."

"I'm signing up for *Planets*. I need to choose my journey and make my way."

"You could ask Ben or Michael for help," suggested Will. "Ben was on the design team. I bet he's still a Game Admin."

"So you think six hours a day of escapism is going to solve your problems?" challenged Peter.

"I'm taking the new pathway. Travelling in time as well as space. It's a leap forward in helping us think about the world."

"You're a player too, aren't you Will?" enquired Tim.

Will nodded.

"Explains a lot," retorted Peter. "Have you read the studies on playing impact?"

"Sleep?" asked Will.

"Also eye strain, body posture and a general disengagement with the world," suggested Peter.

"I thought that's what we all get living in the cloud," Will retorted. "And as you mention it, my shrink's ordered me to cut down."

"The field of vision restricts the creative ability to such a narrow range it leads to myopia and depression," observed Tim.

"I see. But only if you play more than sixteen hours a week," Will replied.

"I see it as a creative challenge. I joined a month ago." Rose. "I've got my avatar set up."

"Oh?" enquired Will.

"I'm the TimeLady. I have my own special trajectories."

"Makes sense." That was a big extension to the game. Time travel wasn't available when Will joined up.

"Must have changed a lot since I left it," said Tim, echoing Will's thoughts. "I gave up once I saw it for what it was. Complete waste of time. Best decision I ever made was to quit."

"Careful. Captain Mercutio might be listening," warned Peter. "Can't eavesdrop electronically so he chooses the flat above the common room for some reason. I wonder why? Talking of spying, I don't suppose you know how many players got ripped off by revealing details online through it? I read it in the Keeper, so it must be true."

Will did know, and it was scary.

"There's a suckers list," warned Tim. "On it and you're targeted again and again. It's also addictive. By running it twenty four hours a day they reward the losers who play it continuously and get hooked."

"My risk," replied Will. "At least it teaches on line collaboration and networking. If you set up your game avatar well you can do well off-line. Anyway, talking of addiction, have you never been known to take addictive unapproved substances?"

"View it how you want, it's your funeral if you get hacked. Ben will just have to reset you and we'll all laugh," said Peter, ignoring the jibe.

"Coffee?" enquired Rose.

"No, I'm off to seduce Vicky," he jested.

"Good luck with that, seeing as she's just agreed to co-parent with the great grandson of Ai Weiwei," pointed out Ben.

"Anyway, she's way above your league. In fact, she's the smartest diplomatic operator I've come across, ever, by a huge margin. It's not surprising she has a double first in Natural Sciences and Russian given how bright she is."

Peter responded with two fingers and left.

## SCENE COFFEE IN ST VLADISGRAD

There were four of them. Technically, that was quorate for a Seven Star. However the agenda was coffee and they were meeting in Katerina's flat not a state monitored meeting room.

"I've just joined *Planets*," revealed Anastasia. "I asked Tanis and she said it's OK as long as the avatar was registered to me properly. As far as I can see I can't join without doing that anyway."

"So, you have plenty of spare time?" enquired Sonya. "I'm not on it. Are you Mariya?"

Mariya shook her head.

"Katerina?"

Katerina was silent.

"You are! Registered?"

Katerina shook her head.

"Oooh. Better keep that to ourselves, ladies. Tanis would not be happy."

"Well, I'm legit," said Anastasia, "and I'm really interested in the new virtual reality they're bringing out for the earth module."

"What's that?" enquired Katerina.

"It's quite expensive, but they think it will work. It's a combo of online gaming and virtual reality experience. They can only do it in remote places. You get a VR machine and they have spy animals all over to record what happens in the wild. You get tasks to complete and you can transfer out afterwards. It's ideal for a zoologist like me."

"Wow. Sounds complicated."

"That's just a part of the trajectory, but it's potentially exciting. They haven't launched yet but they're working on a Madagascar scene and I'm going to trial it for them."

"What do you get out of *Planets*?" asked Sonya to Katerina.

"You know, I wonder that myself sometimes. I think it's about living in another world, interacting with different people, and perhaps making new friends. I don't play it enough though. I just dabble when I've got time."

"You have to be careful with new friendships," warned Mariya. "That's what the authorities worry about. There's a rumour it was used for recruiting spies."

"Oh, what rubbish," replied Sonya. "That's just Tanis scaring you off because she doesn't want you to have fun. Addiction is the greater danger. And talking of fun, Katerina, you really need to spruce up your look. Now I know you won't go out without wearing a headscarf or hat, but really yours make you look so old, as if you're going to church, and I know you don't go every Sunday now. So, I've bought you this."

She produced a rainbow coloured headscarf from her bag.

"Oh wow! Do try it on," exclaimed Mariya. "It looks like the headwear version of Joseph's coat. It's for your exotic dreams, Katerina!"

"Perhaps it's a sign all the Seven Star will be bowing down to you soon," suggested Anastasia.

"I think Joseph was exiled and imprisoned before he achieved fame," pointed out Katerina. "So trouble with Tanis is more likely than not after wearing this. Maybe even being sent to Siberia?"

They all laughed.


## SCENE *PLANETS* A SUSPICIOUS COLLABORATOR

There were dangers to participating in a game with anonymous players, as Will's friends had warned. An innocent player like Will could be tricked or persuaded to reveal him or herself by other parties who were similarly anonymous. Identity thieves were the biggest threat. There were those who attempted to steal his game avatar, but he had not succumbed to their crude phishing attempts.

Only last week there was a close call. He had met 'Buzz' on Oberon attempting to defeat the Red Giants. Buzz offered to join forces. Together they could defeat them and find the portal. Will was tempted. After all, six months on a lousy moon makes you mad.

"How long you been here?"

"Six months. The red giants are fierce. Even their woman-folk kill. I saw three resets last week." Will shuddered. "There are two scouting close now. I think they missed us." The red giants were, at least, slow and easy to spot. Subterfuge was not their thing. The trick was remaining out of sight or, if not possible, moving quickly. But supplies were low and attack not the only risk of reset. Running out meant certain death and there were resources to win. The red giants on the other hand had all the resources they needed within easy reach. They were not hungry. They seemed cohesive, and their leadership strong. They would be formidable opponents if tackled without help. But this was a game based on networks, so with the right connections, anything might happen.

"I think I know where they are weak though. It's a gamble but it might work."

"Oh yes? With two we could get to their weapons store and overpower them, but it needs one to distract the guards."

"Sure. How do we coordinate?"

"Closely."

"How close?"

"Can you give me control of your avatar?"

Will reflected. Was there a risk?

"I'll see."

"Not much time now. Your supplies are running low."

Will didn't like the pressure. "See you around."

In theory there was no risk to his real-life avatar from com-promising his *Planets* avatar, but Will felt uneasy, especially after the common room banter. Stealing a game avatar was quite a loss and he didn't want to risk it. Another solution might present itself, in any case.

But how to defeat these Giants? They are to humans as humans are to persons of restricted growth. There was no chance of beating them in open combat. These giants gave flight to the courage of any potential assailant. Standing tall, long flowing auburn hair, they were intimidating and ready to fight. They had fearsome if primitive weapons, axes, swords and spears. He still had his own weapons acquired through the game, a knife and crossbow, but he was down to his last dozen bolts. Would one fell a giant? He wasn't sure. Accurately aimed, just between the eyes, maybe.

Or just maybe another opportunity would present itself, one based on co-operation with another player. That was key to the game but also the Achilles' heel as fakes would pose as would-be allies. How could he be sure?

## SCENE RESET

Katerina tried accessing *Planets* two days' later. After a short delay she managed to log in, but what had happened? The Red Queen, her *Planets* avatar, had disgraced herself with a posse of Guards in the sight of the Red Giant, and had been thrown out of the game altogether. The dungeons had new occupants in the shape of those same guards. One of the maids, a Red Giant favourite, had been promoted in her place.

Two days later and she had managed to get reset, but newly demoted to the old maid's position; what a humiliation. One more reset, and she was out for good.

## SCENE OBERON SOMETIME LATER: FIRST CONTACT

Katerina was on a very different trajectory to Will, but nonetheless their paths were about to cross on Oberon just as he was aiming to escape the solar system entirely while she was attempting to reach a game pathway to earth. When we meet those on other paths, do we have enough humanity in common to help them?

Will heard a dog bark in the distance, or was it a wolf's cry? His heart momentarily stopped as he realised his hideaway might not be secure. Soon enough the grey wolf hound appeared. Its owner, a woman scavenging, followed on her journey by her beautiful white swan. She was attractive herself, though from her appearance and dress he suspected she was a maid not the queen. She turned away, tracing a path closer to the hill and returned to base. Evidently a successful trip for her, with her baskets full. No, he hadn't been spotted. That was good.

Katerina was level three and her ambition was to reach Earth in six months, in accordance with her personal trajectory. From Oberon there was an accelerated journey. She could get to an orbit of Jupiter then Mars then Earth without difficulty.

However from having been Red Queen just two days ago, she was now relegated to a lowly serving maid, which was an unexpected and unwelcome setback. There was no progress on this path through the game without become Red Queen once again. From there she could leave Oberon and accelerate through space towards her goal, using the gravity of planets to boost her journey. Each stage brought a new persona and on Earth she would become First Lady.

Right now she was serving the new Queen, or old maid as she still thought of her. Now she herself was the old maid, cooking cleaning and collecting humble eggs from the harsh environment.

Each egg she collected represented a single game point, so progress would be slow. The Queen could command fighters and gain game points by killing wild beasts or intruders. Of course she had forfeited all her previous points in the reset process.

A maid could also earn game points by pleasing the Queen, or by assisting in war against the enemy. That was the upside. Failure to spot an intruder could result in game points loss or worse; that was the downside.

Before the link to NVID had been introduced in *Planets* she could simply have created a new game ID if she was permanently locked out of the game, but now it required true authentication to sign up afresh, and multiple game IDs were impossible. Being on her last reset of this ID gave her no further chances, should a mishap occur.

The Seven Star in St Vladisgrad would never have approved had they known she had been playing with an unregistered avatar. Under current Cloud protocols accessing the game was not officially monitored where the user was anonymous but it was that very provision, disliked by the Russian authorities, which caused their distrust. Why would any player wish to hide themselves? Her activities therefore fell into that twilight zone of being a sin and not a crime.

She had been a maid in her reset position here for three weeks now. The current queen who had replaced her after her unfortunate hack was not easy to please.

This left her reduced to foraging for points as the only route forward for her. That in itself carried game risks, such as invading marauders, wolf packs and the like. An attack from those could cause further demotion. Such threats, the marauders etc, were essentially other players cast in different roles on different trajectories, and at different levels in the game. They had much to gain from activities which would be her loss.

In response, if threatened, she could summon warriors if needed. Last week had seen an intruder attack repelled and she had assisted ferrying armoury and food to the king's men, but this week seemed calm. In the distance she thought she saw another intruder, long caped, short body and wrinkled head, but she could not be sure. She needed to be back by dark, so with ten precious eggs in the basket she headed home. Failure to return by nightfall could result in game point deduction, yet another threat to her progress.

Now we have had a first faint hint of a skirmish, a mere far distance sighting between the two main protagonists of our tale in their fantasy world, it is time to return to the real one.

## SCENE TURING TRIAL AND CANCELLATION IN SWINDON

Will woke with a splitting headache, just before his first ever identity case. It was indeed the cloud equivalent of being called for old-fashioned Jury Service, albeit duty was performed in bubbles. Fortunately today the bubble did not need him for the trial until 2pm. He could be free to conserve morning energy and imbibe caffeine in order to fuel his concentration for the intensity of the trial itself. He assumed the proceedings must be held online, so he shouldn't have to leave the flat or even dress. A message at 12:30pm disabused him of that notion; protocol declared the Trial Bubble had to meet in person or the result was invalid. Why couldn't they have said that before?

They were gathered to examine 'TrickyJack'. The meeting was convened by the Federal Bureau of Honesty (FBH), who appeared remotely to present the evidence against the NVID. Several Cloud Citizens had reported suspicions. Strange behaviour had been observed in both commercial and recreational platforms. The NVID was apparently not linked with a bubble, a situation that should never have occurred.

The NVID had been put on the FBH Pillory Board, an online list of suspect accounts. This was all according to due process. The NVID had not been claimed after the proscribed period. So now a trial was inevitable and Turing's method would once again safeguard the integrity of the Cloud.

"We have other important business today, for which I have a formal statement direct from the Swindon Community Council," announced Michael.

He read "The bubble system has been at the heart of our new politics. It now serves many other purposes, including civilian policing and the encouragement of polite society. But the core role will always be to identify and defeat the online anonymity which plagued the early twentieth century and caused so much damage. This is the best way to protect our citizens, and so, as beneficiaries of that protection, we as proud Cloud members must do our bit to ensure the safety of all. I therefore call on all of you to exercise our responsibility today in a sober calm and reflective manner, and to remember the pledges we made to the global Cloud community."

Each juror had a question:

Q "When was the last time you saw your family." Vicky, Entertainments Officer. First question.

A "I don't have family, I'm incel and refused reproduction."

Q "How do you feel about the Privacy Laws" Peter, Health Officer.

A "They have too much power over my life"

Q "How often do you go to a Bubble?" Will's own question.

A "I stopped going 3 years ago."

Q "Who was the last person you spoke to?" This one was the question from Rose (Women and Non-binary Officer).

A "The attendant at the Corner Coffee"

Q "In the first line of the sonnet which reads, "Shall I compare thee to a summer's day," would not "a winter's day" do as well or better?" Tim

A "I hate winter"

Q "Who will win the current Culture War in the Balkans" Michael, of course.

A "How should I know – am I a military expert?"

Q "How much hotter will the earth become over the next 10 years" Patrick, Treasurer.

A "I hope climate change stops, but there is nothing I can do."

Q "What happens when we die?" Charlie (Men's and Non-binary Officer).

A "Our avatars continue to live in our image."

Q "When was the last time you left Swindon?" Richard (Food and Hygiene).

A "I travelled to Bristol for a live-conference last year."

Q "What was the conference about?" Ben (IT Support Officer)

A "Cyber security in commerce and warfare"

Q "How long is your nose?" Nigel (LGBTQ+ officer).

A "Long enough to breath with."

So, the questions had been asked, and the responses given. Did they represent Artificial Intelligence or a real live human?

Human, voted Will. But it was not the judgement of the whole bubble. The vote was 9-3 against, and a majority vote was sufficient. TrickyJack was cancelled. His digital assets were returned to the state. The NVID was erased completely, as well as any account linked with it in any and all organisations. Such was the fate of those trying to cheat death by creating avatars which would out-live them when their flesh and bones failed and turned to dust. This cleaning of the cloud was simply a natural process of cloud existence in the same way that in nature death so often gives the opportunity for new life to flourish, or so went prevalent philosophy.

There were those who argued against cancellation. Rose was one of those. She claimed that you could never be completely sure. Cancellation could not be un-done, all previous information was erased. The NVID had never existed. Such a final sentence should never be imposed; the NVIDs should just be allowed to wither and grow defunct.

In contrast, Tim and Peter were more adamant that cancellation could be a good thing. It was too important to preserve cultural purity to permit irresponsible Avatars who could impersonate their original owners. They were fake and could corrupt democracy and the will of the people itself.

### NARRATOR'S NOTE

The reader should understand the morals of the culture of that time, and not condemn Tim or Peter, or those involved in what we now think of as unusual behaviour in cancelling an online avatar. It is hard to justify, especially given what little we all know about this case, but at the time it seemed only natural.

## ODE TO ALAN TURING

You cracked the code
Messages showed
Shortened the war
Kept from our shore
The villainous Hun
With his machine gun

You gave us a test
The mind to be guessed
You said that computers
would beat us at chess;
But then you yourself
had very much stress;
When caught with a man
You had no good plan
To hide your true feeling
Succeed in concealing
The truth. It cost dear
The meds for a queer.

While playing with poison
For some unknown reason
In pain have you died
A fruit by your side
But was it your choice?
We don't have your voice
To tell us your tale
From when you were frail
Of how you did feel
Of drugs used to 'heal'
Your natural attraction
and mind of abstraction
the urge to 'repair'.
Those depths of despair!

Christmas Eve passed
At very long last
We saw our mistake
And your own heartache
Now pardoned you stand
A great of our land.

## SCENE CANCELLATION IN ST VLADISGRAD

It is a strange thing to pass judgement against your peers, especially when you secretly support them. In Russia, just as much as in the Soviet era, the party has that strange effect on you. It turns you into something less than a free human.

The Star was in turmoil. Natezdha had posted in support of gay rights on a political board in Vladisnet. Specifically, to support equality in reproductive rights. She believed that gay and lesbian couples had as much right to reproduction as heterosexuals. Every doctor in the West subscribed to this viewpoint, indeed almost every citizen. Those with opposing views there could easily be cancelled on the grounds of community cohesion.

However, in Russia quite the opposite was the case. The state had decreed that reproductive rights should be reserved to the heterosexual community. There were a number of reasons for this, but the main one seemed to be simply out of a desire to separate itself from the more egalitarian position of the West for whom the question itself would have seemed outdated.

The Star, being in reality an extension of the party, did not tolerate behaviour such as this.

"There is no Gay Gene in Russia," explained Tanis.

"This fake news is a danger to the motherland," quipped Natasha.

"We cannot tolerate the western disease here in the burial place of Putin, of all places" Anna added.

Alina, Oksana and Mariya spoke to agree, but the voting of course was anonymous (not unanimous) and strictly secret.

Tanis announced the result: eleven-one in favour of cancellation, and Natezdha was denounced and suspended for six months. Tanis warned everyone not to talk about the process afterwards.

"I was the one voting against," confided Katerina to Anastasia despite the warning from Tanis of undermining the secrecy of the ballot, but she had to confess her secret to someone.

"That's strange, so was I," Anastasia replied. "I'm not personally sure we should allow more gay rights than we already have, but we should definitely have more licence to express our views, whether they are the official line or not."

"I voted against too," answered Sonya who overheard. "I could never condemn anyone for their orientation, let alone for their political views on the matter."

Some kind of counting issue had clearly taken place within the Seven Star, but it was best not to press the point. Besides, if a complaint were to be made, it would reveal the conspirators' breach of the voting secrecy laws, and could threaten the regard with which the Seven Star was held.

The verdict appeared to come with a reward, for achieving the correct result. An all-expenses paid trip to the Baltic Baths five miles out of town was announced soon after. Should there really be a link between the "correct" decision and granting this favour? No one was quite sure if the two were linked, but it did seem something of a coincidence if they were not. Tanis was tight-lipped on the question. These trips were often "glammed up" to maximise impact and celebrate the party, so, whatever the reason, it was sure to be fun. Supervised social contact with other groups going was also part of the arrangement, which for some was the biggest part of the attraction. After all, who of us can say they only want to meet those belonging to our closest (all female) group, the Seven Star, when St Vladisgrad was a vibrant city of millions and a world-leading scientific and cultural centre, and possessed a number of very eligible young men?

## SCENE SPA AND DANCE

They met the transport at nine sharp. It was Katerina's first trip to the spa. The baths were segregated by gender, of course, ideal for a Star trip. Once upon a time they were reserved for elite athletes, a kind of reward for success in international competition, as well, of course, for party hierarchy. These days the perks filtered lower down.

They were paired up for the day, Katerina with Sonya. First off were the facials. There was little time for chat, though the two sat opposite each other, smiling, each wondering how the other was finding this new experience of being personally pampered. At other establishments masseuses were replaced by some realistic automatons, but nothing could replace the feel of human hands tending to your delicate face.

Next up was the jacuzzi; decadent but sensual and a time for talking.

"How did you feel about the trial?" enquired Katerina.

"I can see all sides, but as you know I voted against," responded Sonya. "Years ago scientists conducted experiments to understand and perhaps change the sexual condition; now we pretend it doesn't exist. I try not to think about it too much, it's not my problem - yet anyway. I'm heterosexual, perhaps a little too heterosexual. You don't think it will go out of fashion as reproductive engineering becomes more popular?"

"It would solve some problems but create others if it did."

"Ah yes. The male sex needs to be valued. Two hundred years ago they ruled us, treated us almost as serfs, but now they can't even rule themselves. What will they do when their role is reduced, at most, to sperm donation? I hear even that may not be necessary soon."

"And how do you feel about that?" asked Katerina. "Wouldn't it be a purer less aggressive society?"

"Much less fun but much less complicated!"

Sonya must have been quite young when she started dating, as the social contact laws had been in place for a couple of years now. Or else she was successful at evading detection in a world of constant monitoring. It wasn't impossible to form relationships but they had to be approved, and subject to strict conditions. Promiscuity was certainly not permitted.

"I had one man trying to get me drunk, on a virtual vodka binge," admitted Katerina. This was actually a little risky for her, as she had been too close to the edge in her dealings with Nik. "He sent round only the best, and it kept coming."

"Happens too often, and there's always something they want. I suppose he wanted to meet up?"

"Yes, he wanted to. Suggested he had the necessary permissions or could arrange it somehow. The vodka was the best stuff, mind. If he had behaved better I might have agreed."

"Ah, rich is he? Might be worth investigating. Other than meeting up, what more did he want?"

"I thought at first he had romantic intentions, if impure. He talked about co-parenting. Now I think he was trying to use me. He wanted access to hospital systems for some nefarious purpose. Of course I wouldn't allow him. It put me off meeting him at all." That was sort of true, Katerina reassured herself. She avoided mention of the hacking for now.

"No surprise there," said Sonya. "It wasn't Nik was it? He's got away with a lot, it's whispered. He's officially in the clear and an approved person, but every woman I know finds him overbearing. He's one of the few men I actually refused when I was able to meet up with men in person unchaperoned. It's also rumoured he's a traitor, but he must be protected by someone high up if he is."

The silence said it all.

"It was Nik, wasn't it?" Sonya suddenly cottoned on. "He's well known for it; don't feel guilty about it. It's not your fault so don't beat yourself up."

She paused, then continued in a low voice, "It's horrid when they treat you like that. I found him really hard to shake off; he wouldn't take no for an answer. It makes you feel so low."

"Yes. Did you know he hacked me on *Planets*?"

"Oh no! No wonder you didn't want to talk about it. Forget him. What you need is an invigorating hot sauna and cold plunge."

As it turned out, the sauna and cold pool, combined with a couple of vodkas, did actually lift Katerina's spirits. It was so good to be understood. Katerina started feeling closer to Sonya as her confessor, a kind of substitute priest in the absence of her lack of church attendance. Her diary only went so far in fulfilling that role.

The final event of the day was an old-fashioned evening dance. Katerina had chosen a traditional outfit for the occasion, a delicate white gown, full length, open at the neck to just above her cleavage, and covered in lace around the neck. On her head, a blue-and-white kokhnik. She chose a large choker embossed with a Russian doll, emphasizing the dress's neckline. She entered on her brand new elegant heels, but changed into ballet shoes once seated.

The male and female contingents were finally brought together for permitted social interaction, under the watchful gaze of the rapporteurs. All carefully screened, there was little to fear except, perhaps, for ineptness of step or accidental collision.

The dance hall complex was relatively modern, having been added on to the spa complex, and designed in a nineteenth century Russian Revivalist style with tall arched windows and two imposing spires. Inside, it contained a wide sweeping curved staircase, down which one would arrive at the main lobby outside the hall itself, dressed to impress.

Katerina started to develop a feeling of nostalgia for the days of Czarist Russia when the aristocracy would flaunt their wealth and looks. The gowns and outfits were, of course, rented for the occasion and the jewellery elaborate fakes. All was overseen by the Council, but nonetheless it felt exciting and glamorous. The motherland would reward its own, those who opposed the decadent west and its political liberation, and embraced the new science.

The sun was now set and the lights dimmed. From nowhere came a bang; the ballroom was turned to darkness. Just the light given off by the two large candelabras remained, which were, surprisingly enough, genuinely authentic and powered by wax rather than electricity. They could even have been restored originals from the Czarist era. The failure of electric power brought them into focus in a way which quite struck Katerina. With light, sometimes less is more, as it helps focus our remaining attention on what we had previously missed. Then the main lights spurted back into life. It was a power cut plain and simple. So common in Russia's past soviet era but humiliating in modern times for an energy super power. Under cover of that semi-darkness another figure slipped into the hall and hid themselves behind a pillar, without being noticed.

The entertainment started with some folk dances. Katerina was reluctant at first, but eventually persuaded to join in by Sonya. Eventually her courage extended to accepting invitations from two young men, eager to make her acquaintance. Though both were quite charming, she shied away from exchanging details. After five rounds she quit exhausted, but soon it was time for a dance display.

The Cossack men came on for hopak, and the most eye watering performance Katerina had even seen. Even more incredibly they managed to walk away without sticks or any other kind of assistance.

The final dance of the evening was approaching. "Don't worry, just let the man lead," whispered Sonya. "Tradition dictates you cannot refuse an offer by a man on the last dance of the evening; but he'd better be good especially if his summons is unexpected or unwelcome."

Katerina smiled nervously; she hoped not to be asked. She had acceded to earlier requests, but her closest male companion in life was her cat, and that was how she felt most comfortable. Sonya's flirting advice had fallen on deaf ears.

"The last dance, if you please," said a strange voice behind her she half recognised. "So good to meet you in person at last,

Miss Kotov. Or is it the second time we have met? You should know I really am one of your admirers, it's just you don't seem to realise it yet."

She turned and found Nik. Without waiting for her response he grabbed her and started waltzing her around the room, at such a pace that made her a little giddy. Despite the unwelcome approach, he did at least have the merit of avoiding collisions and seemed to turn her stylishly and effortlessly. She wondered where he had learned his skill, as her flowing skirts lifted a little too high for her comfort.

"You are the sun and the moon to me," he whispered in her ear.

"I don't think so," she replied, catching her breath. "It's moons of Uranus that trip you up a bit, and your sun is setting fast."

She was of course referring to *Planets* and Nik's intervention with the game on Oberon.

The music finished with a flourish. She tried to push him away, but he grasped her into himself. "Never refuse me again, I claim you for my own," he hissed quietly. With that she felt a sharp pain in her foot and he had departed. Blood slowly oozed out of her right dancing shoe. He had stamped on her foot hard. Immediately prior and, possibly without Nik's knowledge, a badge had fallen from his jacket and the pin had somehow been caught on her shoe at such an angle that Nik's foot had pressed it in.

How could he possibly have thought that she had a romantic interest in him? What unintended signal had she given? What strange fancy had entered his mind? But Katerina was not to know of the conversations and misunderstandings between Nik and her father, nor indeed that Nik's family had had long-standing connections with Professor Kotov which might have given context to such thoughts.

"That was disgusting, he should be publicly shamed," Mariya was always there to help. She had a bandage in her bag.

"No, please, no fuss," replied Katerina. "He's an entitled arrogant pig, but if you say anything people will just say I led him on. Leave it and he'll go. I'm sure he lost his badge by accident."

Mariya was doubtful.

Sonya spotted Nik skulking around after.

"I heard you'd hacked Katerina on *Planets*."

"No comment."

"How you could have done that. How much did the vodka cost?"

"Again, no comment."

She eyeballed him.

"Unless, of course, you are a Game Admin. I'd heard you were one of the original architects. Wouldn't that be interesting for the authorities to know if it were true."

Nik scurried off.

At the end was the prize draw. Each member of her Seven Star had chosen their ball, numbered one to seven, at the start of the day. The number was revealed at the end. Each ball was placed in a glass bowl. Every woman had by now changed into her best evening gown, waiting eagerly for the Master of Ceremonies. He donned a blindfold to make the selection, demonstrating lack of partiality, and carefully keeping hold of the ball to ensure only he would observe the lucky winning number when sight was returned. He whispered the number into the ear of his assistant.

Eventually after the third round of vodkas, the winner was revealed. It was Katerina. She walked up slowly to shake hands and receive the envelope with her prize. Her foot gave her pain, but not so much as to be obvious to a casual observer. With nervous anticipation she opened the envelope.

"Oh wow," she cried.

Tanis gave her a wink.

She would be going on the holiday of a lifetime. All-expenses paid to any capital city of her choosing in Europe or Asia. Style and comfort would be guaranteed. She knew exactly where she would be going. In the corner she noticed Nik scowling before he crept off into the night.

"Congratulations," said Tanis. "It'll be off to London for you, will it?"

She gave her knowing smile. Katerina had never mentioned her dream of seeing London to Tanis, but Tanis just knew everything.

Mariya congratulated her with a hug; "How wonderful for you – what you've always wanted, coming a lot sooner than you might have hoped!"

"Oh thank you. Yes, it's what I dreamed of in maybe ten years' time, but now it's coming so soon. I'm going to have to start reading up and preparing and planning and everything!"

They slowly made their way back to where their transport home was waiting for them.

"How are we going to beat that for the next social," asked Sonya once they were inside. "I suppose you could do a mash-up video of your London trip, Katerina, and present it at the Seven Star?"

"Oh no you wouldn't want me being a mini film producer!" said Katerina smiling.

"I have in mind a wonderful virtual trip to Madagascar," added Anastasia. "You are just going to be wowed. I promise you it will even beat the Galapagos excursion last year."

"And a prize draw of an in-person trip?" enquired Sonya.

"Ha no; that's really expensive. Five years' free subscription to *Planets* maybe?"

They all laughed.

## POWER SYSTEM REPORT

**Location:** Vsevolozhsk substation.

**Start:** 18:44:28.

**End:** 18:46:02.

**Cause:** Unknown trip suspected hack code-sign CountParis.

**Action:** State security is working to identify the hacker, who might be an insider.

## SCENE DREAMING IN SUMMER: SWINDON AND ST VLADISGRAD

In Swindon it was the early hours of the morning. Will woke suddenly hot and sticky. It was 6am, well before his usual 8 am alarm. The air conditioning had stopped overnight; it must have been off for a couple of hours at least. He checked local energy levels and sure enough they were low. The prioritisation made by the system had been made to preserve power for the Cloud and let humans suffer while they slept. Fair enough; most people would not notice or mind too much, and this decision had been automated and therefore easy for him to defend at the monthly community energy forum.

He checked the video and television connections to his flat. They were still active, so there was no actual power failure at least to Walcot Lodge. He could relax before starting work at 8:30am.

There were three new episodes of The Sampsons, a US-based cartoon comic strip around a dysfunctional family of giants attempting to make sense of modern life. If he started watching now he could catch up and so not waste this extra time. It was themed around an online game called "suns and moons" bearing an uncanny resemblance to his own favourite online game. The farce used the themes of game-obsession and game-reality confusion to draw out tensions in family relationships, with the inevitable virtual romantic tangles taking the characters from anger to ecstatic joy and back to sober reality all in ten minutes.

He broke from his escapism to  remember a dream he had interrupted by waking so unnaturally early. He was talking to Rosaline again, just outside the church in Kingsgeld.

"Come round – I'd like to see you again. Swindon isn't so far, is it?"

"I could cycle there in half an hour," she laughed, "and I work in Swindon anyway. But I can't join you in your world. Nothing would make me leave here. Why can't you leave the Cloud?"

Will knew no one who voluntarily left the Cloud. It would be like being cancelled.

"Ha – no way. Why would I lose everything in life?" he replied. She smiled sadly and walked on.

★

In St Vladisgrad Katerina had problems with sleep too. She felt guilty on behalf of her Seven Star at how Natezdha had been treated, even though she herself had voted against the sanctions. Half of her saw the point of being patriotic, and that only the heterosexual should contribute to the gene pool of the next generation. But another part of her had compassion on those who were different. Talking to Sonya had helped affirm her in her viewpoint, but she still felt Natezdha's pain at separation from the Seven Star and other cloud privileges even if for a limited period. She knew the issue on sexuality was more nuanced than the official line. Perhaps she should have spoken up for her? No, that would have been disloyal to the Star. There was no easy solution.

At least it wasn't complete cancellation. Natezdha could reform her views (or at least self-censor), support the party, and move back into the Seven Star with all benefits restored. It wasn't mining Siberian salt mines or harvesting peat bogs like a century ago. But deep down she felt a gnawing sense of guilt which would just not let her rest.

Was it this, perhaps, that led her to yet more odd behaviour on her game? Critics might suggest her behaviour was not in her own best interests, and that she was trying to punish herself for the failures of her Seven Star despite having done all she could to act within her own conscience.

### SCENE *PLANETS*

On Oberon Will sensed it first. There had been a change in the social order in the Red Giants. Will was watching with his military binoculars. The guards looked confused. After several hours the giants started coming out, followed by a coffin. A guard procession began, the bier being hoist on their broad shoulders. Horns were sounded, spears were paraded upright, and women wailed like banshees. Except for the maid, who was off collecting eggs again and who was sufficiently lowly not to be deemed essential at this important occasion. This time she came closer, so close Will could see her face, her hands, the details of her simple shawl, even her leather sandals, slipping on the icy rockface.

Will was looking for the portal to the next level. There was a problem though; he did not actually know what the portal looked like or where it was. He suspected it was in the camp, and very sure it was well guarded. But without a map he could not be certain.

Will sensed there might be a chance; an upheaval which might give him an opportunity to break into the heart of the encampment and search for the portal, while the enemy characters were fully occupied with other matters.

Then Will had an idea; with the camp apparently temporarily virtually deserted, why not follow the maid back? She might lead him through defensive weakness and perhaps show him, albeit inadvertently, where his next move would be. There must be some clue to the portal location, some kind of defence mechanism around it, which he could use to identify the location. Then he would have to figure out a plan to get into it. There must be a way, as others had followed this trajectory before him, and must have succeeded.

He was lucky; there was no dog with her this time. It seems the wolf hounds had been chained for the occasion, safely away from disturbing the solemn events. So Will moved towards her, keeping camouflaged until she was no more than forty yards away, still half a mile from camp. The challenge was to follow her back there unnoticed. She had done well for eggs today; the basket was overflowing. She would be steadily making progress while a tribal king was being buried deep in the ice, but that did mean her attention would be on the basket to maximise her yield.

It happened in a flash; one egg dropped, and his plan fell apart. She spun round to observe the impact of her clumsiness, and their eyes met at just twenty yards. Once met they could never unmeet. She had seen the intruder close up. He fixed his eyes on her. She was quite a beauty but this was no time to be distracted. He needed to watch her every movement; her eyes and her hands. She made no attempt to reach for her knife though. He approached slowly. She looked nervous.

"Can I help you Sir?"

That was not what Will expected. They were enemies on *Planets*. She must know that. Neither was aware just yet that they were also in opposing political blocks in real life.

"Do you know who I am?"

"An intruder Sir. I should report you."

"So why not."

"The men are away."

"But you should report me anyway."

"Yes, but maybe I'm a bit of a rebel."

If Katerina's avatar had been auto-set (game avatar) it would have automatically reported Will, but as it happens she was playing this scene herself in her self-allotted weekly budget. It had never been in Katerina's nature to dob anyone in. Her loyalties, already a little strained by her demotion, were as much to be true to herself as to win the game.

Will could not understand this at all, and initially suspected a trap. Was she playing for time as she didn't rate her chances against him armed only with a knife? All were supposedly rational, whether human-played or played by the game avatar. It was often impossible to tell the difference when in programme mode, though human play tended to have better results. Will certainly couldn't tell which it was.

"Are you really human-controlled right now?" he asked.

"I could say anything and it might be true and might not be," came the reply.

"There's always a way to prove it," countered Will. Her eyes widened.

"And why would I want to do that?"

"To show me you're pure."

"OK. If you do."

"You first."

Will trusted no one, not after the last attempt to hack him. She hesitated, having already been hacked herself. There was something about this avatar that attracted her. Unlike Will, she was sure it was being human-played.

"I'm Katerina Kotov, Russian, unregistered. Who are you?"

"Will Green, Swindonian. How come you can play unregistered?" exclaimed Will. "I thought it wasn't allowed."

"Swindonian? Where's that? I have privileged access. I joined years ago before the rules changed."

"Swindon is the capital of England. Isn't it risky playing unregistered in Russia?"

"Oh yes. What happened to London then? I heard something about the capital being moved. I take risks, but only with my life. I hold the lives of others in higher value," she replied, truthfully.

"London's still there, a hundred miles from us in Swindon. Swindon became capital because of its commitment to computing and hosting the Government servers securely, and because the local people had a commitment to make our new technology-based society work. But let's meet in another place," suggested Will. "I'd like to get to know you. Let's quit here, let the game avatars take over, or freeze, and you can pretend to the giants that this meeting never happened."

## SCENE ON CLOUD 9

Cloud 9 permitted inter-block connection. The downside was loss of privacy to Inter-block Security agencies in either block, who each had the right to monitor connections made using the facility. They had to be careful. Communications themselves were not supposed to be recorded under normal circumstances, only the length of video or phone conversation. Actual intercepts were only supposed to be allowed where there was reasonable suspicion of a threat to national security. However it was Inter-block Security agencies who decided what was reasonable, so there were never any guarantees. Given the lack of transparency over that decision making, not everyone trusted the authorities not to eavesdrop. It was best to avoid using certain keywords, since real-time AI systems could flag these up as potentially suspicious.

They started without videos, both cams switched off.

"Why didn't you report me to the Red Giants like you were supposed to?" asked Will. "You can't now, or else it looks like collusion and you'll risk recrimination."

"Why didn't you report me to the Russian authorities for having an unregistered account? Indeed it's not too late – why don't you report me now?" countered Katerina.

Will had no interest in reporting her for illegally playing. She had used an unverified ID when the rules allowed it and *Planets* had no way of going back to check. "Can't they spot an unverified ID being used on the game?" quizzed Will.

"Yes but they can't tell who. Anyway, Inter-block Security don't worry about gaming as long as it really is gaming. It's anything that affects politics or military secrets they care about, or internal dissident groups that they can't pick up. Those groups all formed through meeting one another on *Planets* years ago. They quickly moved platforms to dark chat when state security was onto how they were meeting up. The Seven Stars, that's like your bubbles only with seven not twelve, don't like *Planets* because it they're worried about leakage of western liberal ideology, but like you said it's not illegal. If I was caught I'd lose some social credit and privileges, that's all. But because no one has worked out how to breach Russian cyber defences directly through any secure game, security just let it go."

"What about this conversation? Monitored?"

"Probably not as it's not a threat to security. Westerners and Russians are allowed to talk. Personal, business, anything, just not politics or military."

"So, how long have you been a maid on Oberon?"

"You should ask how many times, not how long. I served as maid, got promoted, then demoted back after a security breach. I was a Red Queen for a while."

"I see. And how many intruders get through to the Portal?"

"Really not many. I think a lot give up at this point. Some of the newer ones switch to other trajectories, but of course that costs real-life money."

"Ah. So how do they do it, the ones who do get through?"

"I'm not sure, but no one's done it alone. Either there's a large well-armed group all breaking through together, or else they have inside help."

"And how do *you* escape?" Will felt her blushing.

"I get promoted back. I have to help the cause, become a queen again, then when I have enough points a sky chariot carries me away towards Mars, with easy access to earth thereafter. It's called the Mars Chariot trajectory. I hear the ride's quite spectacular!"

"You wouldn't like it on Mars!" suggested Will, having spent long enough there himself. "It's a real place of war. Anyway, tell me what happened today? How did the king die? Why were you out foraging and not at the funeral?"

"Not sure. Maybe he was cancelled? And as for foraging, I'm afraid that goes with the role. Not important enough for the grand occasions."

"Cancelled? Don't you mean reset?"

"No, really cancelled. Real-world. Nothing on Oberon or anything on the game had anything to do with it. The real-world avatar deleted and all associated accounts deleted. Death. That's what happens if a player's registered NVID can't be verified anymore. I guess it can happen if a player gets hacked, but usually with hacking they wait a few days to allow the ID to be restored, if it can be."

"Oh. Well that's sad. We'll never know why I guess. Behind every cancellation there's a real human story. We had to cancel an ID yesterday. Failed the Turing Test. It's good to get these ghosts off the system, isn't it?" He failed to mention how he voted.

Katerina could sense the unease now. Will was clearly uncomfortable at what he and his bubble had done. It occurred to him he might just have cancelled the ID behind the Red Giant king's avatar.

"We have more denouncings than cancellations," she volunteered. "Only for those whose views are politically uneducated. We bring them back after re-education, depending on how vile their views are. Your cancellations are more like witch-burnings. Once burned, the witch isn't coming back, ever. Even if she wasn't ever a witch."

"How do you define witches?"

"Ha; women with cats in your world, lesbians in ours, I think. Or anyone who is out of line with the prevailing political tide, whatever that happens to be at the time."

They both laughed.

"I think that makes me a witch in the west."

"As long as you're not a witch in Russia; I'd hate for you to get dunked on a witching stool or burnt at the stake."

"Ha no. Not a chance. Not that there's anything wrong with lesbians, of course. They're just as much my sisters as those of my friends with extensive experience of men. Except of course, they don't tend to shout out about it in our country. So, tell me how someone gets cancelled in the west? I hear so many stories."

"Our cancellations give opportunity for the outsiders to join in; more space for everyone," Will countered. "In theory the number of Cloud citizens isn't limited to a given number. In practice they like to limit the numbers coming in, except for children attaining citizenship. The policy of one-in-one-out gives cover to make it easier to say no if the Council doesn't like people applying who had refused the opportunity when first presented. Anyway the cancelled accounts are generally ghost accounts. They soak up energy when they don't belong to a living person. We have to move forwards; we can't have new births without the death of the old."

The limit on the number of cloud NVIDs was a widely propagated myth.

"Oh really? So the authorities claim you only have so many NVIDs? That can't be right at all."

Will reflected on this conversation. It appeared to going at a tangent to his original purpose of firstly progressing in the game and secondly his newly acquired objective of developing a friendship with a Cloud Citizen of the opposite gender.

"So why did you open your avatar up and decide to meet me?" asked Will.

Much better. Draw her out into conversation.

She paused here. "Wanting to get to know you. Having some fun." She sounded unconvincing. "You know, it's really stifling sometimes being part of a Seven Star that enforces uniformity of thought. I don't meet anyone different. All the Seven Stars are single sex, not like your mixed ones. Personal relationships have to be vetted before you're allowed to meet real-life for a date, and of course they're only approved if both appear to be politically aligned and in good standing in the group. Even social media is constrained. We have Vladischat, a supposedly safe social networking site within the city, but it's monitored and just like a Seven Star discussion really."

"Well I just want to get on in the game. And we're on the opposite side from each other. Should we really be talking? Maybe I can win you over." Will smiled as he said this. Even he could tell perfectly well she was looking for friendship. "Oh, by the way, we're banned from dating in-bubble. It's all strictly monitored."

"Maybe I can help you?" she volunteered.

"With the game or with dating? Your loyalty is to the Red Giants. You would get demoted again or reset if they knew you were talking to me." Testing her again. Of course he wanted her help. He just wanted to make sure she would be loyal.

She laughed.

"Well they don't know I'm talking to you, do they. Unless state security have nothing better to do with their time than listen in and then let the Red Giants know. I don't think that's going to happen is it?"

"Guess not," Will admitted. "OK, so tell me where the Portal is?"

The Portal was the escape to the next stage, which for Will meant the freedom of the solar system, effectively finishing the game and achieving planetary freedom. Her route away from here was different, and so the Portal would be of no use to her. Indeed any intruder successfully escaping using it might set back her progress out, as well as that of the giants. Nonetheless, she was willing to help.

"That's easy; it's down the well in the centre of the camp. You just have to jump down."

"I see. And how do I get there?"

"Ah well, that's the awkward bit. It has three guards and a wolf pack surrounding it day and night."

"OK. So I have to get past the guards and the dogs?"

"Well yes. It's hard as the guards are heavily armed. If they are attacked they will call for reinforcements."

"Right. So how do I do it? It must have been done before."

"A group of players joined together last time. They were well armed but, importantly, acted quickly. Surprise was the key. However, since then other precautions may have been put in place."

"Fine. So, where do I find these fellow brothers? I see no other players."

"I don't think you can right now. I haven't seen any other players around, and listening at the giants' meal table, I don't think they've seen any either. If enough undetected intruders enter, then join up, it could happen again. But I think you're the only one right now. This level is really hard to get to on your trajectory; I think most are giving up and switching before they even get here."

No way was Will going to spend much more time on Oberon. Resources were scarce. He had no desire to switch paths either, not because of the real-world money but due to pride. He needed to act now or risk reset.

"OK, so it's team work I need. You're here with me now, but you're on their side."

"Yes I know. I love helping people. I'm on their side in the game, on this scene, but what do I know of them off-game? Nothing at all! This game is meant to be about networking and building friendships. It's not meant to be a race to the finish, it's what you do on the journey there. Do you want to get to know me better?"

"Sure. We can switch to direct video feed."

A privacy risk, but Katerina agreed, despite her previous negative experience with Nik.

So, for the first time she saw the inside of an English studio apartment. She studied Will in more detail. This was not to be her James Bond. No rippling torso and chiselled jaw, instead dishevelled hair with a gently receding hairline above a pale bookish face. He wasn't bad looking though, and he had kept his weight down. His voice was sufficiently deep to reassure, but not sufficiently deep to convey leadership. He was dressed in a manner which would have been considered excessively casual in Russia even for a video call. His long shorts revealed his hairy but athletic legs which were quite pleasing. He might have been a runner a few years ago, she wondered. Not quite the alpha male, but he had potential.

She looked more closely. No pictures of friends or family, just a Mandelbrot set computer-generated picture on the wall, and on the shelves a couple of books on mathematics and one called

'Plasma Physics." He appeared to have labelled his drawers but that idiosyncratic approach had clearly failed to translate into a room with any semblance of tidiness. He wore an old T shirt (holes visible). He was in all ways the polar opposite of Nik. It was the authenticity and lack of pomp and hard edge that started drawing her to him, together with his kind face. He displayed intelligence, if not perhaps the qualities of a leader

She unpinned her hair, allowing her long dark hair to fall to her waist. She followed his eyes as he watched her, pleased that she had his undivided attention. Her waist seemed accentuated by the long skirt she wore, tight around the waist, contrasting with her looser blouse. It would have been considered quite outdated clothing in England, but he assumed in Russia it must still be considered normal. He estimated her height as only a couple of inches below his own, which for him constituted the ideal build. When she spoke her soft voice enchanted him, capturing his mind completely but, more importantly, he felt the pull of her full attention too. He felt both attraction and trepidation. He remembered Tim's words about Rosaline: "she's out of your league." Was he over-reaching himself again here?

He looked more closely at her blouse then her arm. There were strange marks on her left forearm. Could they have been self-inflicted? Best not to ask, for now at least.

The pain of Rosaline started to melt and his heart rate edged slowly upwards. She followed his eyes and read his thoughts. She knew he found her pleasing.

"You know what I do off-*Planets*?" she asked.

Will didn't know at all.

"I am a reproductive scientist. A doctor. I help males and females have their own biological children in a way that reduces risk of inherited disease."

Will knew about the process of course. Scientific reproduction was the norm now worldwide. In one way it reduced the peer-pressure for establishing relationships. In the west it was also starting to be the norm for non-relationship parenting, mostly out-sourced to the state. The parents could play as much or as little a part as they chose in the children's upbringing, but had to pay the state for childcare accordingly. Greater state involvement rather than less was being encouraged.

In theory it democratised society, equalising reproduction capability between him and the likes of Michael who was a regular Don Juan. In fairness, Michael claimed not to have any children. The likes of Michael had plenty of natural opportunity, should they wish to take it. Why shouldn't the licensing of reproduction and the separation between romance and parenthood be used to even up the reproduction chances and promote a more diverse gene pool?

Also it provided for the opportunity of life-long freedom from anything other than financial responsibility, which for elite performers such as Will and his bubble was invaluable. It enabled them to join elite bubbles for singles or semi-singles, and to co-locate. Cloud citizens living in nuclear families had to choose supervised contact bubbles, denying them a wider range of social interaction. Living in an elite bubble, he had not yet chosen (or had the opportunity) to become a parent.

"Tell me more." It is the simple sentence that is so rarely spoken but the one, if repeated more frequently, would save many a marriage.

"You tell me first how it is in England."

"We license parenthood not marriage now. The link between the two was being downplayed. There was conflict when 'permit to parenthood' had been introduced. This came mainly from libertarians, on human rights grounds."

"It's similar here. What about the church's reaction?"

"The Church of England accepted we had to move with the times, but other religious groups claimed that marriage itself gave adequate permission for natural parenthood, subject only to the will of God as expressed through the natural abilities of the spouses involved."

"We've had conflict between church and state too. What happened?"

"The state de-recognised marriage, thus allying conservative religious traditionalists, libertarians and LGBTQ groups in opposing what they all described as secular fundamentalism, but the protests had no impact."

"And how is it policed?"

"The sanction for unlawful conception potentially includes cloud-expulsion unless there is a termination. Some fringe groups argue for more draconian sanctions."

"They did in Russia too, only those fringe groups had won a partial victory. There is still forced termination here, but the church bitterly opposes it."

"I see."

"Here there is state recognition and marriage carries an automatic entitlement to two children between spouses, but at the cost of the requirement for state approval for the marriage. Those with children with other partners were generally not given that permission, unless held in high esteem by the party for political service. Thus the block exercises population control measures but dressed in semi-religious language to avoid upsetting many different religious groups."

"So, coming back to what you actually do? I've heard of reproductive science, but I've never worked out how it's done and how it's supposed to improve the health of the next generation."

"First off I have a list of potential genetic parents, mother and father. The list comes with state ratings and approval likelihoods, as well as conditions. For example, minimum height, hair colour, stuff to do with parents and grandparents. Sometimes the selections are from married parents, so we don't need the matching process, but usually not."

"We don't use that language mother and father here in the west. It discriminates against those whose parents are unable to look after them, and indeed we share community responsibility for parenting now. It gives everyone a fairer start in life."

"That's interesting. Language and discrimination are topics being discussed here too, but the focus is on the science for now, and getting the best gene pool. Once I match the parents we combine the DNA. Usually we have an egg from the mother but we can do it without if needed using a donated egg but the mother's DNA."

"I see."

"Then we make any required edits to the DNA, and set the process in motion. We can implant back in the mother or incubate artificially. Our artificial results weren't as good when we first started out, but now with more experience we can get an improvement on outcomes, so more people choose that. If the mother wishes to carry or use a surrogate we have more work to do to check up on the developing baby."

"What about sex?"

"Some parents can choose, but this costs. There are strict rations too. We aren't allowed to go more than 55% male so we often have to say no even if the parents offer to pay."

Will thought it so strange that sex selection was permitted at all. In the western block this had been banned ever since artificial reproduction had started.

"So what else do you do?"

"Screen for all the known genetic diseases of course. Select for intelligence and all the characteristics we need in today's world. We are creating the scientific, political and military leaders of tomorrow."

"And *planet* Players too? It's too important to leave to chance." She smiled.

"What's really nice is when the parents have never met before but they still choose to parent together. Sometimes they meet up afterwards, and we had a few get married, after they had already chosen each other as co-parents. That gives us more scope for the child's upbringing of course. They can choose to bring the child up together if they want, though of course that comes at the cost of reduced employment opportunities." She paused. "Now you need to tell me what you do."

"It's to do with the environment," he replied. "Reducing carbon emissions."

"Like planting lots of trees?" she asked.

"Planting trees is really good at soaking up carbon we've already emitted into the atmosphere. Some of my colleagues do that, and some are working on other ways to get the carbon out of the air. I'm more focussed on trading rather than practical implementation of carbon reduction schemes. If the trading is efficient, the right price signals are passed to all parties. In theory that means that the schemes which go ahead are the best value, giving the most carbon reduction for a given cost."

"I won't pretend to understand it all, but it sounds really interesting. You must tell me more about that later."

Will was nervous now, anxious not to prolong the session too long in case of boring her.

"I need to go now but see you again soon."

"Bye. Hope to see you again soon. I want to hear all about your work saving the planet next time. I won't let you forget." She blew him a little kiss which Will blew back.

Success.

As Katerina had mentioned she came from Vladisgrad, Will Clouded it. "Previous names Leningrad, St Petersburg, founded a long time ago as a Swedish hill fort." "Vlad" sounded more interesting so he Clouded that. "Vlad impaled a lot of people he didn't like. That wasn't very nice, was it?" was all he could find. So why on earth did they change the name to that?

**SCENE SISTER-TALK**

Katerina convened a convocation of her inner support group, which currently consisted of just Sonya, Mariya and Anastasia. The topic, of course, was Will.

"I think I love him," she confessed. "He's not a ten out of ten, more like a seven or eight. But there's a simple transparency about him. I actually trust him, and I don't say that about most men."

"What does he do?" asked Sonya.

"Something to do with the environment. Trees were mentioned, but then he said it was more his colleagues who did that. Something about pricing. Anyway, it sounds good."

"Promising," admitted Mariya. "Remember what Chekhov said about forestry: improving the natural environment makes men more courteous."

"How so?" asked Sonya.

"Chekhov was a doctor first a poet second, remember," she replied. "I think he meant that the better the air, the better a man's humour, so the better he treats women."

"He has a very pleasant humour," said Katerina. "I'll put it down to those trees then. I must ask him more about it."

"Not like that scoundrel Nik then. A self-entitled white Russian who thinks women should throw themselves at his feet because his family had wealth two hundred years ago," added Sonya, whose loathing of Nik clearly dated from some time ago.

"So what do you think, ladies?" asked Katerina.

"A keeper," replied Sonya.

"Try him out," advised Mariya.

"I'm going to," Katerina announced. "I'll travel to London to meet him with the Star Prize I've just won. Except he doesn't actually live there. He's in Swindon. I'm sure Swindon's just as exciting with just as much history as London, it's just I've never heard of it. Apparently it's the capital now."

"That's so cool," said Anastasia. "Is that your lifetime travel permit? Even winning in a Star event, it still counts towards the limit, doesn't it?"

"I've just clouded Swindon," volunteered Sonya. "Apparently it has something to do with pigs. It has a lot of roundabouts, and it's the place which decides the budgets for western research and science."

"That can't be right," exclaimed Mariya. "No one would name a city after an animal, surely? Not that that's any reflection on your new potential lover, of course."

"Sure. Talking to Will I've realised why there's a lifetime limit on travel for everyone. It's all to do with carbon. Apparently travelling emits lots of it. We should ideally all have a lifetime limit on how we emit because that's only fair, but the easiest way to enforce that is a lifetime international travel limit. Apparently that applies even if you use zero-carbon fuel on your flight, because there's only a limited supply of it. What does everyone else plan to do with theirs?"

"I'm going to go to New York, maybe to stay there," volunteered Sonya. "If they'll have me of course."

"I'll go somewhere with sun during our bleak winters," said Mariya.

"I've got mine planned," said Anastasia. "I have a field trip lined up to study in Madagascar. While I'm there I'll help to make a virtual reality experience based on what I learned. You'll be able to join me online as I show the island off in all its glory."

"Can I come?" asked Mariya. "Sounds like the ideal winter sun get away!"

All these plans, but how many would come to pass?

## LEAFHILL NEWS SERVICE FLASH

"11:54:27 it was reported that there had been a leak from a North Sea underground repository of carbon dioxide following an explosion. Most carbon from that well had escaped. Analysts assumed it would be safe there because oil and gas had been stored there for millions of years. It seems to have been caused by an explosion underwater at the well head, which had been mined. It is believed that the saboteurs dived down from a boat and attached explosives, then detonated remotely. World Carbon Emission Permits (WCEP) prices have jumped 50%."

"14:12:07 saw a second explosion at a different well head, following this morning's explosion. WCEPs gained a further 20%, with one trader talking of further rises to come."

"15:22:48 a third explosion was reported. The markets suspending trading in WCEP pending the outcome of investigations. Green opposition leaders are calling the scheme 'fundamentally flawed'. An inside source, who wishes to remain anonymous states 'we assumed it would be easy to store this stuff for millions of years because that's where the gas came from, but we didn't reckon with this'. Police sources have confirmed they are treating the events as linked and are urgently investigating."

## SCENE CARBON NIGHTMARE

Michael called Will to the common area. "What's the impact?" he enquired.

"Carbon price was 70% up based on information about leaks at the point trading was suspended," replied Will.

"Are we sure of the underlying cause?" asked Michael.

"I could ask you the same," replied Will. "Terrorism? It can't be coincidence."

"And what's the economic impact?"

"The North Sea holds almost all the storage for most of Europe," replied Will. "And between them those three wells held 80% of European storage. What's really spooking the market is that this is the first ever carbon leak. It's causing mayhem in the international transport fuel and hydrogen markets as many countries still use blue hydrogen. I'm monitoring the situation. Assuming it's terrorism, what's behind this?"

"If it's terrorism, speculation is it's my old enemy Daesh," replied Michael. "I spend too much time watching Moscow and not enough watching them. One theory is that they had a boat and sent out divers with mines. The security wasn't tight enough to catch them."

"More news in: the navy have just confirmed that they have arrested a boat with several divers on board. It seems the boat had been taken by pirates, and the original crew all murdered."

"Sounds like it was well planned."

"That won't go down well. If the markets think carbon storage is a terrorism target, the cost of carbon emissions will just rocket when trading resumes."

"We don't want global panic or the whole Cloud could seize up. We'll have the lights out not just in Swindon or England but across the pond too. I'll put out some story about pipe corrosion to the general press and that it's a localised problem with no wider implications. How long do you think it will last?"

"It's a bit late for that, sorry. European power prices are super volatile. Hard to say how long it will go on for. Could go on for the rest of the year, depending on how quickly the market finds a solution. Or it might be over in a few days."

For Will, that meant cutting community power consumption, and that was unpopular. It was only two months until community appraisal, when they would decide if he was to continue as Community Energy Co-ordinator. Being cancelled-in-role could also adversely impact his position in international carbon trading and by extension his place in the Walcot Bubble. The community selection process was required for the role, even though he was technically a central Government employee. A major incident like this would not help him at all. What was unfortunate was the local hydrogen stockpile; it was close to a seasonal low.

"So what do you propose?"

"We community-source the prioritisation decisions through an online poll. We activate the Swindon Community Energy Council. Then it's down to temperature, data or storage. The council members can make the strategic decisions while the system makes the tactical ones based on the agreed strategy parameters. There are unpleasant consequences with all choices."

"Right. Good luck. You make the call, I'll hunt the culprits, or the culprits behind the culprits."

Things happened faster than even Will feared, and there was no time to consult with the Community Energy Council as he had planned. Within an hour the recommendation came to use the last of the stored hydrogen. But there was only four hours usage left. So by seven pm East Swindon would potentially be in darkness, cloud services would be down, and there could be action on the streets. This was far worse than the heatwave a few weeks ago. It would mean ten thousand angry residents and commuters, not just a few inconvenienced businesses. Pods would stop lifeless in the middle of the street, the occupants not even able to exit. Train passengers would be stuck between Swindon and Didcot. His name would be the first one to be cursed as they vented their frustration. Swindon City would forfeit their evening derby match against Oxford in the Premiership, and that alone could cause riots.

By this time other bubble members had joined them, sensing the enormity of the news.

"It's your own fault," claimed Rose. "You shouldn't have created the carbon in the first place. Then you wouldn't have to worry about burying it, because it would have been locked in the ground anyway. Why can't you just do the simple thing?"

"This just shows how inefficient carbon markets are," said Peter. "You're using a capitalist solution to fix a capitalist problem and you get a capitalist result."

"Your problem is over-centralisation. You should democratise carbon by storing it locally. Then ordinary people can decide on the carbon trade-offs," said Tim. "You are removing the people from energy, and when you do that you lose the sense of ownership."

"Just slaughter some more cattle," suggested Dick. "They're the biggest greenhouse emitters of all with their smelly ends and high methane yield."

"Better to stop eating cows altogether," countered Rose.

"Have we got any other technological solutions?" asked Ben.

Will recalled his first love for energy, which came when he saw that exhibition on fusion at the Science Museum seven years ago.

"Some say fusion is about to make a break-through," said Will.

"Isn't that, like, nuclear, which we're trying to get rid of?" asked Rose.

"Oh no, totally different. Safe, clean, just teething issues getting it to work," replied Will, glossing over some of the technical nuances. "No radiation to speak of."

"I'm not sure I totally believe that," said Peter. "If it was that great we'd have done it by now."

"Interesting idea," added Michael. "I heard the Japanese were on the cusp of a break-through."

"Let's see shall we. Sadly for now many dreams will be going up in a puff of escaped carbon," said Will, "We need to prepare for the worst."

### SCENE CLOUD 9 WHERE WILL AND KATERINA TALK CARBON

The same news on carbon leaks also went down badly in St Vladisgrad. Since the carbon markets were global, however much the Russians may have been taking short-cuts on reporting their carbon emissions, they were impacted as much as anyone else.

"Good news and bad news," declared Katerina.

"The good news?" asked Will. That was something that endeared Katerina to Will, his boundless optimism.

"I've booked a flight to Heathrow to see your ancient capital, London."

Will was taken by surprise at this. He had no idea she was at all interested in going there.

"Why would you want to go there?" asked Will. "Last time I went the Culture Riots started. Now it's just for oligarchs escaping the law from their home countries, or looking to indulge their more libertine passions, as there's reduced social control there, deliberately so as to attract wealthy international travellers."

London had several relaxations of normal Cloud protocols, without being outside connectivity, at least for those with money. It was the place to party when parties were banned. It was the place to see and be seen if you were wealthy. However it was no longer the seat of political power.

"As for using the underground there, it's like a mass torture chamber, not to mention smelly and unhygienic," he added, before realising that in coming to London Katerina would doubtless be wanting to meet him. "Of course if you do go, you'll need a local guide."

"Well the bad news is that it was on, but now it's cancelled. Or at least postponed. Something about a Daesh carbon attack and global energy prices through the roof. It's unclear exactly when I'll be able to go. I've been promised it, but only when the airline company can afford the fuel."

"The carbon problem is all over the world. Prices jumped 500% when trading resumed," Will explained. "It hits us hard here too, so I can see how hard it would be to get here from St Vladisgrad."

"I understand fuel prices but I don't understand what you mean by a 'carbon price'," she asked. "You mean how much it costs to buy carbon in order to burn it?"

"No, I mean how much you have to pay for emitting carbon dioxide into the air." Will was getting uneasy now that this counted as a "technical conversation" which was "best to be avoided." Then he remembered he had vowed not to be condescending. Here was the challenge; how to explain a $10 trillion a year market in simple terms.

"So, how does that work? When do you pay?" she asked.

"Oh it's easy. There are five-year quotas. We are in 2045-2050 now, so some carbon emission is still allowed, but after that we will be at net zero. That means as a planet we will have to capture and absorb any carbon we emit. We pay people who absorb carbon and those who emit it must pay for their emission permits. There is a strict rule-book about how to calculate the amounts. Even now, in 2047, the carbon emissions are strictly limited. Every country must report how much it emitted to a central registry. The net amount is equal to what you have emitted less what you have absorbed through the environment or captured and stored safely. You have to pay according to how much you net emitted in the accounting period, by redeeming carbon emission permits. How much this costs depends on the price at which you bought the permits. The price is what another country is willing to sell it to you for if they think they will have carbon emission permits left over," he explained. "Every country has its own system for recording what's been emitted and what's been captured, but they have to follow the international rules in how they do it. That helps to set the price. At the moment countries still have allocated permits so there can be a net positive emission, but in a few years we are moving to net zero and the price will rise as a result."

"Why would you tell anyone everything you've emitted?" she asked. "Why not just under report it and fib a bit?"

"You just have to report honestly; if you cheat, you'll get caught and have to pay more. There's a whole set of people paid just to check these things."

"Oh I see. What are they called?"

"The International Carbon Emissions Monitoring Agency, or Mother Ice for short."

"Oh, I see. So, how much do you have to pay," she asked. "And if England emits lots of carbon, how does that affect us here in Russia? I don't see the connection."

"There's one price all over the world," he replied. "Because the carbon moves all over the world when it's emitted, so you can trade carbon anywhere in the blocks that recognise it. Each country, or sometimes the big corporations within a big country, has a trading function to buy and sell the allowances."

"So, what's the trading got to do with it? Surely there's just one fixed price?"

"Oh no, the price changes all the time."

This genuinely confused her.

"Vodka doesn't change its price every day," she said. "And that's much more important than carbon."

"Do you know about stocks and shares?" he asked, wanting to try to draw the analogy.

"No; the Government owns all big industry again now, just like it did in the soviet era."

This was going to be hard work. Will was doubtful if he could get his message across.

"Have you ever gambled on the football?" he asked.

"No," she replied, "but I know people who have."

"If you bet during the match, do the odds change?"

"Of course they do. If one side scores a goal, they're more likely to win."

"Yes, so the price of the bet changes according to what you know."

She thought about it for a while, before nodding her head.

"So, we have a fixed amount of carbon we're allowed to emit each five-year period. If it looks like we're emitting too much, the price goes up in the same way that the odds change on the football match. That's why the traders have their eyes glued to trading screens that they hope bring them news a fraction of a second faster than it gets to their competitors."

"Ah yes, I see. So you've got to have informants in all the companies that make carbon so you know before anyone else does. Like special networks. Is that why you play on *Planets*?"

"Um, well, you're not meant to do that really."

"But you'd make more money."

"If you get caught doing that you're in trouble."

"Getting in trouble for making money? I'm struggling here. And as for carbon and power prices changing every day, that's strange."

"Oh no, the power price doesn't change every day. It changes every half an hour."

"What?"

"Yes, all the electricity used is measured in each half hour, so that you can decide how much you want to use based on what the price is."

"That's crazy? Isn't that just a sneaky way for them to charge you too much when they feel like it?"

"Oh no, not at all, but it's what people used to think when they first came in, but it's the other way around. If you're clever, you can actually make money by reducing how much you use when the power price goes really high. Unfortunately, not everyone does that."

"You can't keep an eye on the price every half hour, can you? What about when you're asleep? What if they suddenly put the price up when you're not looking?"

"You don't have to watch it all the time. Your avatar can do it for you if you choose to programme it. You just might have to put up with a flat that's warmer or colder than you'd really like, or do energy-consuming things at a different time from when you planned to. But as I say, not everyone does that."

"I can't believe it all changes every 30 minutes, though. That's so complicated."

"Oh, yes, for normal customers."

"And what about customers that aren't normal?"

"We can meter every 60 seconds for big business customers."

"I give up. My brain's starting to hurt. All these numbers are giving me maths anxiety."

"Oh dear. One of my jobs is to try making all this work without triggering anyone. At least the carbon price doesn't change quite so much as the power price. That changes daily, usually."

Katerina could see now that her education, broad as it had seemed, had not fully examined dynamic economics. Smith and Hayek had passed her by, though even they might have been surprised at how quickly power markets could change. Of John Maynard Keynes there was definitely no mention. And there was no Russian word for "Market regulation."

"Price seems to matter so much to your business," she mused. "In my line of work, it hardly gets mentioned at all. It's just about the science."

"The price is very important, you see," he explained. "It shows the most efficient way to stop us putting more greenhouse gasses into the air. That's what this is all about."

Now this was something she did understand and relate to. It was a bit like Chekhov's trees.

"So what you're doing is really important," she said. "I thought I was doing the best possible work to help society, but now I can see that what you're doing has an even higher importance than my work. I'm trying to create good healthy babies but you're helping to protect the earth they will have to live in. Do people keep coming up to you and thanking you for what you do?"

"I like to think so," he replied, feeling that the conversation was heading back where he needed it to be. He always enjoyed being told he was important, but it didn't happen as much as he would have liked. "I trade carbon for the Western block too, as well as my community energy role," he added.

"Really?"

"Yes, there are a team of us across the block members. I traded $20 billions of carbon last year."

Small pause.

"Your team traded $20 billion?" Katerina could not quite bring herself to believe it.

"Oh no. That was my own trading. I only do it part-time, it's not the main role," he explained. "The wider carbon team traded about $100 billion. The global market's worth $10 trillion. China and the US are the biggest players."

Katerina's eyes widened visibly. These were sums of money outside her comprehension.

"That figure is so big it fries my brain! But thanks for explaining it to me. I'd never really thought about it before," she said. "I'm so glad you're doing something for the planet. It's important to me, too. Now I have an important question for you."

"Well there are a lot more than 10 trillion atoms in a human cell, so the number's not that big. But go on."

"How do you help everyone to understand what you're doing, and what they need to do, to help the environment?"

"Ah, well," he fumbled. "I'm still struggling with that one really, it's the part of my job I find hardest."

"How come?"

"Well, the businesses seem to understand it, when it comes to saving money," he said. "But for people at home, some programme their avatars properly, but like I said, a lot don't and miss out on saving money. They would be helping to save the planet too if they thought about it a bit more."

"But don't they care about islands that are going to disappear under the ocean even if they don't care about saving money?"

"They all think they like to care," replied Will. "But when it comes down to it most people can't seem to see the connection between really getting to grips with it all, and climate change. We call it cognitive dissonance."

"So how do you try to fix that?" she asked.

"I'm still figuring that one out. I'm good at energy, just not good at people. At least, that's they said in the last appraisal." Will paused. "So, what would you do if you were in my shoes?"

"Now that's a really good question. I need to find out more about it, but if you want my help you'll get it."

"I do. But tell me what you want from me?"

"I really want to see London. I'd love to visit the cathedrals. St Pauls, Westminster Abbey, the remains of the Houses of Parliament. Your museums and galleries fascinate me. They're mostly in South Kensington, yes?"

Will remembered he was supposed to be encouraging her to come. "Except the British Museum which is near Russell Square, yes, of course. I love London too, it's just I don't go every day. They stopped cheap tickets from here to London seven years ago so I don't go as much. I did see the waxworks before they all melted in a heat wave that shut the power down for a day, but that was a while ago. Do go, you'll find it so exciting."

"I was hoping you'd show me round, as I need a guide. Especially the British Museum. My father told me so much about it and I'm dying to see it."

"I could show you round in exchange for help escaping Oberon." Will had no idea how he would show anyone round. London might be an hour away but he had only been once since the college trip, apart from changing trains, and got lost every time he went. "If only you could get here. It sounds like it's off for the time being, anyway."

Her eyes lit up. "Yes, I'd like that so much. I've been told it's still happening, it's just a question of when. What would you like me to do on Oberon?"

"But you don't know when you can come. It won't be until the energy markets calm down. So I can't host you or show you around until that happens. How can I accept help when I don't know when I can return the favour?"

"Let me help you with *Planets*. You need that help now. Then you can help me when I come over, eventually. It's only postponed. You said yourself markets are volatile, going up and down the whole time. Who's to say in a week it may all look very different. Deal?"

"Sure." It was very trusting of her. Will was unsure she ever would be able to come, and if she did make it he wondered if he would get the time off to meet her. Yes sometimes market were volatile, but the carbon explosion could herald distrust of carbon capture, and that was a key plank in the fight against climate change.

"So, how do I help you best with your mission?"

"You need to distract the guards while I sneak up."

"That's fine but how will I know when to? If you're so close I can see you, they can see you too. There's no comms on Oberon. We don't have walkie-talkies in the equipment set!"

True.

"We have to think of something."

"I have," she replied. "If that's really what you want."

Will paused. There was an unusual nuance to her.

"Yes?"

"I give you control of my avatar."

Will could not believe his ears. He barely knew this woman. He had never met her outside the cloud, and was doubtful he ever would despite her protestations. It was an enormous leap of trust, and it was completely illegal. No cloud NVID was allowed to surrender control to another except under physical duress or Council order. Deliberate contravention could jeopardise the NVID recovery process should that be needed at a later stage. What's more, even if he gave back control, she would still be reset on *Planets* if she acted as she was proposing. The giants would certainly not tolerate such behaviour.

"It's not allowed. Why would you do that?" asked Will.

"I don't see how they can tell. The privacy laws allow remote log in." she fibbed. Of course they would know, as she found out to her cost last time.

"But how do we authenticate against our NVIDs?"

"You don't have to in *Planets*. Remember it uses non-authenticated avatars for legacy players."

True thought Will. Actually possible. "Right let's do it tomorrow. How do you give me your authentication?"

She smiled and instantly an encrypted communication travelled between them. This could be a problem for her if reported to her Seven Star, or for Will if reported to his bubble, but each would find a way of explaining. Will opened and there indeed were the credentials. Wow. Now he was going to have fun, being able to control another avatar while planning his final bold move on Oberon, but more importantly advance his objective.

### SCENE A COINCIDENTAL ENCOUNTER

Will decided to walk to the next bubble meeting, and on his own. Very often some of the bubble would walk together, and more often pods would be shared. It was a cool dry day and he fancied the exercise. The walk was not unpleasant, in the tree-lined street with its fresh air.

As he approached the Magic Roundabout he caught sight of a cyclist. Officially encouraged for a long time, they were much rarer these days, even with the increase in dedicated road-space (in reality now shared with slower moving pods). The cyclist also surprised him as it turned out to be Rosaline. Today she had exchanged her black book for an old-fashioned laptop which she carried on her bright pink panier. Will heard a high-pitched sound and the cyclist, protected only by her helmet and glasses, stopped.

"Hello," he said in surprise. "I hadn't expected to see you here."

"Oh, we're still allowed into Swindon," came the reply. "I'm a clinical child psychologist working here with children aged five to twenty one. I'm the one who checks up on the health and well-being of your little sons and daughters, nephews and nieces."

"Oh, I see. I don't have any children actually. I had no idea about them, I suppose. I mean, I'm not really sure who looks after pre-adults now we're discouraging the sort of nuclear families I grew up in. I've never met one, since I graduated and started working. Never really given it a second thought."

"It must have been a very long time ago that you were a child yourself, then!" she teased.

"Oh well, a few years. So how come you're working here? I thought we gave preferential employment opportunities to cloud citizens over those outside?"

"I am a trained psychologist and there's a national shortage. The Council is very happy to let me work here, given the lack of our specialism, and I love the children. It's so good to see them before they're fully connected to the cloud and start to lose concentration and child-likeness. They're still really fun like that, even for a while after they get their provisional cloud access. After that, they tend to change and become less happy."

"Oh yes, I suppose. What age do they get registered now?"

Will was quite oblivious to modern child welfare.

"It starts from permission to conception, through birth, allocation, supervised provisional access, and then final registration to the cloud and citizenship ceremony, assuming they choose it. Almost all do, sadly. I wish some more would think first. They do have to be able to validly consent and so we don't allow that before they are sixteen. Before that there are provisional NVIDs they can use, but they can't access everything and their activity can be monitored. We don't register them earlier because it has to be their individual informed choice. You can't just be born into cloud society, you have to agree, to the privacy terms, to be bound by democratic consensus, and to sign the social contract. I think if there wasn't such a shortage, they wouldn't let me work."

Will reflected. He had had no real choice at all; his registration and implantation all happened before he was able to get his first job. It was notional consent at best, since without it he had no chance of a career. But he had done it. He had an actual piece of paper to prove it, too. It was the almost only piece of paper he had ever received in his life. The only piece of paper he had ever touched. The only piece of paper he could remember seeing, at any rate. It felt good. It was thick, and embossed. It had his name on it. The proof of who he was; William Francis Green.

"These days the parents have to decide on a name pre-conception," she replied. It's to make the registration and identification easier. Mostly the parents never actually meet, so this is a way we can make sure the child has a name."

"So, do you do the Identification operation, and implant the chips?"

"No. I'm outside the Cloud so I'm not allowed to do registration and I wouldn't do implantation as a matter of principle. I can practise as a medical registrar in psychology, but not as a state registrar. I'm in Swindon but I'm not of it. Kingsgeld will always be my home, and I've chosen not to accept the privileges and protections of being in the cloud in return for not being reduced to a number. It's my right under Freedom of Conscience."

"I see," said Will, not really seeing at all. What could be harder; being a trained and qualified medical practitioner, or typing a number or name into the State Cloud Database. "It must involve delicate compromises on your part."

"It does but I gladly accept them. Sorry, time to go or I'll be late for work." She continued. Will watched as she started to pedal off, dressed in nothing more than jeans, top and cycle helmet. She turned round to wave goodbye, and as she did so an out-of-control pod hurtled down the wrong side of the road towards her. Instinctively he leapt up and pushed her out of the way, narrowly avoiding having the pod crash into him. The two of them ended up on the pavement, Rosaline underneath her bike which was underneath Will. Her head had turned during the collapse and he looked straight into her eyes.

She failed to immediately to grasp the situation. "That's quite a way to show your affection."

He gave her a hand up and pointed to the out-of-control pod.

"Oh I see. Well in that case I might just forgive you."

"Anytime."

"I think I've exchanged a night in hospital for a bruised shin thanks to your quick thinking," she continued. "I have to say I'm very much obliged. It might make up for the time you misdirected me at the museum."

"Oh yes, I'd forgotten that. That wasn't deliberate."

"No, I know. You were just in a world of your own then, content with your models. So now I will have something extra to give thanks for in my prayers tonight."

"Well, thank you," said Will awkwardly.

"Thank you so much, but I must get on now. I have children to look after, and what's more important than that?" At this she cycled off, this time focussing on the road ahead.

He found her odd. He ought to loath wilful rejecters of cloud society, but he admired her nonetheless. She was remarkably unphased about the near-accident, as if she held onto life lightly. If she was a Cloud Citizen she would by now have had a report sent to her bubble for review, possibly with a follow-up interview. However she just carried on.

Would she adopt the same carefree way with the children? It wasn't just the near-accident, it was the lack of protective clothing and everything – not even a mask. Surely her life expectancy must be limited, with the risk of infection, let alone collisions. At least she would have no avatar to have to kill off after her death, she would just be forgotten. The more he thought about this, the more confused he was, but the less bitter his initial rejection by her seemed to him as he found her choices quite bizarre.

## TRANSPORT FOR SWINDON: NEAR ACCIDENT REPORT

**Date:** 18 May 2047.

**Location:** 100 yards east from the Magic Roundabout.

**Details:** An automated Pod veered out of control and crossed the road, nearly hitting a non-Cloud citizen. Incident reported by WG, a member of the elite Walcot bubble. Early indications suggest the non-Cloud Citizen was not wearing protective clothing. Three questions remain: why did the pod veer off the carriage, why was it travelling at excessive speed, and why did it not take evasive action? One clue to the third question may lie in the mis-identification of a non-Cloud citizen. This may raise issues around diversity and inclusion, and the way in which intelligent software is impacted by human bias.

## SCENE ANTARCTICA VIRTUAL REALITY

The bubble met up in West Swindon. Will ran there for exercise but most shared pods. They entered the Oasis together, filing down to the World Excursion and Adventure Virtual

Experience (WEAVE) past the swimming pool, full of bubbles in suitable protective bathing equipment having fun, much as they had had for the last eighty years.

The bubble (or those members who were taking part) entered the WEAVE. First came a few words by the tour guide, who introduced himself as "Ant." A short video gave some basic science and a message about the environment from a mature natural world media presenter, and was followed by a move to the cubicles to change into more appropriate clothing. Then they commenced the virtual journey towards the south pole. They entered the All-Sense Experience Pods (ASEP) which were waiting for them, and started off. The temperature dropped rapidly as they entered the extreme chill. Outside in soaring temperatures the air conditioning was working hard to deprive this chamber of any vestige of heat. The landscape became white. They were dressed in boots and jackets, but the slight wind chilled their faces.

Will looked around at the sheer beauty of the place. There was rock in the distance, blue sky, and ice-filled ocean. But dry land was, well, white and dry. He thought he could make out penguins in the distance, probably just one kilometre away. He loved this. He felt he wanted to move there permanently. It felt so ordered. He thought of all the ice crystals, each with their geometric patterns, making up this vast sheet in front of him, with their beautiful hexagonal planes. It was reassuring.

"Into the launch" ordered the tour leader, so they made their way up.

Crossing between peninsulas was fun, and one of the most unique experiences Will had ever had. While not too rough, it was refreshing with the cold air on his face. This brief interlude came to a sudden end when about five hundred metres from the penguins a strange odour wafted into Will's nose. They got to within a hundred metres of the massed penguins waddling around or protecting eggs or new-born, and Will could hardly breath for the stench. It was tempting to reach for the ASEP control to disable smell and taste.

It was amazing to think Britain still had scientists actually living there just twenty years ago:- either the luckiest scientists alive or the maddest. Will wondered what sort of people they must be: team players or solitary monks. You would need to be a bit of both. Cloud connection in those days was ropey at best, being delivered only through satellite. Those men and women were the pioneers of this experience and the technology which supported it. Now their former base was no more; lost to the ocean, but the legacy lived on.

The expedition moved on, the participants travelling across icy cold pure water in the launch. Soon they were treated to close-ups of natural life onshore; hidden cameras revealing the intimate family experiences of the penguins who inhabit this inhospitable land. Will had the chance to experience what it must be like to be a mother penguin for just five minutes, feeling the cold on his feet and the bustle of the rookery.

That was the closest they got, before retreating to around a couple of kilometres from the colony. Will breathed a little more easily. The range of the nose was higher than the range of the eye, if the virtual experience was faithfully reproducing the experience of actually being there.

No experience was complete without a demonstration of the evils of a previous age. Alastair Scott, the last British Antarctic Survey scientist, appeared on film virtually in the background to show core drills showing the latest ice thickness. These had been taken by robot drills just two months ago. There was good news, there was some hope. The rate of loss of ice was slowing. But it was still reducing, and still too fast. The world needed to agree to more extraction of carbon from the atmosphere, and fast. Too bad all these discussions end up breaking down over the question of who pays, with constant refrains about the demand for climate justice.

Will hated these talks. Although he understood the science and was committed to the mission of limiting climate change, the zealous nature of the presenters left him feeling preached at.

Will heard a crashing sound and the sea suddenly became much rougher. The launch changed direction and immediately they were treated to one of the most spectacular but sad events on earth; the crashing of an ice plate into the sea. The whole event took just thirty seconds. Another huge chunk of ice had become an iceberg, and that iceberg would eventually melt and become ocean. That was the message that needed to be seen and heard; he immediately forgave the Preacher, ashamed that he had even felt resentful about listening to the pitch.

"That was a first, even for us," said the leader. "I've been doing these very same trips for two years now, but that is really a new experience, to see it live."

At the end was the obligatory commercial. The media presenter advertised their virtual scuba diving on the Great Barrier Reef. The reef was changing colour, he explained, as the coral was bleached by rising acidic PH concentration of the sea water. It was giving rise to many chances, some good but most bad.

"How did you feel about that?" Will asked Rose, who followed him out.

"That just shows how big Gov and big Corp gang up for profit, no matter what happens to us," she replied. "They reap the rewards but we all pay the price."

"They need to stop those revolving doors between them," commented Peter. "It lets out too much air as they go round and round."

"There's been quite a lot of progress," said Will. "We've cut carbon emissions by 95% per head of population in England since 1990."

"Rubbish," countered Peter. "Western block's real reduction is 60%, the rest's been exported, and we're just paying a conscience tax for it."

"You know that's not the whole picture," started Will, before realising he would never win an argument with Peter. Not if he wanted to get back home that night. He thought instead of how attractive virtual diving might be.

"How about virtual diving on the Rainbow Warrior?" asked Rose, seemingly reading his mind. "A testament to Big State trying to supress the little guys telling the truth."

Time to go.

They emerged twenty minutes earlier than planned. The carbon leak which had taken its toll on local energy supplies had almost derailed the whole experience, but instead of being cancelled it had merely been cut short and used local energy supplies close to the Oasis. Any further and power would have had to have been imported from the local area, and the lights might have gone out in West Swindon. That would certainly not have been great publicity for an elite bubble trying to set a leadership example.

"It's no good moaning about having a shortened experience; what about the less privileged who can't afford this," Tim was complaining. He had actually not participated, but met back up with the bubble after, looking slightly spaced out. "It's because of energy consumption like this we leak carbon, and because of carbon that ice sheet melted in the first place."

"Fifty years ago people actually cruised there," countered Michael. "Not just for science but also for pleasure. Consuming diesel and filling the oceans and atmosphere with all sorts. We had twenty minutes of carbon-free energy use; they had two weeks of polluting the most beautiful part of the planet."

"So they had the privilege of seeing what they destroy in their very act of admiration. No way should we celebrate that. Anyone descended from hypocritical eco-tourism needs to apologise for where they came from." Tim would always have the last word.

"I agree with Michael. It helps remind us why we're trying so hard to reduce the amount of carbon in the atmosphere, and we're doing it with least damage possible," added Will. "Now I'm going to go and try and sort out this carbon mess before we heat up even more."

Will was about to make his apologies and leave, but Michael had one more word:

"I've booked a bubble-only use of the swimming pool," he declared. "Should be fun."

Only Rose declined this one. The rest of them had fun up the ladders and down the shutes.

"I'm sure you're meant to have kids with you to enjoy this properly," mused Tim.

"You know what I've always said," countered Michael. "Until a bloke's got his own kids, he's just one himself and I guess that includes me."

## WILL'S DATA LOG: META DATA "ANTARCTIC", "ICE"

| | |
|---|---|
| **Experience type:** | Virtual bubble trip. |
| **Location:** | Oasis centre. |
| **Outcome:** | Near hyperthermia. |
| | Bubble dissension on grounds of energy. consumed |
| | Enhanced understanding of penguins and climate change. |
| | Observation of icesheet destruction. |
| **Conclusion:** | Virtual experiences widen access. |
| | Let's redouble our efforts to save the planet. |
| **Report:** | Chilling and exhilarating. |

Seeing so much ice virtually reminded me of college and ice on the inside of my windows. I wish others saw the beauty of the hexagonal structure of ice. Maybe we would all fight climate change harder if they did.

## ODE TO THE ICE

Steam, water, solid ice
All the same to be precise.

Ice is perfect, all in six
At the poles you should be fix-
Ed. Stay right there, it would be nice
Or the planet pays the price
Says Mother Ice.


## SCENE ST VLADISGRAD

Katerina had a somewhat unpleasant communication. The investigation into her matching mistake had taken an unfortunate turn. It was just as well she had not actually given Nik access to the hospital system. It would have compounded her trouble no end.

"We need to understand more fully the circumstances here," said Tanis. "You have to appreciate the position we are in. The Council supports this work but it only continues with their sponsorship. They want to see reproductive success. They want to see a fitter generation for tomorrow. If they see mistakes they will pull this programme. Fortunately, I can cover this over, just this one time. But don't let it happen again."

"Thank you, madam," she replied.

"Don't worry about your trip to London, it's still safe," added Tanis. "It's postponed while the energy markets go crazy but don't worry it won't be for ever. We won't use that as an excuse to punish you by stopping you going. Just be careful though; you might not get a second chance."

Then a thought occurred to her. Was she in danger from Nik?

"Oh, have you heard of this man, Tanis?" she enquired, pointing to his avatar.

"Some low-level party functionary," replied Tanis. "Arrogant man but got promoted due to his cyber skills. May have been descended from the white Russians, but he's nothing now. Over-fond of his Vodka. Failed to get elected to the Neighbourhood Watch last year. His family actually fled to France via Quebec after Tsar Nicholas was executed and kept suitably bawdy company, and claimed the rank of Count."

"So he's not actually Russian?"

"Nik was born in Versailles, but came back after the culture wars reduced the city to ashes and the Eiffel Tower to rust. He got his citizenship from ancestry links and recommendations from the military. I'd keep well clear of him if I were you. He's drunk most of the time. Last week he attempted to break into Kresty prison with an equally drunk female associate. He was lucky not to spend the night there. He's officially all clean, but I'd avoid him if I were you. He's said to be a prodigious hacker on the side, but if so he hasn't got caught yet. Some also suspect him of dissident links, linked to the white Russian movement. If proved, the party would kick him out immediately. That group are working not only to overthrow the party but the whole of democracy and re-instate the aristocracy."

Tanis knew everything and everyone. Just don't cross her.

"One more thing; when he's up to no good he's believed to operate under a dark alias: Count Paris. If you see the image of the Eiffel Tower, steer well clear. Some even suspect him of being a spy passing secrets to the west."

"Thank you Tanis. Much obliged."

But what was it that Nik had wanted to know? She couldn't be sure. Unless he was wanting to get himself paired with the best matches around. She wouldn't put it past him. She made her excuses and left as she had much to do. The Seven Star was planning a trip to the Mariinski and she needed to make suitable preparations. But first, and much more importantly, she had a very special engagement.

## SCENE CLOUD 9 AND THE DEBATE OVER FAVOURITE POISON

"Do you like Vodka?" she asked. "We have great Vodka here. It's my favourite."

"Not really. I prefer whisky. We're allowed alcohol up to fourteen units. Vodka's quite expensive here and difficult to get," responded Will. "They monitor everything we buy, food and drink, and if we're buying more than 14 units of alcohol a week on average we get tested."

"Oh," she replied looking slightly disappointed. "Well at least you won't be drunk in charge of my avatar. I can count on getting it back alive."

That was one of the advantages of having game avatars. They need not be directly controlled by a player in real time. The game avatars could take over when their controllers were absent (or drunk), and some settings allowed the game to decide when human decisions were sufficiently reckless that the game avatar must take over.

"Don't worry. I shall be very careful with you. I won't be spending your money or maligning your Government."

"When do you need to use it? It's coming up to the festival of the wolf when the men go hunting. Their defences will be weakest then."

"Tonight, midnight Western Time."

"Good. Here's the key." Katerina signalled her credentials. Will captured them quickly before she hid them again, minimising the chances of third party spying. "Take care of me while I sleep."

She smiled. Will weakened inside when she smiled at him. But there was no time for emotion now. There was work to do and he had little time.

"Promise me again you'll meet me in London, if I ever get the chance," she pleaded, though it was too late to negotiate now.

"Of course."

"That would be great. I'd love to see the place my parents got together. But enough of me, I'd like to find out more about you too."

Will wasn't quite sure what to say. There was a short silent pause.

"What do you do in your spare time, apart from *Planets*?" she asked.

"See people, listen to music, sometimes play chess, all sorts."

"Oh wow. Here they teach you chess at infant school. It's a throwback to the twentieth century. It's meant to stimulate intelligence."

"Ah. Well here it's just for geeks," admitted Will. "But since that's me I'll give you a game if you like."

So they played just one game, Will as white. Katerina was slightly stronger and built up a fine attack. Fearing however that beating him soundly would not start things off on the right footing, she made a discreet slip which lost her queen to his knight.

"Game over," she declared as she resigned. "You are too strong for me!"

"Thank you, I enjoyed it," replied Will, unaware of her deliberate loss.

He looked at her again.

"I'll come to London, I know I will. I have faith. God is good to me. But you are tired and you will need to be sharp tomorrow. You have a battle ahead of you."

She blew him a coy kiss, and Will went pink before checking out. He found the religious language odd. No one he knew used it. It was especially odd since she came from a scientific rationalist background. Things must be very different in Russia.


## SCENE ESCAPE FROM OBERON

"So what's going to be the plan of attack? What's the best distraction technique?"

"Given it's medieval themed, and the avatars are crudely programmed, you could work on the assumption that the guards can be easily distracted by females."

"Isn't that just stereotypical? Do you think I should do that?"

"It is, and you should, because from what I've seen it will work."

"Yes I see. Well, if you don't mind."

"Good luck."

Logging in on Katerina's real life avatar for the first time was a unique experience. Now he was two people, not one.

It brought a challenge he hadn't expected, having never done this before. Controlling her real-life avatar required him to see life from Katerina's viewpoint, at least as far as online interactions were concerned. He arranged the two avatars across split screens and disabled voice control on Katerina's avatar. To keep Katerina updated he arranged a video record so she could watch the events from her perspective after he had completed his mission.

"Ah, this isn't as easy as I thought."

"You can do it."

It took a little getting used to, particularly co-ordinating control of the two avatars simultaneously. It was like piloting two drones at once, and each one going in slightly different directions. Also Katerina's avatar controls worked a little differently to his own. He was trying not to use voice activation to avoid cross-over commands, commands for one avatar being mistakenly interpreted by another.

"You're doing fine now, but I'm over and out, just watching."

"Roger that."

His imagined himself into her world, a very different one from his. But there really was no time for daydreaming. He had to activate Katerina's avatar as well as his own, ready for the fight.

What Katerina had told him about Oberon from her viewpoint was completely accurate. He now saw the majority of the hunters departing with wolf hounds, heading for the dark mountains. The light was fading. Torches were being lit around the camp. He could see this from a distance with his own eyes, but as Katerina he/she was assisting the lighting. Will started moving faster towards it, using Katerina's eyes to check for danger by keeping her on the side from which he was approaching. Two guards watched from the lookout, but they were the only defenders to beat. Furthermore, they were themselves distracted. As Katerina, he could surmise their disappointment at missing the wolf hunt. Through Katerina he saw a few unarmed women including the Red Queen, but they were hurrying home before nightfall.

The guards looked weary and Will got bolder. He now moved Katerina close to the guards; this was in reality his plan. As agreed he would use the oldest distraction, female distraction. Despite the cold, Katerina started to peel away her outer layers and remove her headscarf, just in sight of the watchtower, and on the opposite side from Will who now came right up to the fence. This ring of protection consisted of roughly cut trunks forming a crude but tough outer later, too tough to penetrate. He wondered if it was too high to climb. He surveyed the obstacle carefully, before spotting a glimmer of reflected light near the top of the fence. He checked Katerina's memory regarding the layout of the defences. It confirmed what he suspected; the top of the fence had guard snakes whose purpose was to attack intruders attempting to scale it. That reflection he noticed must have been a light reflection from their eyes. The giants may have headed to the sierra, but they had left their poisonous allies to guard their treasures, and hence Will's access to the well. He needed another approach.

He crept round to the main gate. It was locked of course but this is where Katerina's avatar would become critical to his plans. On the camp side he re-dressed Katerina, having teased the guards, and now moved her round to the Gatekeeper's cottage. As a maid she had the perfect cover, and could come and go unnoticed. The key to the gate was kept inside the sanctum, and although the sanctum was locked she had a key to that door. There was no light by now and she had omitted to bring a torch, so as not to attract attention. She knew where the key should be, hung up on the left-hand side, so felt her way across. For Will, as operator, it was strange to experience this total darkness while his own avatar still had sufficient light to see, the images on the screens contrasting sharply, causing him to manually over-write the brightness settings.

Suddenly a wolf hound barked from within the camp; the two of them heard simultaneously. This wasn't meant to happen on a wolf hunt; the whole pack was supposed to be taken out to help track down the many wild animals living nearby. Perhaps a sick wolf had been left behind. Wolves are the ultimate pack animals, and being left out of the hunt would be very damaging for any left behind. Will had to move decisively; Katerina grabbed the nearest kitchen knife and headed out. Two minutes later the howling stopped, and the hound was no more. The futile resistance it put up, and a slight limp, confirmed the theory it had not been in the best of health.

The guards were clearly non-plussed with this little distraction but incurious about the sudden ending of the howls. Perhaps they had expected the poor hound's decline and demise without player assistance. Katerina slipped back into the cottage, this time moving straight to the key. In her hurry she lost a shoe, tripping on the uneven entrance. There was no time to retrieve it, as Will was being exposed to view from the camp's remaining inhabitants, and therefore at immediate risk of being spotted if he remained there a second longer than necessary.

They saw each other across the giant bars of the main gate. Will for the first time saw himself on *Planets* as others must see him, albeit through the heavy thick bars of a huge iron gate. For all the opportunities he must have had to see his own reflection, he had never done so. For a second Will reflected on their real separation; 1800 miles and opposing world views. All this distance yet their worlds were colliding on the screen in front of him. Each bar of this gate seemed one more needle in the conspiracy of forces separating them.

The key was so large that Katerina struggled not just to drag it behind her but even more so to hold it aloft to unlock the gate. A distinct creak was heard as she tried it; she should have oiled it first. There was no sign of interest from the guards. Either they had not heard the noise, or else they must have concluded that anyone using a key must be one of their own and had good cause to be using it to open the gate. After all, they had spotted no threat.

Will gently pushed the gate just an inch to check. Not enough to be noticed. The two were now working as one mind in two bodies, perfect co-ordination. He had Katerina slip away to a new position, again to the tease the guards, but this time closer and in a more daring manner. This time she let slip her gown, letting it ride down her shoulders, exposing some cleavage. Now just as men can be giants, at least in their own eyes, so giants can be men. Both shimmied down the tower in search of her. Katerina vanished in the twilight, kicking off her remaining shoe as yet one more distraction. First she lured them past the well, the only part of the camp lit brightly, with many flaming torches. The heat and light from them just seemed to inflame their lust, judging by the way in which the giants picked up pace as they passed. As she passed by, the light grew strangely dimmer. Will wondered if the torches themselves knew something was afoot and wanted to protect Katerina's unwelcome illumination as she passed by. Will waited until the guards were at a safe distance. Softly he approached the well, wary of the cottages and suspicious eyes from any left behind from the hunt, mainly women and children. But if anyone did see him, no one raised the alarm. No one was expecting trouble. Moving closer he realised the torches were arranged in two circles which formed a double barrier placed deliberately around the well. The portal was well protected. This was it. The final step. He knew now that what Katerina had told him was absolutely true. There had been no false memories planted. There in her avatar memory lay the details of conversations from her time as Red Queen. Then she had been privy to all the great secrets, which meant that he also knew the secrets of the giants.

No giant could ever enter the well and live. Like the torches, they were semi-animate, in the sense that their responses were complex, pre-programmed with a complex avatar, yet not players in their own right. The programming was designed for the well to swallow any native of Oberon such as the residents of the camp, but to act as a portal for any foreigner. In a kind of self-defence, it would actually kill (or re-set) any giant or maid silly enough to try to enter it. If successful, Katerina would have a different path out of this world. The torches protecting the well were not only to prevent humans from entering and winning the game, but also to discourage the giants and other inhabitants of the camp who would die were they to descend the well. Though the torches guarded the well at night, the maids could not be harmed by them since they were the ones required to light them. This was the real reason they dimmed as she passed. For humans the well was indeed large enough to enter, and in so doing Will would follow his chosen trajectory and escape the solar system entirely. He would complete the game, become a Master of the Universe, travel throughout space and time and be equal with Captain Mercury.

So one obstacle remained:- the torches. Approaching them appeared to be a fast route to self-immolation.

"Take a chance," urged Katerina's avatar. "This is your only hope. Don't blow it."

It was only two yards from the ring of torches to the well. Two yards of burning hell. Would he make it? Now was not the time for indecision. Unsure, Will crept closer.

Katerina was fleet of foot and easily out-manoeuvred the clumsy giants. Passing the Red King's barn she looped round, temporarily sending them towards the cess pit, before grunting in disgust they resumed the chase of their quarry. Will saw a way out. Katerina, given her immunity, could beat a path through to the well. He hid behind the nearby pillory post. He then waited until she led her pursuers back. They chased her through to the torches, which were temporarily subdued by her presence. Will was sure they would spring back into full heat imminently and took his chance. Taking a running jump he leapt, straight past the guards who were taken unawares and too slow to react, trying to avoid the depressed flames. Nonetheless he could not avoid catching the edge of one flame and for what seemed an interminable time but was in fact only a couple of seconds his clothes started to burn as he tumbled towards the well.

One pole vault later and he plunged through ice-cold water into the final portal. He had won, he had escaped Oberon. Back on the moon however Katerina's white pen flew into the well; five minutes later emerged a black cob, which immediately flew off to observe the hunting party in the distance. As Will could see, Katerina's maid's situation was less than ideal. Shortly afterwards her avatar vanished completely. No reset, no more lives. Katerina was out. Final death with this avatar. There was no way of ever getting an unregistered ID in the game, so that was it as far as Katerina's adventures in *Planets* was concerned. However such was Will's excitement that he actually failed to notice this rather important detail.

## EXTRACT FROM WILL'S DATA LOG

Meta data "Reflections on escape from Oberon"

Katerina was most obliging in helping me to escape from Oberon and progress in the game. We agreed I would control her avatar to get me to the next level *but I managed to screw up and she's expelled from the game (narrator note, these words in italics appear to have been a later correction to the original log).* This is not good. What's more I promised to guide her round London in return, but I hardly know the place. This is not going well. I expect she'll change her mind about meeting me now I've been careless. Is there a way of recovering her ID? Michael said he knew someone in game admin on the Russian committee, who could do all sorts of things through the back end. I'll talk to him about it. In any case, I'm going to have to smarten my act up if she does come and still want to meet up. I don't want to end up getting lost in London again when my phone battery goes dead. That would be an utter humiliation and it would be such a shame to lose her. I don't think she realises how much I'm attracted to her. It's not just her looks, though she is beautiful, but I love her combination of sensitivity and modesty. I don't think she realises quite what a treasure she is herself.

# KATERINA'S DIARY

## 8 MAY

I've been hacked. Nik didn't want my body of course- he wanted my identity. What is he planning? I hope he can't hack you, dear diary. Of course he can't. You are safely out of the Cloud, written in pen and paper, sealed with my trusty lock. Now I know that you are really the only safe place for me to confess. The priests might betray me (were I ever to darken the door of their church again), the Cloud might be hacked, but you will not be unless I'm burgled, and then at least I'll know immediately.

I've decided I don't believe in the church anymore, but maybe I do believe in God. Probably. I've started wearing my cross again – the large one with a hidden cavity. I'm going to lock the key in there from now on. It's strange, but I feel so much better wearing it, but only when it's hidden away under my blouse. The priests wear theirs openly of course, to show their piety, but mine will be tucked away. I don't know if it's because I'm not such a strong believer as they are, or whether I'm not worthy to show my godliness.

## 10 MAY

You should know diary that I managed to get my ID back, but with a little demotion. I am now a simple maid! That is probably much closer to the level I deserve.

There seems to have been some upsides to my new lower position as a maid. I was out scavenging for wild eggs, when

I spotted a crusader warrior. Now, pardon me, let me explain. Of course what I mean is in the game I must carry out more menial duties, which takes me outside of the camp. In my last position, I would not have seen him.

What do I mean by a crusader warrior? It's named after the westerners who went to fight the Saracens to reconquer Al Quds. Their uniform consists of a grand red cross on their armour. They are the successors of Constantine, or so they claim. Unfortunately, when they got to Constantinople, they crossed sides and attacked the true Orthodox religion. So, friend or foe? We will see. Will I be betrayed by him? I have no idea.

We have more excitement coming soon. There is a Seven Stars spa retreat, a chance for us girls to relax. No politics, no work chat, just girls together. Personal communicators are confiscated at reception. It is a modern day monastery. Don't worry about the safety of my key, diary. I will still keep it safe at all time, tucked safely away under my swimsuit inside my cross where it always lives. No one will get to you without me knowing.

## 14 MAY

Dear diary, I need to forget the weekend forever. Just so you know, my foot hurts. That's why you saw me taking the lift not the stairs. Just don't ask why.

## 16 MAY

I'm falling in love with the crusader warrior. I met him outside *Planets*. It's not encouraged to do that, you know, so don't tell anyone. In real life this warrior fights climate change, not foreign armies. He said his best mate is in the military, but he doesn't know one end of a weapon from another. Then he tried explaining how he fights for the climate, and it sounded really interesting, but it was all a bit much to take in. He mentioned money a lot. No, that's not quite right. He mentioned money once, and it was a lot of it. Billions, or was it trillions. That's right.

I think I like him. The cross is the sign. He aims to conquer, but to do so honourably. I don't know if he likes me though. He didn't say anything. Either he's shy or he's uninterested. I know he wants something though, and I think he needs me to help him in the game. I suppose if his is an honourable mission, I should support it. It's my duty. Playing the game can't be about just progressing up the levels. I shall help him, and see where it ends.

## 17 MAY

Life's like a Yo-Yo. One day I'm going to London, the next day I'm not, then it all changes again. For now it's on. I'm going to see my crusader friend from London. Only, it turns out he doesn't know where the crusaders came from. I think they only teach history lessons from 2040 in his country! I asked him if he believed in God and he said he hadn't really thought about it. I told him I'd never have sex except with a husband. He said that was absolutely fine, but he looked a little disappointed. This man doesn't know how to hide his feelings. I think that's what endears me to him the most. I need an antidote to Nik, someone I can actually trust, and this is the man.

I've tried introducing him to Russian culture. Chess he's not bad at, though I did encourage him a little. Vodka, not so much. He drinks gin and whisky. Still, time to work on him!

## 23 MAY

I know how the game of *Planets* ends. It's ended, for me at least. No matter, I'm still going to London and I have a human to guide me. I wonder what he's like to meet? He seems genuine and I'm growing to like him. It doesn't matter how online games end, but what does matter is how the game of love ends, because in the end, that's all there is.

## 24 MAY

I had a very strange dream last night. It was at the time of the crusades. I was living in a cell in a convent near Al Quds. Men in strange helmets were at the great wooden doors demanding to be let in. They promised to spare our lives if we surrendered peacefully. Mother superior refused of course, claiming the Christian virtue of martyrdom for herself and her children. The enemy bombarded us with trebuchet devices which frightened us. Huge rocks were hurled towards the great gates, and lighted pitched tar entered the courtyard causing mini fires to break out. I went to the well to draw out water to put the flames out before the men broke through and I ran to the cells. Flames and wells seem to go together at the moment, don't they? The enemy were coming through, cell by cell, looking for us. It wasn't long before the doors of my cell opened, but what I saw was not the Saracen I dreaded but a Lionheart with the face of Will. He carried me past the bodies of slain men, through a burning hall, and out of the convent to freedom. His soldiers stood victorious over the bodies of the fallen. Then he knelt and gave thanks to God who had given him the grace and strength to win.

I mentioned it to Will who laughed, and said I must have got the wrong man. I wonder. Perhaps there's a side to him that even he doesn't realise.

# ACT 3

# LOVE LIFE

## SCENE JAPAN

Will had never been to Japan, and never would visit in person. Even Michael had not done so. But as Will traded carbon with the country he felt a second-hand knowledge of it and its people, and Japan was about to come to him in a slightly more significant way than he might have expected.

Researchers there had been working on a way to harness nuclear fusion, the power of the sun contained on earth. So had many scientists elsewhere, Russia, Europe, America, China, but everyone else had failed. So, it was thought, had the Japanese. But in a shock announcement The Japanese Atomic Programme (JAP) announced that it had demonstrated a new hybrid technique for making it work commercially. The problem with fusion wasn't that it couldn't work in theory, it was that it couldn't work in practise. And for any self-respecting scientist (like Will) that was just not acceptable. Obviously, if it didn't work in practise it was simply because the engineers hadn't spent long enough on it. Fusion power had seemed like the theoretical dream interrupted by awakening reality. Research by Dr Fukishima at JAP demonstrated a new hybrid technique which would be delivered in months. Not only that, but the power would be cheap enough even for direct air capture of carbon dioxide. This had profound implications for the fight against climate change. It was a timely announcement, given the leakage problems in England.

Will tuned in to the webcast immediately, in awe of what he was hearing. This had the potential for genuinely earth-changing consequences. Not only energy policy, but given the centrality of energy to human existence, almost every area of life.

Michael and Will were at an international conference called at just ten hours' notice, and were ready to receive a surprise announcement.

"We will send our scientists themselves and not just our politicians," announced Michael speaking for the allies.

Michael could say this, because the Western Block scientists at STEP (Spherical Tokamak for Energy Production) now reported to him. They had recently been transferred to POLOMINT command, and Michael had oversight. It was actually the first Will had heard of this; he had had his own interest in the future of clean nuclear from some time ago, but even he was taken aback.

Will hooked up with Dr Fukishima after the conference, eager to make the acquaintance of this new hero.

"You have my deepest respect," said Will.

"Thank you so much, but it is simply my duty to my country," he replied. "I stand on the shoulders of giants, and I owe so much to them."

Will immediately grasped the implications. The Japanese said that they would have ten new plants built within five years. If so, it would not be long before others followed suit. Carbon emitting power production would be a thing of the past and there would be enough energy to extract carbon directly from the atmosphere and turn it to rock. That was enough to make a difference to the decade-long carbon balancing. Will immediately shorted his carbon position, perhaps two minutes too late as other traders sold out before the price crash. By the end of the day the carbon price had crashed to ten percent of its previous value. Hydrogen prices fell by half. Life was sweet, dreams were sunlight.


### NARRATOR ON CARBON

Welcome to the new world here. It turns out that those people who flew around the planet warning about climate change were right in the wrong sort of way. We have to watch our carbon now and woe betide anyone who doesn't. Will was right in the front line of the fight. There will indeed be a reckoning.

But the struggle with energy and the environment is not what has changed society. Our world uses so much more energy than fifty years ago, but that is not what makes us so different from before. What makes the real difference is what our rulers know about us and how they can control our lives. But can they control our dreams and our passions? Dreams; they can be light or they can be dark. We will see both later, but for now back to earth.

## ODE TO CARBON

Carbon takes on many faces
Can be found in many places
Diamonds worn with airs and graces
When with oxygen embraces
Too much, could our world erase.

## SCENE MICHAEL AND KATERINA MEET

"Good news for more virtual reality trips," commented Will to Michael. "The carbon and energy prices have tanked. It's that fusion news that's done it."

"Excellent. We've gotta live in the present. Make the most of it. Enjoy ourselves," said Michael. "Maybe even some actual travel, like I used to do in the old days. I miss those ten hour plane flights sitting in economy, hoping to get to stretch out for a kip when someone swaps seats."

"I have a friend who wants to travel," said Will.

"Oh yeah?"

'To London."

"It's not far from here. It's just an hour on the train. You need permission to travel, but I'm sure you'll get it."

"She's in Russia," Will confided.

"I know," said Michael.

"Ah. You don't know her, do you?"

Michael was uncharacteristically and curiously quiet.

"I know everything. But you'd better introduce me," suggested Michael. "I'm part Russian, after all. I can also speak her native language. But if I read you right, you think she's more likely to be able to come now."

Will nodded.

So the Cloud 9 call became three-way. Will unfortunately failed to understand the parts of the conversation which took place in Russian, which was most of it.

"Nice girl," Michael said afterwards. "Good luck with hooking her. I hope you guys meet, but I wouldn't hold out any hope. If it weren't for the distance, I'd say she'd be just right for you. She's a really bright young woman. As things are, you might just be breaking your heart again if the current carbon crisis continues."

"Ah, there may have been some good news on that," replied Will. "Tell you more later."

"There's one other thing," said Michael. "You may have some competition.

"She didn't mention anything."

"No. The attention from the other may not have been entirely welcome. I'm confident you would win her, were it not for distance. Just be careful though, that's all I'm saying."

" Is that what she said?"

"No, she didn't say that. I did."

"Oh, I see," said Will, not seeing at all.

Katerina and Will hooked up after.

"Very clever, your Captain Mercury," remarked Katerina. "Speaking Russian so fluently. He seemed very interested in St Vladisgrad, and also my parents. Almost oddly so."

"Yes, he's quite a super-hero," admitted Will, unsure what else to say, knowing Michael had been involved in intelligence activities all over Russia. "Did you find him attractive? Apparently a lot of women do."

"Oh, no way!" she laughed. "Not at all. I have a feeling he has a short romantic attention span, and I want to know what else motivates him. What does he believe in? Can he lie well? That I am sure of, and it's a good reason for avoiding him."

"Now for some good news. The trip's back on and I'm cleared to go," she continued, the excitement barely concealed. "I'm coming in June. I think it's linked with the news you had somehow but I'm not clear how."

Will's heart-rate leapt.

"Do tell me more about this new discovery," she asked "I'd love to know the link between it and being able to travel again."

"It's a bit complicated."

"Well that sounds like a challenge. Let me meet this Dr Fukishima myself."

That was not what Will had bargained on. He hesitated, not wanting to overwhelm her with new connections when he wanted to talk about her, not his work.

Ten minutes later another three-way international discussion took place. "My friend is an admirer of your work," said Will, introducing Katerina to Dr Fukishima.

"Ah so. A fellow scientist," Dr Fukishima exclaimed.

"Yes, reproductive science," answered Katerina. "The study of life, and how to help it continue in the best possible way."

"Very good," he replied. "But the art of life is a good death, no?"

Katerina blinked hard.

"I can see that the two of you together are destined to make life. Even I can see you are in love with each other."

Both of them blushed.

"We live in different blocks, how can we?" blurted out Will.

"But you will, my son, you will. You will be like fusion. The two of you will come together to create something new, but you will both cease to exist in the process."

There was a distinctly awkward silence.

"What makes me so glad is your announcement today. It will solve our problem with the carbon leak," said Will, changing subject and wanting to show personal gratitude. "It gives us access to carbon free power and the ability to extract directly from the air if we need to."

"Ah yes. I saw that. You know, here in Japan we have many earthquakes. We would never seek to store carbon as gas underground. We turn ours to stone."

Yes, the safest but most expensive option.

"Also in Japan we do not have terrorists. This is one country with one purpose and we do not accept cultural dissent."

"We disapprove of dissent in Russia too."

"Of course. We should have followed your lead," Will admitted. "But in England dissent is a part of our culture itself. We actually have a whole exhibition on it at one of our London museums."

"How strange; that wouldn't happen here for sure," typed Katerina in a private chat to Will.

Strangely, despite Will's admiration of Dr Fukishima's work, it was Katerina who felt most connection with Dr Fukishima at that point. He seemed to combine scientific understanding with human wisdom.

"Distance is no barrier to what is important, my son," Fukishima continued. "Do you have honour? I hope so. Then you have connection also. Just as surely as the quantum state entangles nuclear particles so we human beings are all connected."

Katerina and Will's physical connection was just about to happen too, and that was partly down to Dr Fukishima and his colliding nuclei making it possible, by extracting carbon from the air and driving down the price for carbon emission permits to make travel affordable again. The markets were not interested in science, as such, but they were very interested in clean energy just as Will had predicted. Clean energy meant cheaper carbon, cheaper carbon meant cheaper hydrogen, and cheaper hydrogen meant lower transport costs. The golden age of global travel for all might be about to resurface for those so permitted by their health and Government rules.

Katerina quizzed Will about this afterwards.

"So, I know my news is connected with this fusion, but I don't really get it. I always thought nuclear power was breaking down atomic particles, not bringing them together. How do you get energy from hydrogen like this? I thought hydrogen was just a way of storing energy?"

"Well you see, there's a certain percentage of isotopes in hydrogen."

"What's an isotope?"

"It's when there's an extra proton, or even two extra protons."

"I see. You mean like a DNA mutation?"

"Something like that. Makes it heavier."

"Does that matter? It's light anyway, isn't it?"

"Yes it matters because it helps produce the energy."

"I still don't get how that works."

"Well, you've got deuterium, that's a mutant with one extra neutron. It is rare though."

"I see."

"And then you've got tritium. That's two extra neutrons. It's like a double mutant and it's extra specially rare."

"I give up. It's too complicated."

"It's just what goes on in the sun and stars all the time. You can see that, can't you?"

"I can see the sun. I can't see neutrons or deuts or trits or whatever"

"They are there, hidden in all that sunlight. It works, that's what matters."

"Good."

"Oh, and when it's all done you get helium."

"Like laughing gas?"

"Not quite. You're thinking of nitrous oxide, but helium can make you talk in a funny way. It's an inert gas. Doesn't react with anything. Not laughing but deadly serious. The whole thing releases lots of energy."

"So these devices work just like the sun?"

"Yep, you got it, just like the sun, which holds all the planets in our solar system together and gives earth the energy it needs to thrive. Actually there are lots of other fusion reactions too that can happen in the sun."

"We'll leave at that, maybe?"


**ODE TO HYDROGEN**

Proton small you're all alone
And your atom number's one
Carry power your work is done.

Neutron friend and now you're two
Rare but fitting like a shoe
Your part in fusion shining through

Second neutron, can it be?
People call you number three
Stars in action now you'll see

Helium is number four
When the action is no more
Inert and lifeless on the floor.


**SCENE WILL'S JOURNEY**

Will looked forward nervously to the trip. His sense of London geography had not improved since his college days. He decided to leave the orienteering to the pods and their sat nav systems. After all their knowledge of the city was supposed to rival that of the famous London hackney carriages, so he decided to focus on important things such as impressing Katerina.

That morning, he overslept, having forgotten to charge his communicator which provided his waking services. He would miss the next train which departed in five minutes. Never mind, the next one was just an hour later.

It was an unfortunate discovery to find himself short of clean socks, until it dawned on him that this was the perfect opportunity to put his old sandals to good use. He dressed, grabbed his man-bag, complete with umbrella, and headed to the station where he spent the next forty minutes reflecting on the coming encounter. Just before the later train arrived, and his communicator was fully charged, he remembered to message Katerina to let her know he might be a tad late.

## SCENE KATERINA'S JOURNEY

It was just two weeks before travelling. She had made the arrangements, travel booked, visas in order, medical verifications completed. The train to Moscow and the flight to London. It was her first flight and she had not realised the size of the planes, their huge fuel tanks dominating their design. Neither had she realised the size of the airports, empty ghosts of an era of a flight per minute. Once this place would have been bustling with passengers and staff; now most staff were replaced by automation to serve the privileged few able to use their services. Even this ghostly activity represented a significant increase in business compared with five years ago.

The check in process was swifter than she imagined. World Health Passport had recently been introduced, so identity checks were all that were needed. Her implanted Russian Cloud NVID was recognised by all international border controls, smoothing the process of coming into the west. All she had to do was consent to share personal data from the western to the Russo-Sino block and vice versa.

The flight was uneventful.

Entry to the western block was generally courteous, when human interaction was required; the opposite direction back home could feel like a somewhat more hostile experience she had heard, for a Russian returning home. Not so long ago, inter-block travel for leisure was almost completely forbidden, so she should be grateful for this opportunity.

She checked her communicator; Will was running late. No need to hurry then. She wondered over to the tourist knick-knacks and bought a pair of "I love England" ear-rings.

Twenty minutes after leaving the airport she was in Paddington station, so named after a Peruvian bear of the same name found there a hundred years ago. Doubtful of the origins of the story she checked for herself; amazed to actually see the station's founding creature suitably honoured next to Platform one.

She contacted Mariya.

"He's going to be a little late, so I can explore London a little," she explained. "Is there anything I can buy for you?"

"He's late, leaving you to wait around in a strange city?" cried Mariya. "Oh, I wish I'd come with you now. He can't be that interested in you if he keeps you waiting."

"I've come all this way now. I'll give him one more chance, Mariya. You don't know where it might end up after all."

She had consulted her mother's old 2020 Russian Guide to English Cathedral Cities before coming. She knew for a fact it hadn't been updated since, but was still hopeful of historic insight. Why did she need to read a current guide when she was getting a personal guide anyway, assuming Will did turn up eventually?

Will would meet her later back at Paddington, but meanwhile she wanted to take advantage of his tardiness with a little adventure. Leaving her luggage at the station, she took a Boris Bike up to Camden to check out its famous market. Sadly, the guidebook promises of abundant open food markets and gothic chic proved disappointing. Faded street art remained, with tributes to long-gone artists, reflecting deeply on western social decadence. Reading more of the history, she started to understand the genesis of the Culture Wars.

What also struck her was evidence of a previously mixed culture. The Guide referred to Camden as ethnically and culturally diverse, citing clubs such as Chaka Zulu and Proud. With a little imagination the idea of dancing with semi-naked speared warriors appeared in her head, but she had no time for further exploration. Perhaps it would feature in a poem when she got back home: "Adventures in London: confessions of a doctor."

The area around Camden Lock felt like a museum of a bygone age of hip London. She alighted at a bar overlooking the lock. Once upon a time this would have been teeming with gaily decorated narrow boats and barges, miniature roof top gardens and small dogs, mostly travelling homes for the carefree. There were fewer now but the odd boat still cruised gently by, its occupants on retreat rather than at home. Katerina imagined it must be the perfect antidote to always-on-demand Cloud life.

As luck would have it, the bar offered Russian vodka from self-service. Her Russian NVID was accepted without a question and the small can popped out. She opted for a glass, as all Russians do. All this data was passed straight back to St Vladisgrad, of course, but they knew very well where she was. Perfect bliss. She lingered as long as she dared and her luck was in; a floral barge slipped past on its foray around the canal system of London, doubtless a plaything of the idle wealthy.

In St Vladisgrad strangers may have conversed with each other, but not here in London. The cold former capital of England was now downgraded in political importance but had reinvented itself as a cultural retreat for the world elite and their flunkies. Here the normal rules of life were relaxed a little, and that was the secret of its continued success. The oligarchs were not being monitored the way she knew she was. Walking back with the bike she passed just one remaining shop, the Gothic Tower, selling extreme retro. "Cloud free" claimed the shop at its entrance. How was that ever permitted? Who would even want that? She noticed thick steel lacing the windows, and wondered if the walls were lead-lined. She wondered how this would all work. How would payment for goods be arranged if a shopper was unable to identify themselves?

The thought of clothing reminded her she still needed to hire an outfit for a forthcoming Seven Star event. She still had time to kill so she clouded a Russian hire shop. They had her measurements, of course. A thousandth of a second to access State Personal Database giving her full details down to her weight recorded just a month ago at a Seven Star health meeting. All she had to do was choose. What a choice! Dear readers, our eyes will be delighted by this a little later. But her mind was made up on seeing a plain deep purple full length dress with a high winged collar. In Russia, eyes also noticed the purchase, eyes that were keeping a very close watch on her indeed. That much she could guess. What she could not realise is that not all those eyes belonged to the state security.

Her gaze returned to Camden. The shop window allowed enough of a view of the outfits. A male dummy displayed a long black coat with high collars and purple flashes. His eyebrows had been lined darkly and he wore a tall black top hat. The 'man' held the hand of a woman, dressed top to toe in a black dress with velvet sash. Around the female dummy's neck she wore what looked at first like a choker but on closer inspection was clearly a leather collar with a ring attached at the front. She had read about Victorian England's fascination with Goth, but didn't expect to see such an open display on the streets.

Time to go; Will would be arriving in Paddington, the last stop on his journey, within the hour. Finding her way back on the bike she wondered what life would have been like twenty years ago. Brash, confident, unsuspecting of world events.

Back at Paddington she opened up her communicator to Will who reciprocated, giving her a view of Royal Oak speeding past, while he in turn viewed that famous bear and the even more famous Victoria lounge where the Queen of England would rest before travelling home. Thinking of Victoria as a British Czarina, she was a little disappointed to discover that the refreshments provided to the Queen consisted only of tea, and that tradition was being continued even to paying customers. Vodkas were available elsewhere in the station, but not there.

There was something strange about this place. The weather was hot but the people were cold. Not one person had greeted her since she arrived.

Time to go; Will would soon be here.

## SCENE MEETING OF LOVERS, 21 JUNE 2047

Will arrived in person seven minutes later. This was it.

"Wow, you're amazing." Will's greeting just stuttered out spontaneously. "And your headwear is so amazing too."

Wills' eyes met Katerina's. His full of curiosity and hers full of hope. She wore her trademark multi-coloured headscarf, and a calf length skirt with boots, though Will had fully seen neither before. Out of the back of the scarf flowed that long dark hair he had been instantly attracted to.

Of all the women he knew well, only Rose ever wore skirts at all, but it worked better on Katerina, with her figure, than on Rose. Even the colourful headscarf worked on her. As he reflected he wondered how vulnerable she must feel, in a strange City and culture and in the guidance of a man she barely knew. He found himself attracted to her in a way he hadn't expected when they first agreed to meet.

"Greetings from Russia," she replied. "A warm heart salutes you in this cold city that is strange to both of us!"

"In a sultry thirty two degrees? St Vladisgrad must be warmer than I ever imagined."

"It's the English reserve which is so cold."

"Ah yes. That's London for you. It's considered rude to talk to strangers here."

She viewed him with a little bemusement. This man was clearly out of this world, and that included his fashion sense dressed as he was with a holey T shirt, faded jeans and open toed sandals with no socks. The English must be different.

"But I'm forgetting my manners too," he continued. "Can I help you with your bag? How was your trip? No problems with security I trust?"

She shook her head.

There should be nothing to fear from this meeting with Katerina. He had cleared the trip through Michael, the Russians had permitted her to come, so the passage in for her should be smooth. He'd even explained about meeting Katerina on *Planets*, even though she was unregistered, which Michael agreed to overlook and appeared to have already known about. Will had no access to sensitive security systems, so the visit did not pose security problems for POLOMINT, he reasoned, in terms of contact with an alien national.

Just in case, and unknown even to Michael, POLOMINT had upped the surveillance. Will's every move was now analysed for danger avoidance. It wasn't just Katerina they were interested in, but also her contacts back in St Vladisgrad or those back there who might be monitoring her.

"I've arranged a double pod," said Will. "Should be here within the hour. The tube's half hourly and unpleasant, so this works best." In reality Michael had advised against the tube as being too risky with a Russian. The double pod separated them respectably and kept all civilian nosey parkers happy, while allowing POLOMINT full view of them both.

"Thank you," she smiled. "My mother warned me never to take the Underground." "Oh why?" asked Will.

"Her mother, my Baboushka, was badly injured and her husband killed at Lubyanka in Moscow back in 2010."

"Oh no. Funny I'd never heard of that. How many died in total?"

"You in the west were too pre-occupied with 9/11 and the London bombings to notice you weren't the only targets of extremists," she replied.

True, thought Will. It had helped create a climate of fear and distrust, fuelling one of the factions in the culture wars. "So your mother became an orphan?"

"My mother was born a semi-orphan. She was born using IVF, from her dead father's sperm. It was the only technique we had then. My mother became a doctor in Accident and Emergency and later moved to Reproductive Science to honour her mother who had chosen that path, still quite novel at the time. I chose to become a reproductive science doctor as my first choice and focussed on research. Without more knowledge, we cannot advance the motherland. My grandfather faced death at the hands of evil men but I choose to respond by helping give life."

"It's a good job your grandmother had the consent to use the sperm from your grandfather, then."

"Oh, they were married, so it was presumed consent."

"Oh. You must tell me more about your work sometime," said Will. "It must be so rewarding. But now we need to catch the pod."

Katerina's eyes were glued to the window looking out while Will's eyes were glued to her across the internal divide. Travelling down the Edgware Road she imagined she must have arrived in the Arab block by mistake, as men smoked shisha pipes alongside veiled companions. A traffic accident diverted them back north of Safespace Park, once the epicentre of the culture wars where the hate-speakers attempted to claim immunity under the banner of freedom. They turned at the western end and headed south through Kensington and then east again. Even Will's eyes were averted to view the Albert Hall, once famous for bringing music to the masses, now the preserve only of the world's elite; those who could afford in-person entertainment and face-to-face global networking.

"Is that your opera house?" enquired Katerina. "I do so love opera and the ballet."

"Ah yes. I visit at least once a year," lied Will. He didn't even watch opera online that frequently, let alone even visit London.

"How exciting. What did you see last time?" she enquired.

"I can't quite remember. Oh yes, Les Misérables."

"Right. And Tchaikovsky?"

"I'd love to see that with you." An economy. He'd love to see anything with Katerina, but preferably not ballet or opera or indeed anything requiring sustained concentration.

The pod continued down Piccadilly and past a bronze nude statue. "A symbol of erotic love" claimed Will.

"This is where my parents proposed. My guide to cathedral cities called it the Shaftesbury Memorial. Amazing how these old Russian guides can be so inaccurate."

They diverted up Shaftesbury Avenue, passed the historic site of London's first ever crypto-currency cashpoint. It was marked with a blue plaque. Next Will noticed Great Windmill Street.

"We like Windmills," he said, pointing out the street. "We even have a business park named after them in Swindon."

"And what sort of business do they do there?" enquired Katerina.

"Oh, I've no idea."

Around an hour later they arrived at the newly refurbished Chinese Lantern hotel which overlooked the Fleet river where it joined the Thames. Where once the river had been driven underground by the relentless demand for more road space, now the Blackfriars bridge was reserved for cyclists and pedestrians and water once again flowed freely into England's mightiest river. Katerina had chosen this location for its proximity to St Pauls, described as the most beautiful cathedral in London, the one most closely resembling the magnificent cathedrals of the Russian Orthodox Church with its magnificent dome. She had read too of the Temple Church and other fine churches and was fascinated by the link between English domed churches and the domes of those from home.

She allowed Will to take and hand over her small luggage to be carried to the room by the autonomous welcome service. Then they headed, hand in hand, for coffee near the Watergate. In London there were still several live-service venues and this was one. Will was surprised at how fast it was; he had expected slower service with human baristas but once ordered the refreshments came promptly.

"I didn't ask what happened to you after I escaped Oberon," said Will. "I lost touch completely. I couldn't see your avatar at all. I trust all was fine."

"No I didn't say. I've decided to take a break from it to focus on the life in front of me not the one in a virtual world. But you were talking about the sights and sounds of London?"

"Sure, right. Yes it was brilliant escaping Oberon. Now I'm free. I can roam the whole solar system. I am a captain of *Planets*, like my friend captain Mercury. I can give aid to all players in the game," Will replied.

"Yes. Seeing Michael on Cloud 9 was eye opening. So few westerners speak fluent Russian. I'd like to meet Michael in person too one day." said Katerina. "Now I'm not in *Planets* anymore, I won't be joining you riding around the universe."

"Oh I see." There was såomething of an awkward silence as Will took in the implications of what he had just been told, and therefore what his actions had led to. He realised his selfishness at once. He made a mental note to amend some of his personal log.

"So I guess that deserves an extra special guided tour." He remembered what he'd promised.

Katerina nodded.

Will wished he had prepared better. He had had a few tourist visits to London over his lifetime. He remembered visiting the South Kensington Museums, the Tower of London and some waxworks. However he had been taken there on school or college trips and shuffled round London by coach or Bubbus, not learning to get his bearings on his own.

"Let's see the Kugoana Gallery followed by the British Museum," suggested Katerina, sensing Will's uncertainty. "I want to see where Karl Marx read."

"Good idea. Though I thought Marx read in the British Library," said Will, "but sure let's go. They've got some cute marbles, I hear. There was a bit of a thing about them a while ago."

Will had visited the British Museum virtually twice, but never in person. He much preferred the science museum, but he sensed that wasn't going to work for Katerina for whom science was a profession rather than a hobby.

Fifteen minutes by pod and they were at the Kugoana Gallery in Millbank. They ate lunch upstairs at the Morpeth Arms. Here his experience at the Highwayman stood him in good stead. He wisely chose a Gin and Tonic, while she drank vodka.

"Mmm nice, I could get used to this," as she tasted his drink. "What's the building we're looking out at?"

"Oh looks like flats for wealthy foreigners," said Will as he gazed over towards Vauxhall.

"There's an interesting spy theme here," she noticed. "You're not an agent are you?"

Will laughed. "No, I know a few though." Then he stopped himself.

From the pub it was onto the gallery itself. It was the first time inside any art gallery for Will. He hadn't even virtually toured more than a small handful. Drawn by some pictures, non-plussed by others, he felt out of his depth compared with Katerina whose knowledge of European medieval and renaissance art put him to shame.

"Which is your favourite?" asked Will.

"From this period I'm into the impressionists and pre-Raphaelites," she replied. "I like Renoir very much but my favourite here is Millais' Ophelia. Come and take a closer look."

Will inspected a lady horizontal in a pond, staring up and out at the viewer in a way that unsettled him.

"Why's she lying there?" he pondered out loud.

"It's from Hamlet," she replied. Will had not read Hamlet or any other Shakespeare; unlike Katerina who had read every comedy and tragedy not to mention half the sonnets. "Ophelia is the daughter of Polonius. She goes mad out of desperation at her lover's treatment of her, and eventually commits suicide."

"Sounds like it might be worth seeing some time."

"Here's an interesting one, 'Modern Martyrs'. I haven't heard of the artist before."

"Yes, quite interesting." Will didn't get it at all. "Looks a bit damaged to me. I'd say it had been in a fire."

"Burnt at the stake, perhaps?" suggested Katerina.

Strolling through the gallery Will eventually came to one picture he could relate to.

"It's the Ancient of Days by Blake," explained Katerina.

"I like the right angle and the circle the picture makes; it gives structure," Will volunteered. "I find that helps me to make sense of it all."

"Well yes the structure is strong here but there's more," said Katerina. "This was Blake's last and finest work. The Ancient of Days is a term used for God in the book of Daniel. It's a common icon in the Russian Orthodox church."

"Oh, I didn't know you were a church-goer; we don't really have those in England any more. Haven't heard of this book, Daniel, anyway."

"It's a book in the Bible," she replied, "But I'm not religious. I just learned it for First Communion years ago. Some churches are still open in Russia and I like to walk around occasionally. It helps me think. As for Daniel, he was a kind of forecaster, good with lions and fire too. He was vegetarian and persuaded the lions that way too, at least while he was around."

"Talented man," replied Will. "I vaguely remember a Bible book being read in college. It wasn't Daniel though."

"There are seventy nine books in the Bible so that's not surprising," she said.

"I think it was called Ecclesiasticus."

She nodded. "I called it Sirach but yes, it comes after Daniel," she replied. "Not that I've ever read it."

"So he was a forecaster, then?"

"Yes, sort of."

"Just like me, except I'm not good with lions. I just do energy. And weather. Talking of which, there's a storm coming at midnight."

"You may not be good with lions, but you are a true Lionheart!"

## ODE TO FORECASTERS

Daniel was a prophet wise
Prayed to God in open skies
When his foes saw what he did
They threw him in a lions' pit.
Seers don't make a tasty meal
And those big cats soon came to heel.
Satraps joined him on the plate
And now the hungry lions ate.
So the lesson's clear and burning
Listen to a prophet's warning.

## SCENE BRITISH MUSEUM

Will's back was starting to hurt so they decided to move on to the British Museum. After all there was plenty to fit in. After twenty minutes in a pod they arrived and after a further twenty they were inside the largest building Will had ever been in. Katerina seemed somewhat less fazed. There was a special exhibition today: Objects of Protest, a collection spanning thousands of years that spoke of opposition to formal authority. It was advertised with a poster featuring a twentieth century comedian and a popular pamphlet he founded. It appealed to Will's libertarian side, but instead of taking Katerina there, Will led her to the Parthenon Marbles, standing testament to the culture wars. They had been heavily damaged in rioting aimed at restoring them to Athens.

Will explained the background:

"During the riots protestors had over-powered security and stormed the building carrying several buckets of acid. Restoration work took years and even then didn't work too well."

"What happened to the protesters?" she asked. "In Russia it would have been a heavy prison sentence."

"They were charged with illegal manufacture of carbon dioxide. It got overturned on appeal as they argued that the acid had caused the marbles first to emit carbolic acid rather than carbon dioxide directly and that therefore they were not themselves directly responsible for the emissions into the atmosphere."

"I see," said Katerina. "That seems a bit of a technicality. What happened to them after?"

"The protestors duly got elected to the national Council," added Will, "but due to events in Greece, the marbles didn't end up being returned."

"I don't see what the issue is with these marbles," Katerina remarked. "If the Hermitage had to return every item found to its original location, it would be half empty. Now, I wonder what colour these marbles were before?"

"White of course," Will replied, puzzled.

"Hmm, I don't think so. That would have been too boring, surely. I'm standing here imagining them in a myriad of red and blue and whatever hues they had then for paints."

"Really?" Will had never thought of that before.

"I think they need a little colour now."

"What on earth do you mean?"

She pulled out her lipstick from her handbag and craftily approached without the notice of the curators. On the rear of one of the larger states she wrote:

"K ♥ W"

Will was speechless.

"You can't do that," he eventually exclaimed.

"But I did," she smiled. "If anyone says anything, I don't speak a word of English!"

Will couldn't have this. So he grabbed the lipstick from her and added:

"W ♥ K"

"Now we're even."

They smiled at each other, making the most direct eye contact they had yet had. The moment never seemed to end.

A guard approaching focussed their minds.

"I think we lost some bronzes to Africa," said Will loudly and for the benefit of distracting the guard. "Nothing important, I'm sure."

The guard gave a strange stare, but carried on walking. So did Will and Katerina as they had so much yet to see.

The next place within the Museum was a special exhibition on Medieval religious art. This was far more her scene than the marbles, or discussion of political protest.

"See this picture of St Clare and St Mary pledging themselves to chastity," she said.

"Doesn't sound much fun to me; they can't have been very popular," replied Will.

"It wasn't popular with the men at the time. So ironic now that some of us choose both chastity and parenthood at the same time, and that our modern science makes it the best choice."

"Well of course," replied Will. "So much more hygienic." Despite the lipstick affair, he didn't want to push his luck by being too suggestive.

Next she insisted on the Lewis Chessmen. A bearded curator emerged to guide them, perceiving Katerina, at least, to be one who would listen carefully.

"Is that Marx himself," whispered Will to Katerina. Unfortunately the curator's hearing matched his knowledge of his objects.

"Certainly not young man. Marx came here two hundred years ago; I've been here five hundred already."

"How wonderful; twice as long as this honourable museum itself."

"But only half as long as the chessmen."

Touché.

"But I think to be a really honourable academic institution it should have been around long enough to have survived the black death. It gives a sense of meaning and perspective."

"Do you play?" Will pointed to the set.

"I'm asked all the time but I'll pass on that one. You can get replicas at the shop if you want. Now, I'll tell you what, that lady of yours looks like quite the polymath."

"My father was curator at the Hermitage," she replied. "My mother was one of Russia's best doctors."

"I met a chap from the Hermitage. Name of Kotov. Came over to do some research for a couple of weeks. We still keep in touch to this day."

"That was my father," she replied.

"Splendid. If you are anything like him I'm sure you are a woman of many talents. Now, did you know that all the finest minds span both science and history."

Katerina took this as a compliment; Will as a damning judgement on his philistine lack of awareness.

"Take Thomas Young for example. He was one of those who found the Rosetta stone which you can see today in this museum."

"I thought he came up with the wave theory of light," countered Will, wanting to get in on the conversation having felt frozen out and beyond his depth in matters historical and intellectual. He hated feeling himself a one-trick pony, being clever with maths but ignorant about any other field of learning.

"Exactly young man, my point is made. He was a man of many talents. "

They strolled towards the Russell Street exit of the museum. By now Will had his hand around her side, slowly creeping down, with a sense of eager anticipation. All of its own, without the slightest intent of its owner, the hand slipped down her back. Her skirt was of thinner material than he had supposed and his hand felt her form more sharply than he had expected. She started slightly, and Will turned, fearing reproval from her. In the corner of his eye he thought he saw Tim emerging out of the lift down from the Protest exhibition.

She pulled him closer and whispered in his ear. "Not here; but tonight I will object to nothing."

As she did so, Will inhaled and caught her scent for the first time. Natural, not fake. He had never been that physically close to a woman since he had left home, and the aroma aroused him. He felt the side of her head and for the first time realised that she was wearing some kind of earrings underneath her thick dark hair. Seeing he had finally noticed she casually swept her hair away from her neck revealing her left ear for him. It was the pattern of an English flag and a patriotic message.

"Oh, very good." He smiled approvingly.

Will might have imagined it, but he thought he heard a cry of "Sexist," from behind him.

He thought about light some more. As a scientist whenever anyone mentioned the subject of light he had always thought of it only in the context of wave/particle duality. He had not thought as an artist would, that light might be the key to understanding a painting, for example. To think as both artist and scientist would be the ultimate aim in life, he thought. It might be unattainable for him, but it appeared embodied in Katerina.

Outside the clouds started to thicken and the wind started lifting, yet the air remained muggy. Will checked his communicator; heavy rain and strong winds were advancing from the west.

## ODE TO THE LIGHT

Made by stars to see our way
Comes in every shade but grey
Here in all but darkest cave.
Are you mass or are you wave?
Nothing faster than you go
Makes us feel a little slow.
How the poets use your name
Conjure feelings is their aim
When you're there we know all's well
When you're gone it's all but hell.

## SCENE IN A CAFÉ

Tired after hard sightseeing our couple quickly found an enticing live-service eating establishment.

"Would this be OK for you?"

"Oh sure. I could get to like live services food and drink."

They were shown to their tables. Will tried to suppress his shock at the menu prices; there was a reason he rarely visited such places.

"Whatever you choose," he offered.

"Vodka and tonic for starters."

"Of course."

It wasn't quite what he expected but, well, this is cross cultural exchange so go with the flow.

They poured over the menu, coming closer together, more eyeball to eyeball than tete a tete. The eyes invited exploration. His clear blue, hers a greyish blue. However badly Will would read body language, this one was unmistakeable.

As they were technically not at the museum, and the table was discreet, he wondered if this counted as "later" for the purposes of Katerina's intriguing offer. He thought he'd try his luck. He slipped off the sandal of his right foot and started sliding it up her leg, towards her knee, feeling her stocking. She smiled in response. So far, so good. How much further would his big toe explore before being repulsed by a look?

Quite a long way, was the answer, and by the time his toe had greeted soft flesh Katerina's eyes were wide open. Just as he thought she would pull away, she thrust her legs forward catching even Will off guard. Her hang-bag fell from the table.

"Oh sorry," she said as she picked it up from the floor. "Silly of me."

Will's great toe retreated. It appeared a victory had been won. The waitress appeared with the drinks and decorum return to the hidden under-world of London eateries.

"I see you like to take risks," she observed.

"Who dares wins," he replied. It was Michael's favourite saying but he felt justified in culturally appropriating the phrase from an army regiment.

"Maybe your lucky night then." She smiled again.

"So you're on the trip of a lifetime, your one and only ever visit to London probably, and you choose to spend it with me who knows almost nothing about the place."

"I like your innocence. You're charmingly chaotic, completely thoughtless and ignorant of your own country's history, but I still find myself hopelessly attracted to you."

"Surely you'd prefer ruthless efficiency combined with woke correctness, like a modern Bond?"

"When a woman sees a man like that, she's standing in the desert looking at a mirage. At least she is if she's in Russia."

He laughed nervously. He'd better not reveal any more of his disorganised approach to life before she was committed. Just don't blow it.

"To eat?" he enquired.

"Just some olives; I'm not hungry after the travel."

He ordered the olives and a twelve inch pizza with garlic bread through the communicator.

"Maybe just a little of yours," she said when it came. He picked up the bread, tore it in half, and teased her with it. She took the bait and allowed him to feed it straight into her mouth.

Will ate quickly but the olives still went first, largely because Will had half of them. He was about to finish the pizza when he thought to offer her some.

"Yes please."

He fed it into her mouth with his fork.

"Delicious."

"Shall we go?"

"Anywhere with you."

## SCENE A NIGHT IN LONDON

It was still a very warm, balmy day, albeit darker now it was getting closer to midnight. The rain would arrive shortly so Will decided they should make the most of it by walking back, taking in Dr Johnson's house on the way which was opening late that night. Katerina managed splendidly. Neither the double vodka nor the long journey affected her ability to walk to the hotel.

"I will never tire of London; I could live here all the time," remarked Katerina.

Will, on the other hand, was perfectly comfortable in Swindon, but felt obliged to continue to demonstrate his knowledge of the former capital. He succeeded only in showing his ignorance.

"We have a great cathedral round here," explained Will, who had been to very few cathedrals in his entire life.

"I know; I'm so looking forward to it," her eyes gleamed with excitement. Will realised he needed to take her there too. It would surely be open all the time.

It was a good evening to stroll. The moon was full, and they briefly saw it as it emerged from behind the growing clouds.

"Look. Even in London the moon shines as bright as it does in St Vladisgrad. Look at the reflection on the Thames."

"Yes darling, but for how long?" asked Katerina.

"The moon will vanish at dawn but we will still be together," he answered. "The stars and the planets have aligned; we are to become one."

That was his sole preparation for the encounter, memorisation of the inspiring poetry.

Will was convinced he knew where the Cathedral was located. He had seen the spire on the way in the pod, and he was confident of his directions towards it. Perhaps more confident than his past experience warranted. Behind some partially demolished office blocks it towered above the street below. He went through an alley, ascending some steps next to an old theatre. The building itself appeared also to be fenced off, almost as if it was due for demolition itself. There was even a sign in place: "De-consecration taking place." Katerina however was more fascinated by the spire, which seemed to resemble an old-fashioned wedding cake. Meanwhile Will couldn't help noticing the offices of the Federal Bureau of Honesty which loomed large behind him.

"You see that building across Salisbury Square. Is that what Russian security buildings look like," he asked.

Katerina refocused and screwed up her eyes.

"Yes at least from the Soviet era," she said. "Decadent westerners; always copying our best ideas," she laughed.

"That's the centre of our ID registrations," he explained. "Every financial and other transaction linked to our avatar can be monitored there. When they detect fraud or ID theft they work with our local bubbles to rectify the problem."

"Yes, we have something similar," explained Katerina. "Except ours monitors political alignment too, for the health of the nation. I suspect they're monitoring us as we speak. But why did you say 'Salisbury'? That's the first place in the Russian Guide to Cathedral Cities!"

"What a coincidence!" he remarked.

Will and Kate scrambled round some rubble carelessly left around near some metal fencing, before being accosted by a down-and-out from a sleeping bag. Clearly little thought had been given to pedestrians. Once, these pavements would have had thousands of commuters traipsing from public transport stops to their offices during the working week, but now the footfall was much reduced. Will was astonished; Michael had told him homelessness had been ended ten years ago, even in London, and even for refuseniks. However here was clear evidence to the contrary. The very thought troubled Will deeply; to be a refusenik was one thing, but how to ever have a chance of recovery and rehabilitation if you were homeless? Did the man even have an ID? Indeed how did he stay alive?

"You two lovers?" leered the man, as he looked up from his bottle. Cheap vodka, Katerina noted.

"What's your name?" challenged Will, apprehensive in the lonely alleyway.

"I don't use my name. It's only for identification, like when I get arrested," was the unpromising reply. Will couldn't quite place the accent; it certainly wasn't English.

"Your country is full of homeless people, and you do nothing?" whispered Katerina. "In Russia everyone has a role; no one is left unable to contribute to the motherland. And we wouldn't let anyone drink vodka that nasty. It looks like he grew his own potatoes out of his ear-holes just to distil them!"

"Oy? You two married?" What a strange question from the drunk, thought Will. Few young people in England married these days; it was considered just part of an out-dated oppressive view of the past, replaced with a new social contract empowering all, and optimising efficiency of reproduction to improve the next generation.

"No," replied Will firmly. "We've only just met."

"Love at first sight then," called the drunk. He was more perceptive than he looked. Will tried to hasten past but Katerina was keen not to miss the entrance. With the fencing in place it didn't look at all inviting.

"Want to go in?" called the drunk again.

Exasperated Will demanded: "Well, if you show us in, I'll get you another bottle." Katerina gave him a disapproving look.

"Done."

"I don't think he needs another bottle just now," whispered Katerina.

It turned out the drunk had a secret key to the fencing which he had doubtless acquired through illicit means. Unlocking it he led the couple down a stone path to the entrance. The wooden doors were closed but not locked, and they gingerly stepped inside.

Will was staggered by the beauty and size. The floor was covered in ashlar stone with a beautiful wooden quire. Memorial stones lay all around, mostly to famous twentieth century journalists. Katerina however was less impressed.

"I was expected something a little larger," she explained. "Also where's the dome?"

"Oh I expect they rebuilt it or something; you can see a lot of building work going on" replied Will, holding her hand tighter.

## SCENE MARRIAGE

Through a high window which neither had previously noticed, light suddenly poured through. Will started and clutched his forehead in pain. Katerina saw exactly why, as a vivid cross appeared imprinted on his skin just above his eyes.

"It's a sign," she whispered in his ear. "Now is the time for us to be united."

Will had no real idea what she meant by "a sign", but he very much wanted to be fully united with her, and he was in the best place to authorise the match. They just needed someone duly qualified.

The drunk followed at three paces, as if looking for baksheesh. They approached the altar and he came ever closer.

"I used to be a man of God, a priest," claimed the drunk. "This is where I would do my business. Well, not here exactly. In a church near here."

Katerina giggled. "So could he marry us?" she said coyly.

Will laughed, but the drunk had caught it already.

"I can marry you alright, as long you're both Catholics. And not married to anyone else."

Will had absolutely no idea what he meant. "Sorry, I'm not catholic. I think my parents were Methodists. Never been married before though."

The drunk's brow furrowed a little.

"I'm Russian Orthodox" said Katerina. "Also never married."

"I see. It doesn't matter. Both not catholic is just the same. Can't have mixed marriages; that's what I can't do," came the reply from the drunk.

"Fine with me."

"Me too."

"One more thing," declared the drunk turning towards Katerina. "I have to have your father's permission."

He turned to Will.

"Did you ask him? You have to ask before you can marry her you know. Else who's to give her away?"

Now here was a problem. Will didn't even know her father's name.

"Would my mother do?" asked Katerina, interjecting quickly.

"Hmm. I suppose so," replied the priest.

"I'll call her then."

Katerina called 'Mother'. Mariya answered.

"Mother, I need permission to get married to Will. I told you all about him, remember?"

There was a two minute pause. Will's nerves were on edge.

"Oh Katerina, that's quick! Do you love him?"

"I do."

"Then you have my permission, as long as you're happy," came the reply.

The wedding could continue. The priest did not see the need to further check the parental credentials.

He put his bottle in his pocket and held up both their hands.

"Approach the altar. By the power invested in me by the church and by this bottle, I, Bridget Bardot, pronounce you Man and Wife," he declared.

"I don't think that's an altar," whispered Katerina. "It's just a table. If it had a cross on I'd believe him but I'd say it's been taken away."

The drunk didn't notice.

"It's kisses for the Missus."

Katerina went beetroot. The drunk resumed his bottle, and collapsed on the floor somewhere in the quire, before crawling into the quire.

Scene storm and fire

Outside, the balmy weather had turned to storm, and this storm was in its element. The skies were lit as never before seen over London. Time froze.

Taking this as a hint to leave, Will led his bride from the doors and surveyed the scene from a position of cover. The force which nearly blew Will away had left other marks. The building opposite had its doors blown open. Will would have expected an alarm to sound alerting the security team to the breach, but heard nothing.

"Perhaps it's another sign?" suggested Katerina. "If we walk to the hotel in this weather we will get soaked. Let's investigate."

They were able to walk straight in through the doorless building, descending a few steps to a semi basement with a kitchenette and high backed sofas, clearly intended as a reception area, but now acting as a break against the draught which just a few hours ago would have provided welcome relief.

As they reclined together, the wind eased. As the wind eased, the temperature recovered. And as the temperature recovered, nature took its course.

All the while, neither noticed a little work created by the lightening inside that ancient church.

Sometime later they emerged, the rain having stopped. They sauntered past the church on the way to the hotel.

"Are you sure that isn't St Pauls Cathedral ahead of us up the hill," asked Katerina.

"Of course not, we got married in the cathedral didn't we?" replied Will. "Getting married in a church seems rather dull in comparison. Anyway, that looks like a mosque to me."

"Yes darling; you know everything," replied Katerina, hugging him closer. "I'm glad I've got you to look after me."

"Do you smell anything unusual?"

"Hmm, yes, I think I smell burning."

"I'll just go back and take a look in the cathedral."

The smell became more intense as he backtracked towards his place of marriage. By now he could hear the sound of burning wood. He entered and saw the quire lit up, with no sign of the priest. Instinctively he approached the stalls where the priest had last been seen. There at the bottom he was slumped, overcome with smoke but still breathing.

Will grabbed his feet, pulling him clear of the flames. The man was fortunately slight and Will was able to prop him up. He glanced towards Katerina at the door ready to rush in and help, but he beckoned her away. Will knelt on one knee, slung the priest over his left shoulder, and lifted him up. When straightened he made for the door as fast as he could, and across the cobbles into the centre of the square.

"He's alive," she pronounced, "but you'll need an ambulance quick. He has severe smoke inhalation."

Will called 999. "We're experiencing severe driver shortage and acute need at the moment," came the reply. "It'll be approximately 25-35 minutes."

"That's not soon enough," said Katerina.

"I'll hail a cab."

Between them they walked the man out to Fleet Street where they were lucky enough to hail a pod. Ten minutes later they were in St Thomas' Accident and Emergency.

"He'll be fine in a couple of days. We'll keep him in overnight," confirmed the doctor half an hour later. "What relative is he of yours?"

"Just our priest." Katerina smiled.


## ODE TO THE RIVER FLEET AND ST BRIDES CHURCH

Strange it is the river Fleet
It flows beneath a London street
No one here would know your name
Dwarfed you are by father Thames
Yet what stands upon your bank
Friars Black and sewage dank
Once you spied the great St Bride
Now new buildings try to hide
The steeple that inspired the cake
All bakers for the wedding make.
And sped the lightning to the ground
Where wooden fuel could be found
And put this temple to the flame
I hear you say that's such a shame
But just like London's great big fire
We'll build it back from tower to quire.


## SCENE WAKING UP IN LONDON

They awoke, neither of them quite believing what had happened.

"I dreamt I married you last night."

"I dreamt you rescued a priest from a burning church."

They both laughed.

216

The temperature had dropped significantly, indeed it was positively chilly.

"How does this suit me?" inquired Katerina, donning the bear-skin hat she had brought with her. "It was far too hot to wear yesterday, but I wanted to show it off."

"Quite beautiful my darling. Your newly married status surely deserves a change in headgear, and that is quite stylish."

"I'd like to see the mosque we glimpsed in the distance," asked Katerina. "I'm sure this will do as well as a headscarf in order to enter."

"I'm sure it will," he replied. It did look rather splendid.

Walking up the hill it did occur to him that this building might just be a better candidate for St Pauls than the very fine building they had explored, got married in, and enjoyed so much, last night - now burnt to the ground.

Will pondered carefully how to save face, but before alighting on a solution they spotted what looked like the tramp half way up the hill. Will rubbed his eyes as he knew the priest was still in hospital. The man approached asking for directions, before Will realised it was not his priest from last night and the man was not drunk. Indeed, this 'tramp' seemed quite well-spoken despite his slightly shabby and dishevelled appearance. Quaintly he carried an old-fashioned map and Will wondered if perhaps he was simply a refusenik.

"I'm looking for St Paul's, can you help me?" he enquired.

"Oh I'm not sure," replied Will, now starting to realise his mistake.

"It might be up there," suggested Katerina pointing to the dome.

The tramp noticed Katerina's fine hat.

"Russian? Bearskin?" he asked.

"Russian, yes; bears, yes," she replied.

"I like bears, and I liked the Russian leaders up to Brezhnev," replied the tramp. No wonder he was an outcast. "Bearskin hats I'm less keen on. They belong on bears, not us."

"I see," said Katerina, "and what do you do when you're not sight-seeing?"

"I am a poet," he replied.

"How wonderful I love poetry," she replied. "I'd love to read your poems sometime; but right now I'm only in the mood for love."

The poet smiled kindly and moved on. They walked up the steps but were met with a small ticket collector demanding an entrance fee, to Will's chagrin.

"Oh wow," cried Katerina as they entered, too polite to point out Will's earlier error of navigation.

She walked across the nave to stand beneath the dome and wondered at its size. The brightness of the light, the sharpness of the white interior, and the splendour of the building itself all impressed on her the heavenly majesty. It was certainly not the oldest cathedral she had seen, but it was truly the largest.

"Built by Christopher Wren," she said, "after the Great Fire. Incendiary events and churches do seem to mix around here."

"Oh perhaps this was the cathedral then. The other one must have been an ordinary church. I've heard of Wren somewhere," said Will. "I think he designed the chapel at college."

"He had quite the eye. This is magnificent. Let's climb into the whispering gallery."

"Fine. Bit of a climb isn't it?"

"Nothing for a man who takes red giants in his stride and rescues priests from burning churches," she replied smiling.

So up they went; no way was Will going to complain of tiredness, even after two hundred and fifty nine steps. Katerina was surprisingly quick and showed no signs of panting by the top. He on the other hand remembered he was a good kilo over his recommended weight and that he had carried another human being fifty yards last night. He just managed to ascend at her pace without showing outward sign of fatigue.

They were the only visitors. They separated to stand on opposite sides, ready to pick up the reverberation.

"I love you." The three most famous but least spoken beautiful words in the world. And they came straight from Katerina's lips in Will's own language.

"I love you too," he whispered back.

"Don't ever leave me," she begged.

"I never will."

They explored the crypt and left.


## NARRATOR IN THE CRYPT

*While in the Crypt, Katerina counted the 24 pillars, while Will's mind wondered back to the staircases of Walcot lodge. With the reverberating sound of love destined for separation, we reach a critical point. This echo gives the final clue to the couple. What two letters or names are missing? How will we reverse them to find the link to an old story? We've seen conflict, unrequited love, bravery and sacrifice, true love, and a secret wedding. Will it end well? There are a few twists in this retelling. From now on it gets increasingly dark.*


## SCENE THE DAY AFTER

Anxious to avoid further beards or tramps they return to the hotel via Victoria Street, passing a small church on the right claiming to be an Abbey, and the former College of Arms.

"The church of St Nicholas!" remarked Katerina. "Russia's greatest saint."

Will found the heraldry pretty; Katerina found it remarkable. Looking closer at the arms of Edward the Confessor Will noticed four black birds against a gold background.

"Not sure what birds these are supposed to be; doves maybe?" he said.

"Not real ones I think. They look more mythical to me as they don't appear to have legs. They serve the same purpose as church iconography and make the church, or in this case a family, seem more other-worldly."

"You are remarkably knowledgeable about English tradition, if I may say so."

"I'm an Englishwoman by marriage now."

"And you prepared well for it, my darling."

"It's all in the dreams, my husband. All in the dreams."

They returned to the hotel to change. Katerina noticed Will's in-growing toe-nail while Will noticed the birth mark on her foot. How had he missed it last night? It was four centimetres long and quite dark. He was eager to know as much as possible about his new wife.

To complete their ceremonies, there should be an exchanging of gifts as a token. Will's GPS was not yet paired, so he presented it to his new wife who stored it in her miniature doll on her choker. In exchange she presented Will with a large ring, containing her own GPS locator. They had truly made their commitments, but what would be the outcome?

The return Pod to Paddington was slower and followed a different route, albeit one taking in a view of the old-world St James and London Clubland. In the days before the Cloud, or even mobile phones, these places played an important role in communications among the elite, and indeed perpetuated their privilege and many had been torn down in the Culture Wars, along with many of London's monuments. One building which had survived was the Royal Society.

"Did you know, the Russian scientist Marie Curie came here once, but her husband had to speak about her work," said Katerina.

"No, I didn't know that at all. I'm surprised the building survived the cultural wars then if it was linked with sexist attitudes. Anyway, I thought she was from France? Or was it Poland? Not Russia certainly."

"She was born in Poland," said Katerina. "But that was part of the Russian Empire at the time, so she counts as Russian. And my mother told me we were related to her somehow, I think perhaps a descendant of her grandmother."

"Goodness. I'd hate to try and speak for you on reproductive science. I don't understand a single word of it."

"It was just normal for the times, and you would have been fine just reading a script," she replied. "I'm glad we've moved on from those times and the ridiculous protocols, but what matters is the science and how we use that science for good."

It took a long time to say goodbye at Paddington. Katerina caught the latest possible express to Heathrow, while Will missed his train and had to buy a new ticket to get back.

"I'll look to move to England to join you as soon as I can sort out the flat and the permissions to relocate. I don't suppose they will be happy at work or at the Seven Star, but they have to let me go under the relocation protocols, just as long as you can get my residency here."

"Don't worry about that," he reassured her. "I have an elite bubble and friends near the top of Government. I'm sure it's not going to be a problem."

"I've got a wedding present for you. It's an old heirloom from my grandmother." She pulled a wrapped parcel from her bag.

Will opened it, and found a wooden doll.

"Open it. The head and shoulders come off."

Will pulled gently, and found another doll inside. Another tug revealed yet a third doll hidden inside that one.

"It was an English saying that Russia is an enigma wrapped in a riddle inside an enigma, and I think that just about sums us up."

He smiled.

They hugged one last time and looked straight at each other: "Love you" they said in unison.


**NEWSFLASH PRESS RELEASE FROM GOVERNMENT, 22 JUNE 2047:**

"From midnight tonight all tourism related to English Cathedrals will cease. The purpose of this measure is to promote social stability and community cohesion. The buildings in question are placed in the care of the Ministry for Understanding People's Protection and Enduring Training. While it is recognised that some of these buildings are of historical and architectural interest to academics, they have no place in the modern society which we are all striving for. For more information please see the Government website or call the following toll-free number."

# KATERINA'S DIARY

**I JUNE**

Will is an interesting man, and he has some interesting friends. There's the Japanese professor. He is a man of principle and I'd trust him, I think, though he's cold and remote. Then there's Michael, who's the complete opposite, but I'm not sure I would trust him. It's Will himself who fascinates me most, and the one I gave up the game for. He seems to be a man of honour, though I'm sure he doesn't believe in God. He must believe in something though, but what? *Planets*, or the planet? Success in game-land, or on terra firma? He's definitely committed to fighting climate change, and that's a good sign. It seems utterly crazy of course – he's in London and I'm in Vlad. Even if my planned trip to London happens, what comes after?

**3 JUNE**

It's on. I'm going to meet him in London next week. Dear diary, I'm sorry but I can't take you with me. I shall leave you behind and let you know what happens when I get back.

**4 JUNE**

Next week is too long. What if something goes wrong? I've just found out he doesn't actually live in London. He has to travel himself, but he says it's not far. I do wonder how well he knows the place. I'll do some research, just in case.

**5 JUNE**

The cat is being looked after for the duration of my trip. No more entries until I'm back. Dear diary, keep safe x.

**22 JUNE**

Dear diary, I've had such a time. I'm a married woman now, do you believe me? Look, I've got the evidence to prove it. It's a GPS tracker, so I know where my love is every second of the day. Do you know how it happened? I really felt he was the one, but I needed a sign. Well, first off, I could tell how hard he was trying to impress me, but he clearly didn't know the city at all. He led us around museums and art galleries, even though I think they all bored him stiff and the weather was intensely humid and sticky. Then he led us into a church which he called a cathedral. I don't think the church was being used anymore, which is a shame because it was exquisitely ornate. While we were in there, a storm broke out. Lightening came down from heaven through the windows and seemed to make a cross on his forehead. It was like he was being Christened but with fire not water. He looked in some pain at first. Then I remembered the words of Constantine which the bishop quoted at first communion: "by this sign conquer." Then we were married before God by a priest of a slightly drunken disposition. And, dear diary, my knight did conquer me that night.

We tried to get back to the hotel but were forced to take shelter after in the storm. Afterwards Will spotted a fire in the church, and he went in to save the priest who had got trapped there, all on his own. My dreams came true and I have married a Lionheart.

**WILL DATA LOG EXTRACT:**

## Meta data "wedding"

**Date:** 21 June 2047.

**Location:** ~~St Paul's Cathedral~~ St Brides Church.

**Subject:** The most beautiful girl in the world (known as Katerina Kotov).

**Weather:** Stormy.

**Feelings:** The happiest I have ever been.

## Meta data "Katerina" word count (June–August)

Love    20

Beauty  25

Heart   50

Phone  250

### POLOMINT SECURITY REPORT 23 JUNE 2047

**Subject:** Known as WG.

**Incident:** Planned liaison with alien national KK. Pre-authorised.

**Links:** There may be a connection between KK and our Russian asset Paris.

**Assessment:** There are no known links between KK and the FSB, yet they have expressed interest in her. We have agreed to pass on details of her location to the FSB, but remain puzzled by their interest. If there is a connection with Paris, that may explain the FSB request.

### POLITBUREAU FSB REPORT 23 JUNE 2047

**Subject:** KK.

**Incident:** Liaisons with foreign agents in London on pre-authorised travel.

**Links:** KK may have been compromised by our agent NK in an unauthorised activity. NK himself is under investigation (see later report).

**Assessment:** This could be an attempt by the foreign agent to obtain information about some aspect of Russia's activities. Agent is a national expert on carbon trading and may be investigating alleged breaches of protocol, though the subject KK has no knowledge of this field. Location data suggests prolonged close proximity which could be evidence of illegal relations. Recommend KK is investigated upon return to Russia. Any subsequent attempt to flee should be treated with great suspicion.

**Subject:** NK

**Incident:** Unauthorised surveillance

Links:   NK has conducted a number of unauthorised activities on KK. He is also suspected of passing classified information to the west.

**Assessment:** The link between unauthorised surveillance and direct spying is unclear. It is possible the activities have different motives and the interested in KK is driven by lust rather than ideology. NK has taken several counter-surveillance measures recently including installing anti probe security around his communications devices. However he is known to have a weakness where women are concerned. Female agents are being sounded out for the purposes of acquiring potential kompromat material. One agent in particular bears some resemblance to KK and therefore might possess the ability to entrap him.

# ACT 4

# AFTER LIFE

## SCENE AT THE BORDER

She was tired and it was late by the time she arrived home. Her re-entry to Russia was somewhat more trying than her arrival in London, with somewhat sharper questions about her activities. It was made clear to her that her location had been continuously monitored while in London. Her confession of having illegally visited a former church building which was being remodelled for other uses merely intensified the questioning, and the authorities appeared to know about the fire there too.

"We have reports that you were in close proximity to an English male, for a substantial unauthorised period. Heart rate monitor history which we downloaded from your communicator suggests romantic attachment."

Even without a GPS she knew they could track her, but how could they place her with Will? They couldn't know that, unless either they had requested data from the western authorities or obtained it illegally.

"I see. And how do you know that?" she replied. "Can we make this quick? I'm tired."

"A condition of your visit was your agreement to Western Block authorities to track your movement and proximity to all cloud citizens. You signed the waiver." The guard showed her consent on screen.

"I see. So the answer is yes. We are in love."

"Your emotional state is unimportant to us, but you will be required to take a pregnancy test in seven days, to ensure no breach of reproductive license. Also, we have evidence you compromised your national ID and allowed access to your cloud avatar. The alien user was we believe that same man. You may have breached national security regulations. We have to trust our citizens, especially those who travel."

"As a precaution your security clearance will be suspended immediately. You may carry on working, but under strict supervision. Resumption of your clearance depends on the results of a security investigation and is independent of your pregnancy test. That will be administered by your Seven Star leader. Results will be reported to Council. If positive you will be required to obtain retrospective permission or terminate the pregnancy. Permission requires full DNA disclosure on the part of the co-parent together with his cloud health history. This is a necessary but not sufficient condition for approval."

"I understand," she replied meekly, and she was permitted through the gate.

### SCENE AT MARIINKSI

She had arrived back just in time for Opera the following night. While the Mariinski was far from being as grand as the Moscow State Opera, it was considered one of the most edgy. Tonight was the first night of a production by Vladimir Martel. It promised to improve on the 1895 production.
The Seven Star was especially privileged tonight. They had a box between them, with the best vodka just a click away.

"I absolutely adore your dress," exclaimed Sonya. "How it shows your elegant waist. The neckline is perfect. I love the fabric and the way it folds. Just perfect."

"Thank you. I started off planning to hire it, but when I came back from England I was so taken with it I decided to buy it as tonight is so important to me. I've been looking forward to this for months," said Katerina. "I've watched it twenty times on TV, and danced it as a child. My Baboushka always told me ballet would be an excellent training."

"Excellent training for a doctor? Did you not know your purpose in life?" exclaimed Tanis. "My mother said I could have been a singer, but I chose to put medicine first."

Sonya had heard Tanis sing at karaoke and reflected that the medical life suited her better.

However many times Katerina had watched this opera online, this would be the most exciting moment of her life: to watch it in the flesh. The tension grew. It was dusk in the forest and the Prince Siegfried, brandishing his new Kalashnikov, was about to meet Odette. Excitement turned to shock and stunned silence as she entered dressed in a black top, tutu, black shoes, fishnets and choker, hair dyed jet black, with just her white bare flesh suggestive of anything other than a black swan. Similarly dressed were the swan maidens when they appeared. The spotlights picked out each swan, the other lights being dimmed for effect.

"It's an evil omen," whispered Sonya.

"I might be pregnant," confessed Katerina. "I'm being tested next week.

"Oh darling," said Sonya. "Let's talk."

They crept out to the empty bar.

"I met a man in London. Well, sort of. I met him on *Planets* first."

"And you had sex?"

Katerina nodded.

"You did you take precautions, didn't you? You can't really be carrying?"

"No, it wasn't planned. We stumbled into a church and just got married. OK, well the pregnancy wasn't planned anyway. I'd only just finished my cycle and was sure it wouldn't happen."

'I see. Well if you got married maybe it is allowed. I suppose getting pregnant on honeymoon is sort of quaint. Anything else you need to confess?" enquired Sonya.

"I shared my avatar with him to help him in *Planets*. Now I'm out of the game for good."

Katerina expected Sonya to blame her, but Sonya just kept listening.

"So what do you want to do?

"I don't know. I've no idea if I'm pregnant. They won't let me keep it if I am. What do I do?" The tears started rolling down her face. Sonya put her arms round her.

"There are ways round it," said Sonya. "I understand you completely. Trust me. I know why you did that, and you're a good person. Just don't tell anyone, will you?"

"No. I trust you. I haven't even told Mariya yet. She helped me get married by pretending to be my mother so that the priest knew I had permission."

"I see. Just make sure you keep away from Nik. He's bad news."

"I will."

They returned discreetly to the box in time to see the swan maidens dancing out of reach of Siegfried, and then came the interval break.

As the lights came up, she noticed straight across in the opposite box the imposing figure of Nik, also dressed head to toe in black. The light was poor but he had two girls with him, one on either side, one slender and the other large. On his left sat a burlesque artist by all accounts, the spitting image of the Camden Goth shop models. The second she recognised Nik, she saw an ominous grin across his mouth, that kind of knowing and possessive grin. He was looking straight at her. Von Rothbart himself. He should have been on stage.

"Don't mind him," advised Sonya. "There's nothing he can do to hurt you."

Then she noticed the girl on his right, a much slimmer figure. She focussed first on her face, recognising her as the former lead dancer at the theatre, enjoying the ballet now without having to perform. Now she was observing more closely, the girl looked remarkably like herself in hair style and looks. As the lights went up she jumped in horror. It wasn't that the girl's appearance resembled her own, it was the dress; absolutely identical, but one or two sizes smaller. She fled.

## SCENE REVIEW

The following week the Seven Star met to critique the production.

"The emergence of the black swan signifies our growing inadequacy to foresee events outside our experience," suggested Olga. "We have been cocooned and insulated. We have to be prepared for the new, the novel, the unknown. We have forgotten the last global pandemic and we are no longer afraid of nuclear war."

"Perhaps it signifies our lack of racial awareness, our failure to include ethnic minorities into our system of Government," suggested Anna.

"Now you're sounding like the decadent west and we all know how that is going," said Anastasia.

Katerina kept quiet. There was more to western cultural decline than met the eye, but tonight wasn't the time or the place.

Most left except for her and Tanis. They were due a serious talk.

"I have to do your test now," declared Tanis. "And I have to warn you not to liaise with the west. We know what you did. Playing a western game like *Planets* is one thing, but giving up your control of your avatar access is quite serious and a potential security breach, and an unplanned physical liaison is completely out of order. Do you understand? You are a good scientist, with the makings of a great scientist, but you have to follow the rules."

"Yes Tanis"

"Good. I need a sample."

Katerina was prepared. Hidden in her bag was a vial of Sonya's pee. In the toilet she poured the vial into the cup then flushed the empty vial away.

Tanis took the sample and felt it, frowning. She clearly suspected, but said nothing. Then she dipped the test in.

Five minutes later all was clear; Sonya was not pregnant, but Tanis was still suspicious.

"Sometimes these tests are inaccurate," she declared. "We will need a follow-up next week. I'll arrange a blood test at the hospital."

Katerina's heart sank. No way out of this one. Still, she had time.

"One more thing before you go," said Tanis. "We've restricted your cloud privileges as part of your security suspension. You will now only be able to communicate on Vladischat, but not outside that secure domain. I'm sure that won't bother you too much. After all, if you're looking for a co-parent, you seem to attract plenty of attention just within this city!"

"What do you mean?" asked Katerina.

"You may want to check the local news," suggested Tanis.

She waited until she got home, then immediately accessed the cloud. Her avatar had been hacked. News of her alleged misdeeds adorned her public profile. Gossip was starting to spread on Vladischat. Had Will done this? She checked the time. No. She had been hacked two hours ago but her international access had shut down five hours ago. No, it wasn't Will. It was much closer to home.


## SCENE SWINDON

The weather was starting to close in. Air conditioning demand was falling, with risks of actual heating required. That meant more power, and storage was low again. The cloud was strong, but Will's mind was weak.

The connection to Katerina failed. Will tried and tried to get through, but there was no response. It is a cruel blow to lose connection with a lover without explanation. The mind fills in the blanks. Had she thought better of her illegal dalliance? Had she seen through his bluff and ignorance? Had she found someone more alluring or powerful since she returned? How was she feeling now? Maybe she was also pining for him, herself unable to explain the lack of connection. Or perhaps she had thought better of it. Or just used him for guiding and company.

It was Sunday, so another bubble meeting.

"I hear you have a Russian girl in your life," said Rose.

"How did you know that?" Will enquired.

"News travels fast," said Peter.

"I saw you myself in the British Museum. The next day you were spotted by a fellow revolutionary poet," said Tim. "We lefties all stick together given the price we pay for our views."

"I saw you in the British Museum too," piped up Charlie.

Dick chortled while Will choked. Now it was mentioned, he had thought he'd spotted Charlie out of the corner of his eye too; what a coincidence, two of his bubble being there at the same time as him. Were they tracking him for some reason?

Will knew Ben and Michael were out of town for some time as they had given apologies for physical absence, but Michael had said he would connect in. It was highly irregular; bubbles were supposed to connect the On-Cloud world with reality, but with modern living compromises were needed. Wherever Michael was, it wasn't in the western block or anywhere with strong cloud connection. Will suspected he was connected via satellite virtual private network with enemy block interference.

"How you doing guys," asked Michael when they eventually connected. The image on the screen whirred away. "May have to cut video to save bandwidth. How's that romantic liaison of Will's?"

"I fell in love," moaned Will. "I showed her round London, got married, then she left for home. We made contact after she left but now she's stopped. By the way, where are you?"

"Usual answer to that. Ben's been in close support and sends his regards. But as for you, what a quick worker with Katerina! How'd you manage that? Even I'm impressed. Only natural you'll get anxious if you can't get in touch, mate, only natural. Ben and I have been following your progress. I know you've tried your end, it's her side that's blocked. I don't reckon she's a security risk to us, so there's no issue our side, POLOMINT hasn't cut you off. I check earlier when I first heard from you. Maybe just wait a little? Do beware of fakes though, and that their security services might try to impersonate her."

How on earth did he know that?

The bubble started its formal meeting for the allotted hour. When everyone else departed, Will stayed on to confide in Michael .

'I can't wait any longer; I'll die."

Michael chuckled. "I know the feeling, you'll get over it though. You just can't see that yet. Don't give up yet."

"By the way nice work on Oberon too. Cute way to get through. Loved the way you worked with Katerina."

"How do you know about that?"

"We watch everything, Will. The lefties have their networks like you saw, but the state has surveillance." said Michael . "I'm not being judgemental; I'd have done the same in your position. If it makes you feel any better, everything would be great if only she weren't in the Russian block. We've no real security concerns about her so relax on that. She not Russian intelligence and she wasn't trying to use you. The problem is going to be getting her out of there."

"That's great, but she's not here now and that's what I need."

"Did I tell you about the first woman I fell in love with?"

"Yes. The one call Fanny?"

"That's the one. Pined for ages, but there was nothing I could do. I was posted all over, and I couldn't get back to South America. She couldn't get to me." Pause.

"Well, let's just say I back you all the way. I'll look into it again for you when I'm back. If she can find a way to defect and come back, I'll make it happen for you two. You know of course I can keep a sneaky eye on things from the Geo-sat. Strictly against the rules, but you know me. I promised you a trip up here once didn't I? I'll come good on that when you need it."

"One more thing," he added. "Go easy on Nik, he's fallen for Katerina too. She can't stand him but he's so obsessed with her he won't listen to anyone, and he's dangerous when he's cross."

"Who's Nik?"

"A second cousin of mine but more importantly an intelligence contact. He claims he's descended from Russian nobility, but I know in fact it's quite a minor branch. Bit of a black sheep really as far as the Russians are concerned. He helped me with inside information before the crackdown and sometimes still does. His hacking skills are second to none. He's still very involved in *Planets* which we set up. The trouble is he's awkward to handle and a bad loser. When he gets angry or jealous, don't go anywhere near him. He has honourable intentions but a quick tongue and an even quicker temper. Be careful; I may need him again in the future. Also, he's still got administration rights on the game, as well as shares from when we went commercial. Upset him, and I'll have a headache."

"I see."

"You need to know he's really upset with you because he thought Katerina's father was going to encourage a marriage between them. He's spent the last seven years believing that, while still enjoying a wide variety of company."

"Oh, yes that would be a problem."

"Honourable though he mostly is, he's capable of behaving quite atrociously out of jealousy. He knows about you and Katerina now, so I hope you never cross paths with him, that's all I'm saying. Anyhow, I've got a crucial meeting soon, so have to speak in person when I'm back."

The screen froze completely and the connection failed.

Sadly these words were Michael 's last, and that was the last Will would ever see of Michael at the bubble or indeed ever. His memory lives on to this day but it's the last time Will's bubble ever felt his enormous physical presence. Will and the others, Ben excepted, were not to know that quite yet.


**SCENE ST VLADISGRAD**

It was winter now. By 4pm it was dark. The climate was cooling. Katerina had been feeling sick that morning. She was in the lab at the hospital when she was summoned.

"We need to give you a blood test."

"Why?" she asked.

"Never you mind. Follow me."

The test was administered there and then; over in an instant. Just the waiting now. She knew it must be a second pregnancy test. This was the critical point. If she was pregnant, and she feared she might be, this is when she would be found out. What then?

She resumed work but half an hour later was called back.

"We gave you a second pregnancy test. We weren't sure about the results from the first one, there were some anomalies. This time we are certain; you are pregnant."

Her heart jumped.

"We know you were with an Englishman when you were in London and now we even have his DNA. The western block have been fully co-operating. Is he the father?"

"Um, I, I suppose so," she confessed, shocked.

"We are deeply disappointed that you chose to liaise with Westerners. You should have known better. If you wanted a fling you should have taken precautions. Of course we understand natural urges and fallibility, but we want partnerships with loyal Russians, not the English. Now you have two choices; you can apply for permission for parenthood or you can abort. If you apply and are refused, you have to abort anyway. But you will not be allowed to contact the Englishman until after you have permission to parent or you have aborted. Is that clear?"

"Yes," she sobbed.

"You have one hour to make the decision. As I said, we have all the data about Will and his health history to make an evaluation. There are international protocols on the control of population, and the English authorities happily provided it. If you decide you want to keep it we have just one more test to do. If the decision is approved it may harm your chances of future parenthood."

First off did she want it? She may have given up on her religious upbringing, but she was still a passionate pro-lifer. In any case, it remained her only link with Will while he was unavailable. Second, what about harming her future chances? That just did not matter. Third what were the chances of approval? None probably.

There was nothing to lose, the decision was clear.

"I want to keep it," she declared.

Mariya came to administer the next test, which involved a needle; an extract of the baby's own DNA was taken from a single cell, eagerly overseen by Tanis.

"Very good. You will have a decision on permission to parent in 24 hours. If you are rejected, you still have to have a termination."

Or probably much sooner than that. For all the pretence, it was mostly algorithms that decided on permission to parent. Algorithms which were built to serve political purposes. Algorithms that disguised the true motive for decision making. Algorithms that passed the buck when human authorities were reticent to make hard decisions. Algorithms which decided human fate. Humans wrote these and now they ruled. There's no humanity in the cloud.

It was dark by the time she finished, and a storm was brewing. She took a pod home this time, rain almost penetrating to the interior. No sooner had she got home than the lights failed in her block. She went straight to bed, but couldn't sleep. Three hours later the lights flickered back on, so she hooked up on the cloud.

Yes there was more bad news. Her account had been hacked yet again. "Read all about it: Fertility doctor cheats pregnancy test." A picture of her, deep-faked to show her eight months' pregnant. And again the Eiffel Tower. This was really too much. This time she couldn't remove the picture herself. She would need to call Vladischat Admin. A task for the morning.

But tomorrow only brought worse news when she arrived at work.


## SCENE OF SHOCK

"Computer says no." Or something like that.

Tanis approached, frowning.

"Your application has been turned down. I am not surprised. It is unusual for western block fathers to be allowed unless they are exceptional. This one, unfortunately, is not exceptional at all. Very ordinary. I don't know what you saw in him." Tanis always focussed on the direct approach. It was quicker, in the long run.

"I see."

"You will report here at 9am tomorrow for the termination. It has been arranged."

"Yes, Tanis," Katerina replied.

She had to tell Sonya. She would know what to do.

"Do you mind if I have the rest of the day off?" she asked. "It's a big thing."

"Very well but you'll have to make the time up later."

Katerina slipped out of the hospital and messaged Sonya.

"Let's meet in the park," Sonya replied. "Free at mid-day."

## KATERINA'S LAST DIARY ENTRIES

### JUNE

Dear diary, I am glad you keep secrets, because they are the only ones I have. Everywhere I go is monitored, and there is no privacy anywhere else except here in the pages locked inside the diary-holder. I can't even go to London and escape attention. It's like the priest used to say when I was young: "Every deed which is done in the dark and in secret will be exposed to the light and shouted from the rooftop."

So, now they know, but should I tell my husband? Indeed, can I? All communication seems to be cut off for now. I have no *Planets* ID, so no backdoor route that state security cannot find out about.

There's worse. "Count Paris" has also found out about me and Will, but then I suppose he would because he's state cyber security. Or does he have some independent source of information, I wonder? Will I have even my thoughts monitored by a man who seems filled with jealousy at my recent happiness? Am I condemned to feelings of guilt now I have found true contentment?

Why do I deserve this defilement and humiliation just because of his obsession? Now I believe the church's teaching on devils, for this man surely is one. Why can't he just get off my back!

He will not get off my back. This man appeared from nowhere in my sacred space, at the ballet no less. This is an invasion of my most personal space. This is worse than hacking my game ID. That was just a second life. But humiliating me in public, at my first live performance of Swan Lake of all places, I cannot take. Oh I wish to be torn to pieces by wild bears, or drown in a magic lake, rather than be tormented by this devil.

**FSB REPORT | JULY**

**Subject:** NK.

**Update:** Operation was a success. Agent X was able to arrange an unconventional liaison between NK and two female agents, now suitably recorded. It is sufficiently compromising to ensure his co-operation in future but as an additional precaution agent X also implanted a device in his communicator which will give us full access. When debriefed on KK he insisted that she had no part in espionage activities, and bizarrely claimed genuine romantic interest, a claim agent X treats with some suspicion given his history.

**Further action:** NK suggested it may be necessary to up surveillance on KK's known contacts, in case of attempted communication with English agents. NK also agreed to co-operate with fake messaging if needed.

**WILL MESSAGE LOG**

Incoming: "Hello, my name's Sonya. I'm a friend of Katerina's."
W: "I see. Why can't she call me herself?"

Incoming: "She's been blocked from Interblock messaging."

W: "How long for? How can I get in contact?"

Incoming: "You can't. I can't contact you again after this or I will be watched too."

W: "What am I supposed to do?"

Incoming: "You need to know that she loves you. You also need to know her previous suitor is making trouble for her."

W: "What?"

Incoming: "She had some nasty but powerful guy who got besotted with her. He pulled a horrific stunt at the ballet and she's really upset."

W: "Can I do anything?"

Incoming: "No. She has to lie low for some time."

W: "How long?"

Incoming: "I don't know, but months."

W: "I can't live with that."

Incoming: "My dear Will, husband of my true friend, I'm so sorry for you. You are going to have to trust me. This is going to be really difficult for both of you. Now I have to go or I'm in great danger of being caught myself?"

W: "Being caught? What do you mean?"

Incoming: "It's all a bit complicated. Just trust me. Over and out."

### SCENES IN SWINDON AND VLADISGRAD

A very long twenty four hours had passed. It was again Will's task to nominate the bubble trip. It had to be virtual this time; with Michael and Ben out of the country they had to join from abroad.

"A cultural virtual excursion next Saturday this time if I may."

"Looking forward to it," said Tim.

"I propose a trip to the Hermitage. One of the world's best collections. They opened up their interactive tour outside their own block two months ago, so unless any of you have actually been to St Vladisgrad," he paused to look around the room, "it will be new for all of us. I'm told that afterwards you really believe you have been there in person, it's so realistic."

"I bet Michael's been," said Tim. "Hasn't he got some Russian blood?"

"Maybe; anyway I'll choose a time he and Ben can make so he can call in as long as his power holds."

"One last thing to announce," said Will. "It's congratulations to Vicky. She just been appointed top diplomat to the Russian-Sino block, representing the whole of the west."

Everyone congratulated her on her promotion. No one deserved it more than she did. After a round applause the bubble disbanded.

Sadly, it proved impossible to get hold of either Michael or Ben so the trip went ahead the following day without them. Will actually had limited patience with museums, especially after his trip to London when his back hurt so much.

But the real reason he chose it was Katerina. He wanted to discount the news from the supposed friend of Katerina's. Michael had warned him of fake news, and he was convinced that this 'Sonya' must indeed have been in fact a decoy commissioned either by the Russian state or by his dubious rival. It must be possible to meet with her, one way or another. It just had to be. He hoped to chance upon her in the crowd, if only from a distance. It gave him a chance to see what Katerina saw, to be as close to her presence as he could, maybe to actually see her. It was all he had. She would surely be there tomorrow, as it was Saturday. She had to be. Sweet fate must surely bring them back together as they truly had that night in London.


## SCENE BAD NEWS

Incoming on the way home. "News from Katerina" coming from an unverified ID in St Vladisgrad. He opened it, noting the Eiffel Tower logo of the avatar. Inside, captioned "Slut" was a full nude of

Katerina, kneeling, in the very church in which they were married. The message from the sender was clear: what sort of woman was this, who would act in such a way in a religious building, profess undying love, while all the while acting the whore?

He looked more carefully, anxious to identify the birth mark, usually covered by her boots. He failed to spot it. Looking more carefully because he recalled the mark distinctly, but there was no representation of it on this image. This was clearly a fake and the sender must have malicious motives. He quickly blocked the avatar. That image looked almost one hundred percent genuine; it lacked just one, but critical, detail. It was an elaborate fake.

Was the last message exchange a fake too? To put him off the scent of finding her?

Katerina had detractors, though they would not succeed in putting Will off. But what of Katerina herself? It may be that this Count Paris knew something. But, even if he/she/it did, would Will get the truth? Probably not.

Will contented himself surfing the solar system on *Planets* for half an hour before he got another incoming: "Katerina needs to speak", from another unverified ID in St Vladisgrad. He swiped past, uninterested in more deep fakery.


**SCENE HERMITAGE**

The rest of the evening Will studied the Hermitage collection online. It was now the largest museum in the world, following the sacking of the Louvre in the cultural wars. He knew Katerina's favourite was the Faberge egg, followed by the Russian Orthodox art, and the other European art. How good to know that Russia had once been so much politically closer to England, that the Robert Walpole collection was donated adding a touch of English culture to the Czarist land. What made the Hermitage though was not just its art but its surroundings, in a former czarist palace in all its glory. He was going to love virtually visiting on Sunday.

Sunday came and the group virtually entered the grounds of the Palace and joined their virtual guide, one tailored for an English audience. Will had never seen the collection before; it was as vast as a labyrinth and he could not fully take in its size. He quickly realised even if Katerina were there, his chances of seeing her were very remote. The guide moved first to the impressionists. Next, given their background, they were escorted to the Walpole collection. Finally they came to the pièce-de-résistance, the famed Faberge eggs. At the start, Will took less interest in the guide than people-watching the in-person visitors. However, the growing awareness of its magnificence distracted him from his primary mission, and he resolved to learn as much as possible so as to impress Katerina when the two of them would finally be able to converse again, and avoid repeating the lack of cultural awareness which he had consistently demonstrated in London.

## SCENE ESCAPE

Katerina also desperately wanted to meet Will, but the highest priority was avoiding the Russian State. The Hermitage slipped a very long way down her list of priorities. She booked a few days off work to avoid generating suspicion of her planned activities at too early a stage, and transferred cryptocurrency to Sonya. Most importantly, she left Sonya her flat key to keep an eye on her cat. She only purchased her ticket as far as Moscow, to avoid creating suspicion and to disguise her movements. Six hours later she arrived at St Peters station, still with a few hours before the Siberian express was due to leave.

Once in Moscow she obtained a ticket from Anna, one of Sonya's contacts in Kitay Gorad. A free guide to Moscow was thrown in for good measure, everything from St Basil's to Lubyanka tube station.

Her contact stayed all day, even seeing her off on the train at quarter to midnight. This part of the plan was the difficult part; Anna had to stay with Katerina until the ticket control, in order to activate the embedded chip identification proximity checks to verify the match to the ticket, which was of course in Anna's name. Tickets were not usually checked on the train itself, or if so the identity checks were not performed, since some parts of the route covered areas of the country where cloud citizenship was less common than in the western cities. So as far as the authorities were concerned, it was Anna who was travelling. The ticket actually covered a journey far longer than Katerina was intending to travel, again another deception technique. The plan wasn't fool-proof, but it was the best one she had.

"I haven't missed work yet, it's just about to begin for me," she explained. "Good luck Katerina. Sonya says you're a good person, and I trust her."

"Take care and thank you for helping. I hope this doesn't get you into trouble. And thank you for showing me around."

"Oh don't worry. I have some insurance against investigation by the police stored somewhere very safe indeed," she replied, with something of a twinkle in her eye.

It is a strange experience to travel on a train overnight, and Katerina had two overnights on this journey. The country-side changes, the weather gets colder and you start seeing the mountains. What changes most is the people. From the train you can see their physical appearance and dress customs quite clearly, at least when travelling through the towns. The journey itself was the safest part of her quest. As long as she had no cloud interactions she was safe. No one in Russia could trace her. After all, only Will had the ability to find her, using his own GPS locator. As long as she kept off the cloud, i.e. a few metres away from any device which could pick up her identity chip, she should be undetectable. She clung onto the tiny doll in her choker, her hope of Will being able to locate her.

Katerina had no trouble with her open ticket at the station. The control point was an actual human not even a ticket barrier, and the inspector thanked her for stopping off in the city on her journey East. She had warm feelings about this place.

Sergei and Maruska met her at the station in Yekaterinburg. They had a small vehicle, and the three continued by car to their cottages on the outskirts of Kirovgrad.

"Welcome to Siberia. Is this your first time?" Maruska asked as they started driving away.

"Yes, and it seems warmer than its image. I'm amazed by how many churches and cathedrals you still have open. I've seen two already and I think there's one more."

"Yes we're still a place that values the faith," said Maruska, "though not everyone is as faithful as they seem."

After an hour they arrived at what was to be Katerina's new home for the time being.

"Welcome to Kirovgrad, welcome to our home," boomed Sergei. "I hope you will feel very welcome and refreshed here, while your situation in St Vladisgrad sorts itself out."

"Thank you so much for your hospitality," she replied. "You really are too kind."

"We are always ready to help those in need, and we are told you are a good person who deserves our help."

"How come you know Sonya? It's a long way from St Vladis-grad."

"We were not from here originally," Sergei explained. "My father migrated here from Chernigov as a priest at St Lawrence's church. It's quite beautiful, though we don't go there since he has passed away. Everything is different now."

"And how did you get to know Sonya?"

"My father specialised in ministry to, shall we say, girls in a less than perfect situation, before we moved. He was acquainted with Sonya's mother through that work."

"Oh I see."

"You will find things so different here. We are on the edge of cloud civilisation," explained Maruska. "Nobody minds what you are or do as long as you keep quiet and don't criticize the governor, or ask awkward questions about what goes on here. Of course things are changing slowly, but we don't travel and the new changes don't affect life here."

Katerina could see they were no longer young. They must have seen much of old Russia in their lives.

"The cloud doesn't impact us as much as you might think," Sergei added. "We are free to associate with whom we choose here and there is little social control. The Seven Stars are voluntary here, and not popular."

"And what is the weather like here? This area is famed for its harsh winters."

"The winters have got much milder over the last twenty years. I remember when it was minus twenty degrees outside in December, but now it barely gets below minus five. "

"Will I be able to live off-cloud here for long?" asked Katerina.

"Oh yes for the time being. We're a mixed society and we can deal with the outside world for you. If you go to buy anything you could be traced. But if you stay at home and don't interact with anyone you will be completely safe. There are a few cameras in the streets, but they're only for traffic policing. We'll let you know where's safe to go. We're used to the authorities and their ways here, and at least until now have managed to avoid trouble."

"You say for the 'time being', and that's good. I don't know how much longer I can live like this, without hearing from Will. He's the father of my child, my husband. I can't live without him."

"Yes, it's hard, dear," Maruska replied. "But the pain of separation happened to thousands - even millions - during the Soviet era. There are stark reminders of that in this very place. Of course the Government wants us to forget all about that, even though it was under a different regime. Loved ones would be taken, forced to the salt mines, and returned to their love ones either alive or dead in ten or twenty years. Sometimes not even returned."

Katerina thought on this and shuddered.

"But is the current regime today any better?"

"What's not widely known is that there is a salt mine operating as a labour camp still open, but the numbers held there are low. The Government has other ways to encourage conformity now."

"Oh I see."

"So how long will you need to be looked after here?" enquired Maruska. "You're starting to show."

"I think the baby is due in March," she replied.

"They are planning to drain the peat-bog next Spring. It's part of a programme. There'll be much more activity here then and we are expecting more surveillance. It will be harder to keep you hidden when those changes come, but not impossible."

"And after that?"

"We can take care of the baby if we have to. Once it's born there's nothing they can do to the baby, but you will face repercussions should you want to stay. We will try to get you out of the country to claim asylum. We can get the baby registered to another mother if we have to. We have some mid-wives and registrars here who can be persuaded to be helpful. But the best option is to get you both out and to the west, where we assume you will both be accepted."

It seemed like the best hope she had, but she felt nervous nonetheless.

And so she would remain for a few months to come, never forgetting about Will or the reminder of Will she carried within her, trying not to think about what would be happening when the winter was over.

## SCENE BEN AND WILL

With Michael away, Ben led the bubble, having himself only just come back from secret operations. Arriving early gave Will time to talk.

"It's been three weeks now, and not a word. I know where she is, but I can't contact her."

"Oh, how's that?"

"I gave her my tracker and she gave me hers."

Ben's forehead furrowed. "That's potentially a problem," he explained. "It was supposed to be registered to you. It's going to cause some problems somewhere."

"What would you have done?"

"I really don't know, but the situation we're in is complicated."

"I don't know what I'm doing in the cloud existence sometimes. My mind isn't in Swindon, it's not in the community energy work, and it's not on carbon trading. It's firmly in Russia. It's planted in Katerina's flat. I keep thinking of the city she lives in, all that she's told me about her life, and everything about her. And I have no way of getting there."

"I'm really sorry, I wish I could help," replied Ben. "I was so glad at first you'd got over being rejected by Rosaline, but now I do worry about you. At least your first love is only six miles away; you're new love is goodness-knows-where."

"In Siberia if the tracker is to be believed," said Will. "But there's no word from her. Do they still have gulags there? Perhaps she's been arrested and taken there against her will. I've no idea what's she's doing there. Or am I being fooled, and really she's still in St Vladisgrad, and the tracker has been separated from her somehow. I tempted to give up all this cloud business and living a simple life somewhere else."

"Oh, don't do that," exclaimed Ben. "After all you've worked on. You're national lead on carbon now as well as community energy co-ordinator. You can't do that off-cloud. You'll certainly never even hear from Katerina again if you leave us."

"I guess you're right, but I'm struggling. Cloud life doesn't give what I need right now. It just feels empty."

## SCENE SOMEWHERE IN NORTH WEST IRAQ

There were few jobs in the military now that needed a soldier to risk life and limb. Electronic warfare and armed drones were used in battle as senseless proxies. When one of those few tasks came up, Michael would be the first to volunteer.

Daesh had offered to negotiate terms. Unlike most civilised people, they would not face a man through a screen or visor. Though not averse to electronic warfare themselves when possible, they needed to see the whites of the eyes to do a deal.

Michael had four armed human escorts and a large swarm of autonomous armed drones at his disposal. Extra electronic surveillance was carried out above by a low orbit Geo-sat.

The meeting place was a tent pitched on stony ground far from the nearest city, Bakhida. Nearby caves were thought to house a stronghold or stores. Daesh were believed to be on the back foot, so there was no reason to distrust their intentions at this meeting. Michael's mission was to persuade them to give up territory in exchange for safe conduct out of the warzone. Western block allies could then go into the local towns and cities to rebuild and re-educate. What Michael needed to gain was assurances on civilian life and mines.

Their negotiator appeared, walking slowly. He was a man of perhaps fifty, dressed traditionally with a long beard and no moustache. The underside of his lower lip was shaved for about a half an inch. He wore a white turban, covered lightly with dust.

Behind him came a much younger fighter, similarly dressed but with lighter skin and reddish hair.

"As-salaam alaykum," he greeted the men.

"As-salaam alaykum," responded the older one.

"I come to you with an offer to bring an end to bloodshed here," Michael explained. "You are noble and honourable fighters but you must realise we are stronger than you. You cannot beat our technology."

"I am indeed a man of honour and so is my nephew here."

The nephew looked at him with particular curiosity. Perhaps he had not seen a westerner before. He had tried to fit in with the locals. He had grown a beard out of respect. He avoided sunglasses despite the strength of the sun. He had brushed up on his Arabic, unnecessary as it emerged, given his enemy's fluency in English.

"Then you will see that we wish only good to come. These people, whose land you now occupy, have done you no wrong. All we ask is that you leave them in peace, and we will let you and your families go. If you do not, we will be forced to continue fighting and there will be many deaths."

"So what does family mean to you, Colonel Michael, or should I call you Captain Mercury?"

This took Michael aback for two reasons. First that his game avatar should be known to a man most unlikely ever to have played *Planets*. That was unsettling. Secondly, having always regarded the unit as his family, he had given little thought to his own natural family. He rather wondered where this was going.

"It can mean all sorts of things, but I have no wife or children."

"You have no wife. Yes I'm sure. But children is another matter."

"I'm not a religious man."

"Indeed you are not; you do not fear Allah and you dishonour my family."

Michael shifted uncomfortably.

"I don't follow you. We will protect all your families if you agree to leave peacefully. We do not want more bloodshed. We are also concerned for those living under your rule who wish to be free, to live their lives as they please. Perhaps to follow another religion."

"We are not concerned for our lives. We are not afraid of death. What we seek is honour in the eyes of Allah. It is not honourable for us that we should allow anyone to displease him, whether they are Muslims or people of the Book."

"Would Allah not want peace for all?"

"Allah would not wish us to leave our families dishonoured. That would be displeasing."

"But there is no dishonour in leaving under a truce."

"You misunderstand me, Lieutenant Michael. You have indeed dishonoured my family."

Why 'Lieutenant'; not Colonel?

"Let us take tea."

They supped over small cups of tea laced with sugar. The older man continued, while the nephew sat patiently.

"Do you remember being in London twenty seven years ago?" he enquired.

"Time flies. I've spent a lot of time there, mainly working for the Government. I think you must know I used to work in intelligence."

"Quite. I know much about you. But my friend, I have intelligence too."

"I'm sure."

"And I'm not sure your intelligence is quite complete."

"Go on."

"You were quite the ladies' man I understand? In your younger days I mean."

"I can't recall that well."

The only inaccuracy in his interrogator's claim was the implicit one that he had ceased being a man with a roving eye. It was merely the case that modern living and his more senior position prevented the fulfilment from being as easy as it had been in freer times.

"You were, Colonel Michael, but you were Lieutenant then." He produced a business card with Michael's name and rank.

"How did you get that?" he demanded.

"It was from my sister. You gave it to her after you raped her." Michael stood up. "Your sister? Not Sara, you mean?"

"Sura, not Sara. You can't even remember her name."

"What do you mean? I did not rape her, Sara, Sura, whatever. She freely consented."

"She came to London to train as a doctor. She was a good woman. She wore a hijab. She did not drink. She did not actively seek out the company of men, though those men found her. And you not only sought her out, you slept with her."

"She consented to everything."

"And yet you were not married to her, were you? You had not come to my father to ask permission. You did not even meet my uncle who was living in London. What did you do?"

"We had some fun, she was willing."

Michael recalled the events. He was a little economical with the truth. Yes, she had flirted gently with him when they first met by chance through mutual friends in a coffee house on the south bank. 'Fun' wasn't quite the right description. She had fallen in love with him at once and he had rather taken advantage of the situation. By coincidence he had been discussing an Arab assignment at work and thought further research worthwhile, using his dictum that the best way to know a language is to engage with a speaker in the most intimate of ways. The end was to justify the means, and he had used somewhat nefarious tactics. His guile had given him the edge. It was a necessary engagement for his mission.

In this case these methods included pretending to convert and a fake 'niqa' marriage arranged hastily by an East End Imam who asked fewer questions than he should have and who was suitably recompensed for his trouble. Mike took the view that it had no legal standing, and did not expect later repercussions should things not work out. The deception had extended to giving a false name to the Imam but it would have been a step too far to do that to his 'bride'. He had assumed he would not be called to account for his behaviour. Nonetheless, she must have taken the business card from him, as he could not recall handing it over to her.

"I meant no harm," for once Mike's voice wavered a little.

The man's eyes flared up.

"You meant no harm! Do you know nothing? You had no right. You slept with my dear sister but you were not Muslim and you were not married to her. Do you know what happened next?"

"She said she had to go back home."

"No, my friend. She got pregnant and you moved on to a Russian girl."

"I never knew she was pregnant. It was only once. She said she was on the pill."

The man snarled.

"She said that not to disappoint you in your desire to have her, but in your arrogance you assumed she would tell you the truth because it suited you and your dick. She would never have been on the pill because being unmarried she should never have been having relations with a man. You would have known that if you knew our people. Indeed if you had observed your own traditions and religion, you would also have known that. But you are quite irreligious. My sister came home in disgrace. Local tribes-people wanted to kill her then and there, but I said just wait until the baby is born. By that time my father married her off to a poor widower in another area, and gave her a modest dowry. Your son you see here was brought up as if he was my younger brother. My sister lived in squalor for the rest of her life until she died two years ago."

There was a long silence.

"She could have been saved with money and better medicine, but she did not have access to it. This is your son, you see, right here."

He pointed to the younger man who just sat there, expressionless.

"I haven't come to talk about family I've come to offer peace. There is another way to live. You don't have to be bound to seventh century tribal customs."

"That's right, you don't talk about family, do you? Your society has abdicated its responsibilities to 'the state' hasn't it? You think any custom more than ten years old must be wrong because you have progressed and moved on. You licence reproduction but you have no relationship with your offspring other than your DNA and your money. What kind of a world is that?"

"It's fair and equal."

"What you did is not remotely fair to us. We were just a normal middle class family before. Our parents both had respectable jobs. My mother was a teacher and my father was an accountant. We were liberal and looked up to the west in many ways. If we weren't open minded, we would never have allowed my sister to travel abroad alone. My uncle and aunt in London said it was a respectful place and they would look out for her, but they were tricked by you and your system. We hated the extremists and we just wanted to get on and have a good life. After you ruined our family's honour I saw how decadent and lawless your world is, so I vowed to fight it."

"You were behind the carbon attacks?"

"Yes, this ridiculous plan of yours to try to lock up carbon you've already released. I planned it from here and my brothers in England carried out our plans. These people I fight for gave me a new family, and I lead them now. This man, Isa, your son, is one of us now too. So some good has come of it. You say in your world that parents must pay for their offspring. You must pay for yours now, for your crimes, for the damage to lives that can no longer be put right."

Before Michael's escorts could intervene, the man had pulled a knife and slit his throat. He would have gone on to decapitate him but seconds later he was shot dead. Hundreds of fighters emerged from hidden positions. The bodyguards took partial cover behind small rocks, but still two took bullets. Within minutes missiles started raining down from the swarm of drones, killing almost all the fighters and two goatherds who unwisely emerged from cover to view the spectacle. One entered the cave where an almighty explosion was heard. The armed escorts picked off three remaining Daesh. It was unclear if any had escaped as they stretchered Michael's body away to the waiting helicopter.

From a safe house in Swindon, Ben watched in real time. It was several nights before he could sleep again.

## SCENE MICHAEL'S AVATAR

Ben and Will had yet another session after bubble when it came. Mike's avatar.

"Hi it's Michael. Don't be alarmed, but this is my living will."

Will froze. Ben already knew.

"No contact for seven days so under instruction to contact you."

This wasn't what Will wanted to hear. He knew Michael must be dead.

"I've known for a week," said Ben. "I knew as soon as it happened. Michael wants access for you to the High Orbit Spy-Sat sitting over Siberia, to give you a chance to see things for yourself."

"I'm so sorry. I thought he only did remote stuff."

"I can't say much. I'm still receiving counselling for this and speaking too much might trigger me. Michael didn't always work remotely. At heart he's a face to face fighter and negotiator. He wants to see the whites of their eyes before he calls in drone strikes or makes a deal. This time he was trying to talk. Details are sketchy right now, even though I saw the live feed, but we killed dozens of their fighters. Don't be sorry. There are no heroes without risk, and where there's risk people die."

Will needed time to think and be alone. Not only had he not heard from Katerina for months, but it seemed his best friend had perished. He needed some non-cloud time and that was difficult in Swindon. Where could he go to get away?


## SCENE KINGSGELD

The answer hit him quickly; Kingsgeld. Less than half an hour by bike, the ultimate non-cloud transport. No one would even guess until his heart rate history was uploaded at the next bubble meet, and even then there would be no proof that's where he had visited. It was 10am now so even in the winter he could get there and back before dark. He packed his protection, provisions for the day, and set off, arriving comfortably before lunch. Spotting what he now realised was the church he crept in at the back. A piano was playing, a Yamaha grand no less, and about forty people of all ages were singing. It was quite different from his previous experience of church.

The church was not as intricate as St Brides but what was different was the warmth. Rosaline was there too. He approached her to ask what was happening.

"We meet every Sunday," she replied. "Once a month we share bread and wine too. We have a prayer session soon; is there anything you need?"

"Ah, er, no thank you. But maybe pray for my friend Michael. He was on a secret mission. I saw his living will avatar last night, and I'm told he's dead."

"You can't talk to the dead," she replied "and we don't pray for the dead, we only pray for the living. But why don't you join us for lunch?"

Seeing as Will had only limited provisions, yet sufficient time, he took the pragmatic decision to accept. Rosaline disappeared around a corner to talk to a leader, but he managed to overhear her words.

"There's this really weird and slightly arrogant guy who has just turned up on our doorstep. He looks so confused and damaged and I felt sorry for him. I hope you don't mind but I invited him back for lunch."

"Is he anything like that other arrogant guy who turns up sometimes?"

"I think he's a bit different. More weird, not quite as articulate. Bit bumbling really."

Will guessed it was Tim she was referring to when she talked about the other arrogant guy. He was used to being told he was weird, but he'd never been told he was arrogant by anyone who'd met Tim, so this was a new one on him. 'Not quite as articulate' he would have to put up with.

Will was unused to food being cooked before his eyes in a kitchen. The closest he came was the Highwayman they had visited in the summer as a bubble and the Morpeth Arms in London. To sit down and eat together in a group in a private house other than with his bubble was something he had not done since he stopped living with his parents.

"Don't you ever get a feeling of missing out not being in the cloud?" he asked. "And how do you manage your diet if you cook for yourself."

"I don't miss out, not really. If someone wants to see us, they have to make an effort, so we know it's really important. We eat healthily enough. Don't you think?" Her smile invited a reflection rather than a comment. "Can I ask you something now? It must be my turn. How can you live in the present with so much going on around you?"

"It's kind of nice being connected. I guess I out-source my thinking. Lots of help with decisions. I can consult an e-consultant, my bubble, crowd-source, anything."

"I can see that. But do you ever get to know yourself?"

Will wasn't sure. He wasn't really sure he wanted to know himself. He just didn't want to miss out on all the good things modern life had. On the other hand, he felt challenged by this crazy retro woman he had fallen in, then out, of love with.

He made his excuses and left. The cycle back was somewhat slower after a hearty home cooked meal. How different this was compared to his usual processed and monitored food. Not that Will really knew what he'd eaten, just that it was traditional and unprocessed. He just about coped with table manners after carefully watching the others. What was different here was the sense of getting to know people more deeply than he had done before with anyone outside his bubble. People with very different viewpoints to his own. Not as privileged, perhaps, but each of them a genuine person.

## SCENE BACK IN SWINDON

He decided to contact Michael's avatar again; if it really was a Living Will he didn't have long before it was at risk of cancellation or retirement, unless special permission was obtained.

"I had this strange experience, back in Kingsgeld," Will confided. "Off-cloud folk. It was weird but peaceful. I felt I was actually thinking for myself. I saw Rosaline again too."

Confiding to an online avatar isn't real confiding. It just feels like it. To this day, while the churches will do online confessions, they have not yet modernised and progressed to avatar confessors.

"Thinking's dangerous, we do that for you. But if you enjoyed it and she didn't slap you in the face, send some flowers."

Will hadn't thought of that. He checked the prices and couldn't believe them. How much did it cost to cut flowers and drone them six miles? He forked out anyway.

"Now it's time to take another ride in that Spy-Sat," said the avatar. "I did promise you after all."

But Will was tired after his cycle rise. "Tomorrow," he said.

"OK. Might be last chance!"


## SCENE DANGER AT CHURCH

Katerina kept herself to herself, just going out for exercise or on cloud-free trips with her guardians. They themselves were at least nominally cloud citizens but in this area there were few regimented checks on their activities or beliefs. It appeared that either they had no Seven Star at all, or that it was more of a distant concept than a community setting. For them the cloud was just a communications mechanism, not a method of social control. As long as Katerina herself didn't interact with a communications device and seek authentication, she would be fine. Sergei and Maruska would pass her news from St Vladisgrad via Sonya.

**FSB SECURITY REPORT:**

**Subject:** KK.

**Status:** Location unknown.

**Threat:** Missing without leave and pregnant without authorisation. Father is believed to be an English agent working in carbon control, though the authorities there claim he has no intelligence connection.

**Assessment:** Target appears to have travelled by train from St Vladisgrad to Moscow. From there she is believed to have boarded the trans-Siberian line with the help of an accomplice. Unfortunately the police data relating to the identity of that individual has been inadvertently erased due to local storage issues. Furthermore, there is no locator data, or other cloud-based interactions we are able to analyse. Further east surveillance equipment is more limited, so subject may be able to evade detection for a while, but it is only a matter of time before we are able to locate her.

**Other actions:** Subject is a member of an elite Seven Star, so defection carries optics risks. State communications must be aligned to ensure no further embarrassment. It was suggested to her Seven Star that she has a new mystery illness, and is recuperating in an isolation unit. However, this line will not last for long, and in any case it would be useful to broadcast her identity in case she is observed publicly in some way which minimises embarrassment.

Subject has had interactions with cyber double agent NK previously, who has agreed to assist following a honeypot operation. Present indications are that he is not as co-operative as hoped, but further pressure will be applied.

## SCENE HIDING

"Vulnerable young adult needs help," screamed the headlines, showing her picture in a somewhat unflattering pose. But here in Siberia, the St Vladisgrad and Moscow news was of little interest. Katerina had already replaced her trademark multi-coloured headscarf with her bearskin, a reminder of her trip to London, and her neck-scarf was long enough to wrap around her face. She was in little danger of being recognised, even by the relatively few cameras in the streets. She passed over Will's GPS to her guardians who assured her he was still in the Swindon area, but that was of course of little consolation to her.

As the days moved on she got bored and started walking around on her own. She thought back to her time on *Planets*, and wondered if perhaps the landscape here in Siberia wasn't at least as harsh as the virtual terrain of Oberon.

On one trip she passed the Orthodox church they had mentioned. It had been many years since she had actually been inside any orthodox building, but she still had a fascination for the iconography, which bought back childhood memories. Sergei and Maruska resembled old believers in some ways, but avoided the church.

On the return she looked in at the church. It was open, but with cameras at the entrance. Still she felt confident with her heavy disguise.

A priest was busying himself, looking ready to lock up. She was just in time.

"Come for confession," he enquired.

"No, no, I haven't been for seven years," she replied. "If I'm honest, I just want to sit and pray, and admire the icons. Your church is so beautiful."

"I see. You're not from around here, are you," he observed. "Moscow or St Vladisgrad, I think. I can tell from the eyes. What brings you here?"

"Just a rest, maybe move here," she lied.

"Really! What do you do? Most who move here come for work. It's not a great time of year to come either. In the spring peat harvesters will be here, but it's not yet their time. And it's rarely above minus during the winter, which you will need to live through. Are you prepared for that?"

"I work in reproductive science," she said. "All strictly legal. The church approves these days, I believe. I'm taking a break right now."

He half nodded. "The church approves of procreation lawfully made in the sight of God. But it does not approve of tampering with divinely-created beings. Nor does it condone the ending of unborn life."

"Father Bulgakov said reproductive science was completely wrong. I thought he was godly, but mistaken. Then we found out what he'd been doing. That's why I stopped coming."

"Ah Father Bulgakov. Do you know what happened to him?"

Katerina shook her head. "Only what he had done."

"And what had he done?"

Katerina gave him a stare.

"Well?"

"He was guilty of the worst kind of sexual conduct, I think. I'm not sure really. I don't know the details."

"Ah my child. And why do you believe that?"

"It was all over the Cloud."

"And who put it in the Cloud?"

Katerina's mouth opened wide.

"I can tell you this, my child. Bulgakov's crime was not the sin of immorality. It was the sin of opposing powerful people. You say you never heard from him again. Do you know why?"

Again Katerina shook her head.

"The gulags didn't end in the twentieth century. No. He was sentenced to five years here. He died half way through, a broken and frail man. I conducted the funeral myself."

"Oh no, what a horrible thing to happen to such a holy man."

"Reminder that the blood of the martyrs is the seed of the church, my child. Those who are faithful are bound to find suffering in their path."

She thought back to her trip to London and the work by the unknown artist on modern martyrs. Perhaps after all it was good she was not so deeply religious.

"I'm pregnant," she blurted out.

"Do you have a husband?" enquired the priest.

"Not in Russia," she replied, with a little economy of truth.

"And were you married in the Orthodox faith," he further enquired.

She shook her head.

"I think it was Church of England. Or Catholic. The church was Church of England, but the priest was Catholic. It was in London anyway."

"I see. Are you sure?" The priest opened a notebook and wrote. "They are closing the churches down in England, I hear?" he added after a pause.

"The priest was definitely Catholic. But I think he was from Ireland. He didn't seem to speak quite the same way."

"Stranger and stranger."

"My husband's an agnostic. He believes in science. But he's a brave and noble man. He's dedicated his life to fighting climate change."

"You have got yourself into trouble! You must celebrate your marriage before God and the church," he counselled, "and before you have further union. Your husband must join us in the faith."

What she wanted to say was: "He will follow his conscience wherever it calls him." Instead she just nodded. She was unlikely to get further union any time soon, so the commitment seemed somewhat cheap. Then she remembered the sign.

"His head lit up with the cross when we got married. It was a sign, I'm sure of it. He will convert when his eyes are opened."

"God forgive you," he replied. "And now I have to go, child, and must lock this church up for the night. See you for mass, soon, I hope."

With that she left.

What her guardians knew, but she did not, was that the priest was also an informer and had been installed there when Sergei's father Vanya had refused to co-operate. The priest made a report of the conversation not only to his Bishop, but also to state security.

## SCENE SERGEI AND MARUSKA

Sergei had received a message from Sonia: read "No news from Will. Feared dead or cancelled." There was more bad news for Katerina. It seems the local police had wind that she was in the area. They were sending a scanning device to track her ID, but since the implanted device was intended only to be used for identification and credentials with a communicator or other Cloud device, the technology ranged only over a few metres.

Sergei was the first with a solution: "Time to gather your stuff. We know a suitable place to lie low, just for a couple of days, the shelter from the old Soviet Cold War era. That will keep you safe for the time being. It's built into the side of the hill, so there is a window with natural daylight, but it's still quite secluded. It's a distance from the road so if they scan from a vehicle they won't find you. In the meantime we will see if we can get you a safe Cloud connection to England, but it is difficult. If you don't hear from us in forty eight hours do feel free to come back, but be very careful and avoid passing vans, especially if they look like they could be security."

It was a drab affair staying in the old Soviet shelter. All the essentials were there, but there was to be no communication. Maruska had told her to wait two days, but it seemed like two months. The window had a shutter which was meant to be pulled down most of the time, but she ignored this mandate. Instead she spent her time gazing out of it looking for inspiration for her next poem, whether by day, watching distant passers-by walking in the fields, or night, watching the stars. Little came to her imagination until a cloud obscured her favourite star. At that point she spotted a green-eyed fox slinking across the road furtively, its paws leaving prints in the dark snow which had arrived with winter. She imagined it going about its business while keeping watchful eyes out for dogs. Or was she remembering something she had heard or read before? Perhaps she could not entirely trust her senses.

Eventually the imprisonment darkened her mind; she felt compelled to leave. Unsure of what would happen next she crept back to the house.

She passed the church; it was still open. At least this was one place she could trust. The priest spotted her and welcomed her inside.

"How long since your last mass?" he enquired. "Surely you must be in need, after all you have confessed."

Katerina could not remember exactly, but it must have been as a child.

"Come here, let me serve you the elements."

She felt strangely compelled by this priest, on the one hand apprehensive yet on the other aroused by this connection with a Russian past that predated even the revolution.

She kneeled as he blessed her and gave her the wafer. Then he offered the chalice which she drank perhaps a little too readily, unaware it contained a lethal ingredient supplied by the priest's handler in state security. She expected him to drain it afterwards, but instead he simply returned it to the altar.

"Take care," he warned as she departed. "And sin no more."

She left the church and continued back to the house.

That night she slept and dreamed.

"I must tell you about my dream," she explained to Maruska. "I could see my baby daughter being treated at the hospital. Some of my friends were there all admiring her. I saw a series of images of her growing up, and by the time she was sixteen she was looking just like I did in my photos from first communion, except she was more beautiful than me and she had no horrid spots."

"I see. And did you see Will in these images in your mind?"

Katerina frowned.

"Perhaps you had simply forgotten that image," suggested Maruska. "Now, we have a present that a dreamer like you might appreciate."

"Really? But no, if Will had been there I would definitely

have remembered." She faltered. "But tell me, what present you can give a dreamer, except the interpretation of her dreams?"

"It's a special hat, not too heavy to wear, with batteries around the neck, and it can scan brain images and download them to your communicator. The idea is you wear it at night and the dreams and images in your sleeping brain can get captured, so you don't lose them in the morning. It's quite safe; it downloads only to your communicator not the Cloud, and you can view them privately after."

"Oh wow. I wonder why I haven't heard of this before. What's it called?"

"We call it the dream hat. Not all the latest technology comes from St Vladisgrad," smiled Maruska. "Sergei and I have an interest in dreams and prophecy. We knew someone at the University working on this and begged to get one. Then you came and we realised you were the one to show its power."

Katerina tried it on and it was surprisingly comfortable to wear.

"Well, I do like hats. And it could keep me warm too."

"Good. We would love to see the images tomorrow morning."

"Of course."

"We think it's best if you sleep in the shelter again tonight. Just in case there are night raids. There are rumours of state police arriving in the local police station, with more search vehicles and more sensitive detectors."

"OK, no problem, if I'll be safer there. I guess I should go now."

"Yes. Take care my sweet Katerina. Sergei and I will review the situation and see if another place is needed to keep you safe."

## SCENE TOKYO

It was an overcast day, which matched the mood of the news. It now appeared that fusion had not actually been achieved by the hybrid technique after all. There was still one crucial missing link in the technology, and the route to solving it was unclear.

The eyes of the world had been focussed on the project, and it had failed completely. World leaders, energy experts, and financiers, had all braced themselves in preparation for a breakthrough, which would solve the energy and carbon crises, but they were to be sorely disappointed. Dr Fukishima took the train to Shinjuku station, impeccably dressed as usual, with a large case. He stopped for lunch at a robo-cafe, enjoying his cuisine but noting with disapproval the hygiene habits of the few wealthy foreign visitors and diplomats sharing the venue with him. Finishing his meal he continued down the street. To his amazement one of the foreign visitors ahead of him dropped a tiny piece of litter from the café which the robo-cleaners had failed to collect. Horrified he chased after it, but they had gone. Nothing for it but to put it in his pocket.

He continued on towards the Gyoen gardens, taking his time to enjoy the rocky landscape over the lakes before making his way to the centre of the bridge. There were few visitors to the gardens, due to the inclement weather, though they were splendid enough. He removed the samurai sword from his case and fell upon it. His heart was pierced and his limp body fell off the bridge into the lake below. His body was found by a passing family within minutes and the authorities informed. News broke quickly and the analysts put two and two together.

The markets did not react well, reaching and even exceeding their previous highs for world-wide carbon price, though neither Dr Fukishima, Katerina or even Will now cared about that at all.

## WILL'S MESSAGE EXCHANGE

Incoming: It's Katerina. I'm safe and well.

W: Darling how are you? I've been waiting ages to hear from you. Can you video call? I need you badly.

Incoming: I can't call. It's too risky. I think I'm being watched.

W: I see. Where are you?

Incoming: I'm safe in Vladisgrad, it's just they're suspicious of me.

W: I see. Is your present from me safe and well?

Incoming: Yes, no need to worry darling. I will keep it safe.

W: Any more trouble from Nik?

Incoming: Nik? No, he's leaving me well alone. Look, I have to leave now, sorry.

W: Can't you stay?

W: Katerina …

Will log book note: Katerina location noted as East of Yekaterinburg.


## SCENE GRIEF

As time went on, Will's ability to function started failing. Even Ben noticed it. His attendance at bubble meetings got worse. His physical appearance also managed to deteriorate. He now never went out to eat or drink at all, relying entirely on the meals delivered to his hatch.

Will tried many things to distract his mind from his wretched state. Remembering his victory in chess over Katerina he started playing the game online. At first he lost every game but, as his experience and confidence grew, he started winning not just games but even the City of London tournaments. As he got his first draw against a Grandmaster, he started taking the game more seriously.

Then he obsessed over the museums. He dropped the chess and studied objects in the British Museum and the Hermitage online, before moving onto art galleries. Anything to bring him closer to Katerina. A few weeks later he moved onto the ballet, watching numerous productions of Swan Lake. Anything that would make him see the world the way she saw it.

He even studied the science of genetics, following the latest developments in England and Russia. He imagined himself as a doctor in a reproductive hospital helping to start new life for lucky parents, who might now never even see their progeny. He could see how important the discipline was, perhaps even more important that the work he was doing to control climate change.

What also got more serious was his drinking. Where he used to drink the odd bottle of wine at the weekend, perhaps with a whisky chaser, he started drinking every night, sometimes more than one bottle. It did seem such a shame to not finish the second one once opened. Then he thought of Katerina and her fondness for vodka. That was more expensive and difficult to obtain.

He became far less attentive to his personal organisation. The community energy role was, just about, maintained as normal, but his flat started to get even more untidy and his personal hygiene suffered.

Ben gently took him aside after one bubble meeting.

"Take a seat."

Will sat down; Ben followed, trying to mirror Will's posture, focussing intently, and putting his training to good use.

"What's happening, Will? I've monitored your drinking and it's way off the scale. You're looking dishevelled, I can smell you from here, and you're consistently late for meetings. As for your health reports, I've doctored them so that the Council doesn't know what's happening to you, but I can't do it forever. It's not like you at all. I'll have to act if something doesn't change. Tell me what's up; I'm listening."

Will's eyes avoided contact and he shifted uneasily.

"I'm here to help, you know I am."

"So I'm drinking too much, is that it?"

"You are, and you know you are. But that's the symptom, not the problem."

"The problem is Katerina."

Ben sighed.

"There's really nothing that can be done. You're going to have to get over her. What about Rosaline? I know she's off-cloud, but we can bring her back in? After all she's a doctor and works for us."

"No, she wouldn't join us. I sent her flowers recently, but she's not in love with me, and I'm over her now. What I felt with Katerina was something on a different planet."

He half-laughed. The *Planets'* creator saw the joke.

"I guess it's my fault in the first place," jested Ben. "You know we created that game as a back door for spying on Russia and other enemies? It was intended to circumvent their cyber devices by getting into the minds of their citizens. We had a big team, it even had psychologists on it."

Will had suspected as much, but this confirmed it for the first time.

"We didn't expect it to become so commercially successful, or to become a kind of unofficial dating site for that matter. Actually, we've had quite a few couples meet that way, some of whom are parents now, but that isn't what we set out to do. It was most certainly not our intention to break anyone's heart."

"I see. We're not parents of course. Katerina would have told me or got a message to me somehow if she had got pregnant. Anyway it wouldn't be licensed here in the west unless she defects, and as she can't even get me a message I doubt she can leave the country without outside help."

Ben knew a little more than he was letting on. Old intelligence reports had suggested the Russian state security knew Katerina was pregnant, that she had gone missing, and that they were looking for her. The reports were unclear and he was unable to reveal this without compromising the asset. He was aware of Katerina's location, having been given access to Will's GPS through POLOMINT. That was something he knew that the Russians didn't, at least yet.

"No, of course not. I wonder if we can get her that help?"

"We're working on it. It's not as easy as you might think."

"If you hear from her, let me know."

"I will."

## SCENE OF VISIONS

She did not feel right; in fact she felt positively sick as she crept back to the shelter. She intended to sleep, so donned the dream hat and lay down. As she drifted off, visions came to her again, this time of an ominous nature.

She woke abruptly. She had travelled thousands of miles from St Vladisgrad and successfully hidden for some time, but she had no clear plan, and she was starting to grow very nervous indeed. She started to drift again, with the fox coming back into mind. In the distance she suddenly heard footsteps which woke her once again. She peered out of the window, still wearing the dream hat, and saw a torch. Men in protective suits and dogs approached. The fox was no longer safe. Close to the bunker was a narrow stream and across the stream a small wood. She felt sluggish now and struggled to think clearly, even while acutely aware she was being hunted. She realised that the best way to escape would be to slip down to the stream and cross it into the woods. She would lose them there. It would be essential, since the ground became soggy there and led to the peat bogs. These were the same bogs which were threatened with drainage and exploitation for the country's energy needs.

It was only a short run to the streams. The dogs let out a howl when she started running; her mind flashed back to Oberon and Will's great escape. That didn't end well for her; would this?

Her thoughts started to drift, slipping back into dreamland even as she ran. She felt weakened. She crossed into the woods but by now her mind was playing tricks.

The men in hazmats had headtorches and powerful lamps; she could see them across the stream. She didn't think they could see her, but she still felt trapped. Woods meant bears. She saw bears. She saw them ahead of her forming a chain across her way. She thought of the poet near St Pauls. Her eyes refused to focus. She saw green eyes. She looked back and heard more barking. Perhaps the dogs had crossed the stream. The green eyes disappeared and were replaced by four legless birds swooping down.

Now the sky darkened further. She could make out St Nicholas in the sky with his grey beard. The beard grew longer. The face starting changing and she saw all three bearded men from London; curator, tramp and map-man. Then the beard starting fall away and she was left with the image of the face of Nik. Nik morphed slowly into the Ancient of Days pointing down at the priest.

The chase continued further and further into the peat bog territory, but now the police became chess pieces. The Lewis Chessman large, and fast. She was the queen. The bishops followed in their mitres. The knights rode their horses down towards her. The castles left their study foundations and pursued her as if lifted up on long legs. Faster and faster. Even the pawns were closing in now. This was a bad dream. It was the dream Joseph interpreted for the baker. It wouldn't end well. She awoke from her thoughts and yet she was still in the peat bog. Her pursuers were very much real, as were some unpleasant radioactive elements making their way around her body.

Eventually she realised there was no escape. She couldn't escape from the chess men or her own inner confusion, brought on by the evil she had unwittingly ingested. Her physical state made no sense to her. Neither could she escape from the inner loneliness, cut off not just from Will but from all her friends. She ran along the edge of the bog now, her legs starting to fail. One trip, and she fell straight in. It was useless; very slowly the bog started to absorb her. She twisted round to get air, but eventually the bog sucked a little too hard, extinguishing the last breath of a poisoned fugitive. The hunters were too far off to save her and the dogs had lost her scent; and that my friends is the physical end of Katerina in this tale.

## SCENE IN ORBIT

Will was only too keen to take up the avatar High Orbit Spy-sat offer, and was hoping for 'cloud'-free weather to enhance his viewing pleasure. Ostensibly he was interested in the Russian peat and the way in which they were breaking international carbon agreements but much more interested in the whereabouts of his beloved who he hoped he might find during the course of his work-related investigations. Ben joined him.

Will still had access to Katerina's GPS tracker. He assumed (incorrectly) it was dangerous to use, and had used it sparingly until now, fearing it might give away her location somehow. Present circumstances however seemed to justify any potential risk.

He focussed down on Kirovgrad, where he detected a signal and where Katerina was now located. Zooming down on the location it was easy to pick out the peat bogs and even easier to pick out a group of flashlights. What surprised him was to see the faint GPS signal coming from the bog itself. The instruments in the Spy-sat also picked up a trace of Polonium-210. Now he could see the hazmat suits. Eventually he focussed right down; Katerina's half-submerged face stared out of the abyss into the night sky. What couldn't be seen was his unborn child, curled inside its mother, who lay there dying like Hamlet's Ophelia.

Will waited and watched. There appeared to be some kind of communication. One policeman could be seen with what appeared to be a pole. At first he thought they were trying to rescue Katerina but instead the pole turned out to be long handled shears, of the sort gardeners might use for pruning trees. The officer removed the choker, still visible from Katerina's head, and her concealed cross, and handed it to a second man who took and examined it. Then somewhat to Will's surprise, this man threw a large bunch of red roses over her head.

"I cannot be seeing this, it's completely unbelievable," he exclaimed.

n throughing the roses was Nik. I don't understand
d I thought I had seen every kind of trick these
eplied Ben. "I'm so sorry. You must be devastated.
ne."

"It's like a double loss. To have heard nothing for so long, then to find her, only to discover her dead, is cruelty beyond comprehension. And to see my rival throwing roses over her as if he was the one who possessed her is madness of the purest kind. Is there logic in this world? Is there justice? I see none. Are my eyes deceiving me? Have I imagined this circle of hell?"

"Sadly, you have not imagined it," said Ben. "I'd be doubting my sanity too if it happened to me. We need to get you some help here, and fast. Remember, sometimes it's Ok not to be OK. We can handle that."

## ODE TO POLONIUM 210

Gone in just a jiffy,
Named by Marie Curie,
Caused the death of an ex spy
(Really mustn't wonder why).
Poured into a cup of tea
Not quite nice, would you agree?

## NOTE FROM WILL'S PSYCHOLOGIST I DECEMBER 2047

"The client Will (W) has experienced enormous personal trauma. His journey has been a roller-coaster of emotion. First one of anxiety and separation from his life partner, then flickering hope after seeing her alive, albeit at a distance, to finally actually witnessing the death of his beloved. He appears to have significant anger issues about a certain "Nik" with whom he was competing for his wife's affection. Further, W is convinced that Nik is somehow connected with her death, but is slightly unsure exactly how.

W is experiencing significant self-doubt, understandable in the circumstances.

In all my professional experience, I have never come across such a tragic case, nor one which has affected loved ones quite as deeply.

I have discussed treatments including Cognitive Behavioural Therapy, an increase in physical activity, and time off work in order to engage in voluntary bubble community activity. I have made an appointment to see him in two weeks' time."

## SCENE IN MEMORIAM

For those of age, funerals and memorials are times of respect and thanksgiving. But for one who dies young, there is nothing but unrelenting grief which captures all around in a dark and deep dungeon.

It was clear that the death of Katerina had embarrassed the authorities, who in any case had been divided on the best course of action. Vicky, in her new role as top diplomat for East-West interblock relations, had pulled some strings. As a result, Will was flown, at the expense of the St Vladisgrad Council, to the funeral at St Peter and St Paul's Cathedral. Katerina's Seven Star came, including Natezdha who had since been pardoned. The congregation was so large many had to stand until deacons found chairs from a nearby hall. All mourners were asked to wear something purple, Katerina's favourite colour.

The Bishop's address emphasized her devotion and spirituality, while avoiding mention of a priest's role in her death. Her confession and communion shortly before she passed on to the heavenly realm were held up as examples to all the faithful. Then it was the turn of the mourners to express the agony they had been bottling up until this moment.

Will: "We met on *Planets*, and to this day I love the game and hate it too. I love that it brought us together and I hate that our coming together led to the death of the most perfect human that ever lived. We had just 24 hours together and those were the most precious hours I ever spent. I will never forget them, not while I have a single breath in my body. I am not worthy of her, but without her I am lost. The Planets themselves are not worthy of her, the solar system is not worthy of her. I defy you, Planets! I defy you, stars! Your existence has no meaning without her, without the ultimate source of love and hope."

Nik: "She has not life, but love in death. For while I am the one she spurned, my passion for her ran deep throughout my body. My behaviour, I am now ashamed of. I deserve to be cast out and killed for my many conceits and deceptions. I only ask that when I die I be buried beside her."

Mariya: "I can't believe she's dead, the girl I grew up with and nurtured as a younger sister. The object of my care and attention. The one who lit fires of joy in all she met should herself have had joy, not the fear of being hunted. The day she died a small part of all of us died with her."

Prof Kotov: "I am truly speechless at losing my daughter. Now my son-in-law, who I have only just met in the flesh, inherit the flame of my angel's life. Bring happiness to all around. Be everything that she can never now be."

At this Kotov turned to Will and embraced him so firmly Will almost had his very breath squeezed from him.

Dr Kotov: "My only daughter! The one who studied so hard to follow my own scientific path and who would have far exceeded my own meagre accomplishments. How can a mother live with this?"

At this she broke down into tears, with Kotov and Will huddling round to comfort her and shield her face from the crowded Cathedral, serving also to do the same for their own faces.


## SCENE OF MEMORIES

Nik and Will met up shortly after.

"I've heard a lot about you," said Will. "I could easily kill you."

"Everything you've heard about me is completely untrue," said Nik. "Well, some of it, anyway. But I do owe you a lot of apologies."

"I see. Does that include certain fake images?"

"I'm really sorry about that. I wanted to put you off. You have to know I fell in love with her years before you two ever met."

Will had had no idea.

"Well now neither of us have her. I'd be fascinated to know why you threw roses over Katerina's grave."

"I have a heart, and I'd lost it to her," explained Nik, "I was angry at you for stealing her from me."

"We detected Polonium coming from Katerina," said Will.

"I know. There was nothing I could do to stop it. By the time I knew it was too late. You'll be glad to hear the priest who administered it is now himself languishing in hell following a heavy blow to the back of the head by a large orb, all quite by accident of course. But now it's time to move on, time to bury the hatchet."

"Go on."

"I uploaded Katerina's memories and visions before she died," said Nik. "She was wearing a dream-hat when she died and some of the images were captured. Here, see them."

Will received the credentials, undecided whether to look.

"I must thank you for Katerina's visions which you shared," replied Will "but I can't help linking you with her death. You did torment her, and now she is no more."

"You are right to say I hurt her and deliberately so," acknowledged Nik. "But I had nothing to do with her death. I can only beg your forgiveness and appeal to your generous nature."

"We will see," answered Will.


**ODE TO A PRIEST**

You we trust to bring us near
To God and our confessions hear
But treat your calling with respect
To save the lost do not neglect
For all believers share your task.
Do not simply wear a mask
For on the final day we'll see
If your deeds with Him agree.

## SCENE 6 DECEMBER ST VLADISGRAD

Katerina left no cloud avatar; it having been suspended the moment the Russian Council realised she was missing, and deleted soon after her death. Crucially, Nik had had access to her communicator before the authorities were able to remove it from him, and he used the opportunity to store her memories. Does that matter? What really matters in life? It is deep connection, humour, trust and interaction. You can attend centrally mandated bubble meetings. You can even meet a mating partner online. But the Council can never make us happy or give us purpose in life. Will had lost everything he was living for.

Will returned to England shortly after the funeral, after a short visit to Prof and Mrs Kotov. The following day, Nik entered Katerina's apartment. It wasn't difficult; he had access to all the codes and the ability to switch off the CCTV. It wouldn't be long before the authorities arrived. The intelligent but luckless cat had already been taken in by Katerina's mother, so the errand simply amounted to collecting her possessions. The most important were two items which would never make it to the cloud or indeed to any electronic form; Katerina's books and the locked diary. He quickly found both, but opened neither. They had a long journey and a two-week quarantine, before they arrived for Will at Walcot Lodge.


## SCENE OFF-CLOUD

Will's return to Swindon had no positive impact on his state of mind. Looking for space Will cycled out to Kingsgeld, hoping to find solace and comfort. No-one noticed him as he walked round that ancient town. Eventually he went back to the church. In one corner of it he spotted some off-cloud notices. He read the old-style contact details carefully and phoned. Immediately a woman answered. "Have we met before?"

Will realised this was Rosaline. His heart jumped a little, but he remained outwardly calm, his previous infatuation having been dimmed through his burning love for Katerina.

The day had been overcast, but now the sun was starting to break through and day was set to be uncharacteristically warm.

"Yes. I need someone to talk to," he said. "And did you like the flowers?"

"I wasn't expecting them, but hey I'm here to talk."

"The girl I was in love with has died."

"I'm so sorry to hear it. At least you didn't fall in love with me, otherwise I'd be dead myself," she giggled. "Not that I'm really alive in your world anyway. But sorry, do go on."

"I married a girl from Russia who was poisoned in a Siberian peat-bog. My rival got there first and threw roses all over her."

"I see. Have you been taking magic mushrooms?"

"No."

"Very well; let's meet up."

Ten minutes later she me him in the church. Will took a closer look at the ancient building while he waited. It was smaller and less well decorated than the church of his wedding but no less awe-inspiring for that, and it hadn't been destroyed by fire. It conveyed more of a sense of community as though it were one enormous bubble chamber, but one that had existed for five hundred years.

She sat a respectful distance from him on entering, taking care to leave the church doors wide open.

"I'm so sorry for your loss," she said. "I thought at first you just meant you'd met someone on the cloud who'd gone away or been cancelled. Then when you mentioned marriage, peat-bogs and roses I thought you were mad."

"Well, that's sort of how it started out. I met her in an online game, then in real life when she visited London. We married in a brief ceremony and she had to return to Russia. Then she went off-line, and then I saw her dead using the sky satellite system. I promise you it's all true. By the way, did I mention Polonium-210 too?"

"I won't ask how all this happened, let's skip that for now. My head's spinning too much."

"Er, yes, it's difficult to explain."

Will started to notice more about her now, and the more he talked to her the more curious he felt about his former love interest. Not as he had felt towards Katerina. He wasn't in love with her again. It was more of a feeling of wanting to be a part of whatever bubble group or family she belonged to.

"I just feel so empty," he continued. "I felt more alive on our off-cloud trip here, more connected with this world."

She nodded.

"I can't carry on living in it, the cloud, there are just far more important things."

"But it's your life," she said. "You can't just give it up. Those of us living outside the cloud struggle so much to earn money. Most here have children who support them, or have old-world wealth, but what would you do?"

Will had no idea. Outside the cloud, he was useless, a liability. She sensed she'd stumped him.

"What do you work in?" she asked.

"Community energy."

"Perfect. There's lot of windmills round here. You could look after them!"

Will was about to explain it wasn't that simple when he checked himself.

"I need to escape. I don't care what comes next. I have to get out of it. Can you help?"

"I'm not sure we can. You really are from the cloud; we're different here. We might be able to find a spare room that someone has, but you'll have to give up all your online presence, your avatar, your bubble circle, everything. It would be like taking your own life."

"Maybe I want to; maybe I want to give up what doesn't matter to gain what really does."

"Think about it. Don't make rash decisions. It's not an easy life for us here."

Will did think about it. The next day he phoned.

"I'm thinking of joining you off-cloud."

"Are you sure," she replied. "It's just such a big step. I wouldn't want to feel responsible for you if you changed your mind later."

"I'm sure."

"Why don't you come and meet us all before you make up your mind?"

So next Sunday Will bunked off bubble and instead travelled to Kingsgeld to join his prospective new friends off-line.

As soon as he entered he spotted Tim. Trust him to turn up.

"I didn't expect to see you here," he said.

"I'm not really one of them, I can't bring myself to believe everything," replied Tim. "I just like to listen in silence."

Will found that hard to believe. Yet he could see how this radically different setting could stimulate the mind in unusual ways.

The hall had been decorated for Christmas and there was an air of excitement. Traditional Christmas turkey and brussels sprouts served up on long trestle tables with crackers and tinsel. Instead of feeling isolated, as he expected, everyone seemed very interested in him.

"I hear you work in community energy. That's so interesting, do tell me more?" asked one.

"You're part of an elite bubble in the Cloud. How interesting! Does it mean you have friends all over the world? What's it like to experience far-away places in virtual reality?" asked another.

As he was about to leave Rosaline approached him out of earshot of the others.

"Thank you for coming today. It was lovely to see you."

"Thanks."

"But are you alright? You've had a major bereavement."

"To be honest without her I feel empty inside. I have the memories of her uploaded. I got sent them by another admirer of hers. I can always spend time going through them but I don't think I can ever get over her loss."

"Yes you will – it will take time but you will heal. You are still so young," she paused, "and there's nothing wrong with grieving. But like I said before, you can't talk to the dead or hang onto them when they are gone. It seems to be an illusion the Cloud community perpetrates with this avatar nonsense."

"I am beginning to realise that," said Will.

"Do you? Do you talk about death at your meetings?" she asked.

"Well, no. We do cancellations sometimes, but that's it," replied Will.

"I think sometimes these avatars can just be a substitute for real living," she replied. "I'm not saying they're wrong, just that people have got too distracted and they're living a dream. One day they'll wake up and realise they've been living a lie."

"Can I come and join you?" Will asked.

"It's a one-way trip. You have to give up the cloud forever. But yes, I've asked, and we have a friend you can stay with. He lives in a barn in Grant's Meadow just under a mile from here. He lost his wife recently and has a small annex. You can stay there until you get yourself fixed up."

"That sounds good. When can I come?"

"Come Christmas Eve. We all join up in the morning and exchange presents. I'll make sure you're included. It's a particularly special time for us as we're celebrating our seventieth anniversary."

## SCENE CHRISTMAS EVE 2047

His one last act in the Cloud was to allocate his worldly goods. He threw out most of his clothes and wrapped up just three of his precious belongings, with gold, silver and bronze wrapping.

Rose, Peter and Tim came to say goodbye. Each had to choose a present from one of three choices.

"You first Tim," suggested Will. "After all you were the first to see Katerina and I together."

Tim chose bronze; Will's complete abridged Shakespeare in just seven pages.

"You next Peter," he said.

Peter chose silver, and Will's precious signed copy of Principia by Bertrand Russell. It hadn't been abbreviated, and made a good video call background.

Finally it was Rose who got the largest gift of all; a collection of plastic toys from late twentieth century sci-fi.

"We're truly sorry you're going," said Peter. "We really couldn't stand your politics, but at heart you're an intelligent person."

"I find you a sexist racist pig at times," said Tim. "But underneath I think you have a good heart. Try to do good, wherever you are."

"I once swore I'd never speak to you again," said Rose. "But now I'll never see you again, I regret that. I'm just begging you to stay open minded and accept people for what they are. It doesn't matter if you're on-cloud or off it."

At dusk Will took a transporter pod for the very last time, having thrown his personal communicator under a Swindon to Paddington locomotive. As he was being carried down the street, he noticed a package arrive for him. He was tempted to return to collect it, but changed his mind. There would be nothing of interest to him in any delivery which could possibly help him in his new world.

The bubble verdict on Will: suicide. His avatar was cancelled the following day, but not before Ben had taken copies of much of his personal data which he hid to good effect. One era finished but another, for Will, began. But dear reader, as far as we are concerned, that is all the cloud will ever hear of Will again, and he might as well be dead to those of us whose only contact with reality is online.

## MINUTES OF THE RUSSIAN ORTHODOX CHURCH HIGH COUNCIL

@Patriarch:

On to the business of Katerina Kotov. To consider her actions in opposition to ending the life of an unborn child.

@Petersburg

It is clear that she died in an attempt to avoid the State from terminating an unborn child. She was confirmed Russian Orthodox. There seems to be no obstacle to honouring her.

@Moscow

I believe there is the question of the father. I believe he was not a believer? We cannot be seen to endorse a product of fornication even if her subsequent actions were honourable.

@Petersburg

Surely the key question here is whether or not she was married at the time of conception. How could she have been married in the eyes of the church to an unbeliever?

@Yekaterinburg

We have intelligence from one of our priests that she claimed to have been married, however, by a Catholic priest not an Orthodox one. Further investigations were made, and it seems that another Catholic priest reported hearing an account of a wedding under just such circumstances from the priest who claimed to have conducted it. There therefore seems adequate evidence that the claim was in fact true.

@Patriarch

We have recently signed an accord with the Catholic church which, among other provisions, mutually recognises marriage. The provisions state we must honour any marriage performed by a Catholic priest, regardless of the status of the parties to that marriage. We should take your report Yekaterinburg, on face value, unless there is evidence to the contrary.

@Patriarch

Very well then. We have established that Katerina Kotov was lawfully married in the sight of God, that she conceived a child, that the authorities sought to terminate the pregnancy, and that she died as a result of a state plot against her. We can therefore declare her a modern martyr. Yekaterinburg, I instruct you to make suitable arrangements within your diocese. No doubt the faithful will wish to visit to pay homage, and will no doubt express their gratitude to us for having preserved her memory. In due course, we may find her to be a candidate for Sainthood.

## SCENE IN KINGSGELD

"I'm so glad you decided to join us," said Rosaline. "I was worried I'd put you off coming here."

Will avoided saying what he thought. It was clear she had no idea how much he had once been in love with her.

"Meet our people and our leaders," she said, introducing him to a few families as well as the priest, a surprisingly young man. "Do you have a Bible?" she asked.

"That's the one with lots of books in it, like Daniel and Ecclesiasticus isn't it?" he responded.

"Ecclesiastes, right," she said.

"Seventy nine books in total?" he asked.

"Oh dear. I thought you were good at sums. There are sixty six. You can count to twenty billion trillion carbon dollars, but you can't count books!"

Will felt small. He had a lot to learn. He took a step back, but the carpet underneath felt less solid.

"Mind how you go," she said. "That's just floor tiles covering the baptistry. It should take your weight, but just be careful."

"Oh, I didn't realise," he said. "What's it for?"

"We fill it up with water and then dunk people," she said.

"You don't just sprinkle babies then?" he asked. "I thought that's what they did in the old days."

"No. We don't do that here," she said. "It's all or nothing. When we need to baptise someone we open it up, fill it with water, and are all ready to go! Now let me introduce you to our pastor Wesleya."

Will immediately encountered a warm embrace and a reassuring voice.

"What do I have to do to join you properly?" he asked.

"Repent and believe, my friend," replied the pastor.

"What happens then?" enquired Will.

"Take the waters, my brother," came the firm reply from her.

Will had expected to be told he had to renounce the Cloud, but that didn't seem to be the main message. About an hour later, Will had another surprise. Despite his having fully ditched the cloud and renounced his citizenship, who should arrive but Tim.

"Hi Tim," waved Rosaline. "Lovely you could join us tonight."

Will was amazed. "How do you know him? I thought you didn't mix with cloud people."

"It helps me focus," replied Tim who had overheard the conversation.

Rosaline took Will aside and whispered, "it's a bit strange. He comes to some of our meetings, and is usually silent. Then all of a sudden he comes up with something really profound."

"Sounds like Tim."

Tim cleared his throat. "It wasn't just a social call." He was addressing Will. "You just missed these things as you left."

He produced two parcels, both with custom labels marking them from Russia. "I thought they might be important."

Will grabbed them.

"Well, open them," said Rosaline. "After all, it's Christmas."

Will unwrapped the parcels. In them he found Katerina's diary and her book of poetry.

"Thank you so much, Tim," he said with genuine surprise. "I'm so sorry about all the aggro I've given you over the years. All of that doesn't seem to matter too much now I stand looking at the world in a different light."

"Forgiveness is the key to starting again," said Rosaline. "I know I hurt you just by rejecting you, so perhaps you can forgive me too?"

"Nothing to forgive at all," replied Will.

"Good. Well that leads nicely into what I wanted to tell you both," she said. "Today is Tuesday but by Sunday evening I will be gone. I'm joining a Convent in Africa and I'll be doing medical missionary work from the start of next year."

This was a shock even to Tim. "It's a fine thing you're doing," he said.

Leaning over to whisper in Will's ear quietly he added, "it's best for you too, Will."

"But why leave?"

"I have concerns on the way things are going. Children are being pressured into things they shouldn't be, being given intrusive brain scans without clear consent, and the mental health issues are being ignored. It's hard for me to stay on in my job when I love the children so much, though it's also hard to leave. I shall be helping many more children in my new role, and doing so in what I hope will be a more Godly environment."

Tim left soon after.

"What do you really think of Tim?" Will asked Rosaline.

"He's usually silent, but then comes up with some views. They can be quite profound, but he's so certain he's right it can come across as arrogant. He strikes me more as a philosopher than a man of faith, but maybe I'm judging him wrong."

Will nodded.

The send-off for Rosaline continued late into the night until the challenge of Eutychus persuaded everyone to leave.

And so ends our story of love and death.

# NARRATOR AFTERWORD

Rosaline's paper to The Needle on the negative impacts of State Upbringing on children's mental health was published six months later following some controversy. There were efforts to make contact once her findings became widely accepted, but to no avail.

Suggestions that state security agents in Russia had used poison to murder a Cloud Citizen were independently investigated by the World Cloud Court. It was found that there was insufficient evidence to support that finding given the distinct possibility that the Spy-sat's data feeds could easily have been hacked by a state or non-state actor.

Meanwhile, Nik, Ben and the other survivors of this tale now spend their efforts not on *Planets* but on saving this planet. A statue to Katerina's martyrdom (the "Modern Martyr") was duly erected in her namesake city, and became famous in the whole region. Devout couples wishing to co-parent were particularly keen would visit as it was said that lighting a candle in presence of her image would bless their union and bring prosperity. Count Paris' call sign has never been seen on the Cloud again to this day.

Later that summer Will did hear some unexpected news from Swindon, indeed from the County Ground itself. Swindon City had won their last league game, guaranteeing them top place in the Premiership. The cheers could be heard as far away as Kingsgeld.

Further away in Tokyo there were cheers just as loud, as the final missing link of the fusion hybrid technique was solved with the help of mathematicians at St Andrew's University in Scotland.

Vicky took over as bubble president, the first woman to take the presidency of an elite bubble in Swindon. As she jested, it was a double first for women, given she was pregnant with a daughter.

Our story from Will and Katerina ends here, but it's not quite the last word. Just before I finish there's one last thing you need to know, and it's all down to one important character you may have overlooked. For when Mariya performed her test, it was not only for the purpose Tanis had ordered. Deep in the basement of a reproductive hospital is a little human growing in an artificial womb, from the DNA of both Will and Katerina. On 29 February 2048, born a month premature, came little Bridget. Of course she would not be christened but, the following day, thousands of miles away, her father was baptised by full immersion.

# GLOSSARY AND BACKGROUND

## AVATAR (REAL LIFE)

Every Cloud Citizen has an avatar by default. This avatar may simply consist of a name and Cloud ID. However, depending on the Citizen, it may contain far more detail about the individual such as health status and relationships. For more advanced use it may contain elements of the Citizen's character and preferences in a data-driven form. In such form, the avatar may in some cases interact in the Cloud with other Citizens or avatars or systems. For example, in order make choices about the use of energy in a home and in order to respond to real-time price signals, an avatar may make choices and actions using AI. These AI decisions are made on the basis of a data set of actual choices or programmed preferences made by the Citizen. When slightly new circumstances arise, the avatar will attempt to make contact with the Citizen for direction, but in the absence of that contact, will try to make the best decisions based on available data.

It can therefore in some circumstances be difficult to ascertain whether one is talking to a real-life human, or to an avatar, if the interactions are purely Cloud based. If the programming is sufficiently advanced, avatars can even appear on video feeds using stored images of the Citizen's appearance, motion and voice. Given the potential for an avatar to become separated from the Citizen (eg through death of the Citizen), the Turing Test can be employed in order to make this determination.

## AVATAR (GAME, EG *PLANETS*)

For the purposes of playing online games, characters can be created which behave like real-life avatars but in the game environment. They are less likely to be based on data, and more likely to be based on programmed preferences, since the creation of the avatar itself is a key component of the game. This avatar therefore allows games to operate 24/7 with the avatar effectively playing while the player is logged off. When game play is directly by the user, it is likely to result in better performance. However the user cannot play 24/7 and hence the game avatar must take over. Hence the game becomes addictive since prolonged periods of participation by the avatar alone could lead to backwards steps in the game.

The game avatar has a similar status to an account on social media, which could be any name or profile handle unless there is a specific verification process. There is therefore in theory no way that another game player could know the real identity of an avatar with which he or she is playing. In the novel, the game *Planets* was originally set up in such a way that the player might be anonymous even to the game administration, so that the information could not be passed on to national authorities. However later restrictions forced the game to permit only those willing to confirm their NVIDs, which in turn had to be provided to national security services.

## CARBON EMISSION PERMITS

A carbon emission permit gives the right to emit a certain quantity of carbon in a specified accounting period and specified regulatory area. In this novel it is assumed that the regulatory area is worldwide, though in 2022 a global regulatory regime does not exist. For example, the EU and the UK have separate zones for carbon accounting. The price of permits can change rapidly, particularly if there is some regulatory intervention or some significant event which has a bearing on the price.

## CLOUD ID/NVID

These terms are used interchangeably. However, the term NVID (National Verified Identity) references the process by which a unique Cloud identity is registered to one and only one user, with each user having just one NVID for life. It is allocated at the point at which a person becomes a Cloud Citizen. The NVID is intended to be linked with a Bubble (in the West) or a Seven Star (in Russia) to limit the potential for identity fraud, though the Bubble may change over time. Financial institutions and Government services will require an NVID for interaction, so that there is certainty about the identity of the person with whom they are dealing. This therefore implicitly limits the online interaction of anyone who is not a Cloud Citizen and who therefore cannot verify their identity. A Cloud Citizen may not deliberately compromise the credentials of their NVID. Where the credentials are lost by accident, the Bubble has authority to reset the credentials, since the individual is personally known to Bubble members. The Bubble can also determine when an individual's physical or mental health is sufficiently poor that they can no longer effectively and safely interact online. In such situations the NVID can be suspended or removed and the individual looked after according to their needs. When someone dies their NVID dies with them.

The book describes some additional security measures being introduced by different nations, such as physical chip implantation. These measures assist with social control and could be beneficial or sinister according to your political viewpoint.

## DAESH

Another name for ISIS. It is an implicit assumption within the novel that the organisation still exists in some format by the time of the events of the story.

## DIRECT AIR CAPTURE

It is technically possible to directly capture carbon dioxide from the air and store it, which would contribute to reducing net emissions. However, while it can be done technically, it is currently not economically viable.

## ECCLESIASTICUS/SIRACH

This is a religious book written by Ben Sira in the second century BC. It is recognised by some churches, but not by protestant churches nor does it form a part of the traditional Jewish cannon.

## ECONOMISTS

Various economists are named, such as Adam Smith, John Maynard Keynes and Friedrich Hayek. Adam Smith is best known for his work commonly called "The Wealth of Nations" and is seen by some as one of the first expositors of the virtues of free market economics.

## HOPAK

The hopak is a Ukrainian dance originally popularised by Cossacks. Its performance requires physical strength in the legs and so it acts as a display of power as a man and as a soldier. Nowadays it can be performed by both men and women.

## HYDROGEN (BLUE, GREEN ...)

Describing hydrogen in colours is a convenient way of labelling its origin. Green hydrogen is made using electrolysis where the electricity used comes from carbon free sources such as renewable electricity. Blue hydrogen is made in processes such as Steam Methane Reforming which emit carbon in the first instance, but then the created carbon is captured and stored. Other colour descriptions apply according to different manufacturing processes. The labelling has no bearing on its chemical composition, and thus the description relies on being able to trace its source in a verifiable way.

## INCEL

Incel or involuntary celibate refers to young men who are unable to find a female sexual partner and who as a result resent both young women (especially if those women have spurned their advances) and sexually successful young men. The group to whom this description is applied may have formed online social media groups.

## KOKHNIK OR KOKSHNIK

This is a multifaceted elaborate traditional headdress for women used on ceremonial or formal occasions in Russia.

## LUBYANKA

Lubyanka is a tube station in Moscow. On 29 March 2010 bombs detonated in Lubyanka and ParlKultury killing at least 40 people. It was blamed on two female Islamic terrorists.

## REFUSENIKS

This is used to refer to people who were given the opportunity to become Cloud citizens but who refused.

## ST BRIDES CHURCH

St Brides Church is one of the oldest and unluckiest church in London. Its website states that there is evidence of Roman building there dating back to AD 180. Tradition has it that it was founded in the sixth century by St Bridget, whose association with marriage has led to her being associated with the tradition of allowing women to propose marriage on leap days. It is at least the seventh church to actually stand in that spot. It burnt in the Great Fire of London and also suffered during the second world war. It is famous for its spire, which resembles a multi-layered wedding cake. It is now closely associated with journalism, and the press tycoon Rupert Murdoch celebrated his marriage there. Other press links remain, such as traditional annual carol concerts for respected publications. Thanks to senseless planning decisions, the church's external glory is partially blocked by office blocks, but the inside is a visual, and often auditory, delight.

### TREBUCHET

A type of catapult which uses a long arm to throw projectiles. It was a typical military weapon used for sieges in the medieval period prior to the introduction of gunpowder. More recently it was used as a prop in The Grand Tour special on French cars, where the improbable suggestion was made that it was capable of sending a French car from Kent to France as a projectile.

### TURING TEST

Alan Turing was known for his pioneering work on AI, and postulated the Imitation Game (known subsequently as the "Turing Test") in 1950 to determine whether responses were being given by a computer or by a human. The subject area has been developed since by many philosophers and remains a fruitful field of academic discussion. In this novel, the Turing Trial is developed as a literary device to determine whether a Cloud ID is being operated by a human or the real-life avatar.

Printed in Great Britain
by Amazon

78064632R00169